Baseball Man

Charles Puccia

Baseball Man
Copyright © 2016 Charles Puccia
www.charlespuccia.com

Published by Carduna Publications

ISBN: 978-0-9963234-3-7

Edited by Ben Way (benjaminway.co.uk)
Copy Edit and Proofreading by Ian Howe
Typesetting and cover design by FormattingExperts.com

* * *

If you enjoyed reading *Baseball Man*, please rate this book and leave a review for other readers. It means a lot to me—and to Vinnie, who is busy investigating crimes and complicating his relationships with Ben, Dan, and Ginny. Thank you!

Remember to sign up to my email list at charlespuccia.com for pre-release information on Vinnie's next story.

Sincerely,
Charles J. Puccia
vbstories2@gmail.com
www.charlespuccia.com

Contents

Chapter 1

Bus Stop

The black and white Boston terrier exited the bus's bifold doors and ran to the man standing curbside. Vinnie had waited five minutes for the eight a.m. bus. The unaccompanied dog, called Ralph, didn't surprise him; the next passenger to exit, Kaelin, Vinnie's neighbor, was a surprise. She was unmistakable from one hundred yards: the Purple Lady, as neighborhood kids called her—she almost always wore purple, and today she had on her purple pant suit, a purple blouse, and matching purple sneakers.

Al waved from the driver's seat, but Kaelin's appearance had shocked Vinnie, so he didn't respond with the usual "Howya' doin?" in his strong New Yorker's accent unmodulated one smidgen after nearly three years' San Francisco residency.

In all his times waiting for Ralph he had never seen Kaelin on the bus. Vinnie didn't like changes to life's daily routines. He called it bad karma, and his best friend José Rivas, better known as Slider, agreed. For the ten months since Kaelin Peterson and her partner Grace Lee became his next-door neighbors, neither had been on the early morning commuter bus.

Ralph sat next to Vinnie waiting for his leash to be attached to his collar. If not for Al tacitly agreeing to Ralph's bus journey everything would be different. A single complaint would have nixed Ralph's weekday excursion. No Ralph meant no Slider, for the simple reason that Slider had stayed around to dog-sit Ralph.

Otherwise, he would have moved, as this was his way to avoid police complaints by local residents over the homeless vagrant in the park. And no Slider would have made Vinnie's transplanted life in San Francisco even more isolated.

Vinnie stared up at Kaelin, attaching the leash. *Bad fuckin' karma. Now what's going to happen?* He didn't like the way she stood—she seemed listless and her eyes were red.

Leaving New York City had not been Vinnie's idea, but the mob's—a consequence of another bad karma day. A bad, bad, bad karma day that resulted in murders. The mob gave him no choice: leave town to avoid the New York District Attorney serving him a subpoena. Vinnie knew too much: who planned the murders; who paid for them; and who attacked him. Exile was an offer he couldn't refuse. Only Ben Hausen knew his whereabouts, the man he had hoped to make his life partner, his new family—the family he should have had.

Ralph pulled on the leash as Vinnie took Kaelin's midwife trolley. At five foot seven, the attractive Kaelin Peterson was lean, fit, and capable of handling her own medical kit, yet Vinnie took her trolley and offered her his elbow. Kaelin grabbed hold of Vinnie's muscular arm; his one-inch height advantage seemed even bigger as he stood upright in designer jogging pants and a tight synthetic workout T-shirt. Vinnie thought Kaelin's cheeks puffed out. She sniffled before Al shut the doors and drove the bus away.

"Hi, Kaelin. Late night? Difficult delivery? No taxi?" *Yeah, give her a big smile, show her the teeth, pretend happy.* Vinnie often had trouble reading Kaelin, but not today with her red-rimmed eyes and runny nose.

Kaelin and Grace as next-door neighbors were his catalyst for hope. Not even Ralph and Slider prevented Vinnie's sudden feelings of loneliness, despair, and recurring reflections on his teenage years, his first exile. He could not forget the day he had been thrown out of the house by his homophobic father and

2

a bullying older brother. He loved his family, until they turned on him. He pleaded with his mother, who was sympathetic but had no choice for the sake of her daughters, the big sisters he hugged. He and the women sobbed as he went out the front door with a single suitcase. And now he had left Ben, as good as gone. Vinnie had lost all hope of being part of a family. Sure, he had Slider's friendship, but Slider would never be like a family, not with his problems. Vinnie wore morose like his favorite Ralph Lauren sweater. He sulked until the day Kaelin and Grace became his neighbors.

The two walked along in silence. Vinnie restrained himself. He wanted to begin an interrogation, but knew that with Kaelin he had to wait for her cue. Kaelin looked at Vinnie's startled face and explained. "I took a detour, and the bus was convenient." She moved to the middle of the sidewalk as traffic passed by.

Ralph tugged harder at the leash. "Come on, Ralph has his business. You can explain in the park."

Almost upon Kaelin and Grace's arrival ten months earlier Vinnie sought a close friendship. With each shared barbecue he felt that closeness grow. And then came the day Kaelin smiled at him, a beguiling congeniality. She bubbled with enthusiasm over midwifery, and seeped into her description her planning for Grace's delivery.

Vinnie had clapped at the unexpected announcement. He felt thrilled by the excitement of Grace's pregnancy. He felt the baby would make a family for the women—and him. He asked to attend one of Kaelin's midwife births to learn about delivering babies. Her reply slapped him down: "Not only would it be inappropriate but sometimes things go wrong." Vinnie's knack of overstepping boundaries was known by his friends, and he accepted their gentle admonishments. Kaelin was not subtle nor kind, and he learned to approach her with wary footing.

That night Vinnie replayed Kaelin's response. Was it the request or something more? He'd been rebuked before, maybe not as harshly. His mind sought answers to vague questions. Why did the announcement of the pregnancy give him joy? Was he so desperate for a family that even vicarious would suffice? Had he misjudged his neighbor's friendship? It was if Grace's pregnancy was an unknown lure, as if he had a sudden desire to skydive, something that would never have crossed his mind. He could not explain his feelings. Did he possess some kind of gay maternal instinct? Or had the lonely exile awoken painful memories of his teenage years devoid of family? Was this his subconscious psychological survival strategy?

A half-block away, they walked through the only entrance in the six-foot high, ornate wrought-iron fence that enclosed the park. Ralph led them to Slider, sitting at his usual corner bench. After petting the dog, Slider unleashed him. With his new freedom, Ralph ran to the farthest corner from the entrance, and Vinnie mumbled his disapproval.

"Hey, Chime. Hiya, Plum. How y'all doing this mighty fine day?" Slider's Texan drawl greased his words.

Vinnie placed Kaelin next to Slider before pulling a plastic bag from his pocket and heading after Ralph. He walked the two sides of the pathway rather than take the diagonal shortcut across the center grass between four juxtaposed rose trellises.

The area outside the pathway varied in width from ten to fourteen feet before abutting the fence. This zone, with its large shrubs and trees, buffered the park from traffic and pedestrians; in some areas, bushes ran three rows deep for added seclusion. Ralph's business took place on the edge of these thick bushes, between two enormous begonias.

Disposing of the bag in the nearest poop bin, Vinnie reattached the leash to Ralph's collar and held it out for Slider, who deliberately let it drop to the ground. Slider's intentional defiance of San Francisco's leash law caused him and Vinnie to bicker like a married couple. Today was not the day to continue their debate, so Vinnie held his tongue and picked up Ralph's leash without a word.

"Move over, we have to talk to Kaelin." Slider and Kaelin shifted, providing Vinnie space on the end. Vinnie patted her arm and sat, placing Kaelin inside the man-sandwich. "So what's the problem?"

With one hand scratching the back of the other as if writing her words before speaking, Kaelin's voice fluttered on the exhale. "I don't know where to begin." The muffled sound of passing cars penetrated the silence. "Why are people so deceptive?"

Slider nodded as if shaking off a fly.

"Dunno? Anyone in particular?" said Vinnie, a slow-circling wrist moving his cupped hand as a non-verbal signal for her to continue.

"This morning, after my delivery, I went to the clinic to find out about Grace's checkup. She's at four months and she's said nothing." Kaelin's backhand wiped her eye.

Slider leaned forward. "Take your time, we've all day. Right, Chime?"

Vinnie gently squeezed her arm and whispered, "Uh-huh."

"We've wanted this for so long. Me the most. I wanted to carry the baby but... well, you know about my problem." Kaelin stopped, shook her head, and her voice became stronger. "That's history. So Grace became pregnant without telling me, but this isn't news, is it?"

Slider bent forward to hold Kaelin's hand. "She meant it as a gift, I'm sure."

"Sure, yet I wish she'd have... it doesn't matter, not now. We should have asked one of you."

Slider smiled and squeezed Kaelin's hand again. "Well, it would have to be a takeaway; we're not suited to direct deposit, are we, Chime?"

Vinnie slapped his head. *Is Slider off his meds again? Fuckin' convoluted analogy. I better check his pillbox.*

"So what's upset you?" Vinnie took Kaelin's other hand and

imitated Slider's gentle patting, only he jiggled his leg. Vinnie's voice dropped. "Is the baby okay?"

"The baby's fine."

"There you go, good news. The baby's health is all that matters, right?" Vinnie's words tumbled out. *Now I'm spouting fuckin' idiotic clichés.*

"Of course the baby's health comes first, except—"

Vinnie's hand tightened on Kaelin's. Her voice strengthened. "I asked about the donor like I've done before. The receptionist was a temp, and either she saw my midwife bag or she made a mistake, but whatever the reason she assumed I had full rights and read me Grace's file." Kaelin inhaled. "God, I can't stop thinking about it."

"Just tell us. You can't keep us in suspense. I mean I'm about to fuckin' explode." When anxious, Vinnie tended to pepper-spray expletives throughout his speech. His former boss and dearest friend, Dan Livorno, had helped him overcome this habit, one that had nearly cost him his job at Del Vecchio & Neale, Inc. That had been New York, far away, a place forbidden to him after the DV&N murders and nearly his own. Now he had himself a mountain of compensation money from DV&N—blood money, he called it—and for some reason his proclivity to curse, primarily the F-word, had returned. Out of loyalty to Dan—or for something to do, he wasn't sure which—he made a half-hearted attempt to control the foul language. But now the words rose like bile churning in his stomach.

"Vinnie, it's nothing."

"No, it's not. You need to fu—fudging tell us!"

Slider nodded encouragement. "I agree. Even Ralph's all ears." He held up Ralph's ears, and the dog tilted his head to receive a nanosecond smile from Kaelin.

"The temp said there was no donor. Grace's pregnancy was through intercourse."

"What! She's wrong." Vinnie leaped up, causing Ralph to

bark in alarm. "The temp doesn't know how to read the fuckin' charts!"

"I thought the same, so I asked to speak with the head nurse, who gave the temp hell for her breach of confidentiality. We argued until I had confirmation. Grace is not pregnant from clinical insemination." Kaelin flicked at a tear sliding down her cheek.

The two men looked at each other, then to Ralph sniffing the grass as Kaelin chewed her words before spitting them out. "You know this means Grace had sex. With who I don't know. Not yet." A finger flick wasn't enough now to stem her tears.

Vinnie handed Kaelin a tissue he had retrieved from his pocket. "I understand why you're upset but wait until you have all the facts. There will be a good explanation, I'm sure." *What's fuckin' wrong with me? I can't stop spouting fuckin' clichés.* Vinnie tugged at his ear.

Kaelin fumed. With her parting words—"Why would she do this?"—Vinnie watched her leave the park, cross the street, and disappear behind his house. He foresaw the battle when Grace returned home.

And right there Vinnie decided he would investigate. He would apply his private investigator skills, learned over the Internet. Even as an unlicensed amateur, there were things he could do. He already knew that if Grace had hidden how she became pregnant from Kaelin, then she was probably hiding a lot more. What? And why?

Chapter 2

Friends in the Making

Slider released Ralph's leash, increasing the dog's scavenging area, which Vinnie ignored.

Do I start with how Grace became pregnant? Or Kaelin's question—why she did it? She could have been impregnated at a different clinic, but then why continue to visit the first? And her records would show that too.

Vinnie's fascination had grown in tandem with Grace's belly. He felt drawn to a family in the making. He loved Grace's glow. He touched her tummy like an obstetrician checking on a baby's health. If Grace sniffled, carried a heavy bag, or stubbed her toe, he worried.

A bark distracted him from his daydreaming, to which he soon resumed.

He had met Slider two and a half years before on this park bench. He had been surprised by Slider's Texan staccato greeting. "Howdy, y'all. You'un like my dawg? Y'all came out of nowhere. Now take a load off. You fixin' to stay awhile?"

With elbows on his knees and hands cupping his chin, Vinnie contemplated the last couple of years. Slider's slang had become commonplace. His big Texan's laugh, his guffawing like the time he found Ralph wandering unaccompanied in the park and saw him as easy reward money, never imagining it would yield a dog-sitting job and companion.

Slider's hardest knee-slapping laugh came with Ralph's original name, Whitey Garcia. The white-pawed terrier's real owners, Mark and Alice Datone, San Francisco State University professors, were Deadhead admirers of Jerry Garcia, San Francisco's legendary hippie musician. Mark had confirmed Slider's story, including Slider's circuitous nicknames.

Slider spent his childhood either throwing a baseball or watching TV reruns of *The Honeymooners.* He loved Jackie Gleason's bus driver character Ralph Kramden, which was how Whitey's name changed.

Mark became Books for his extensive library, and Alice was Ivy due to her Mount Holyoke degree.

Yet Mark's follow-up to Slider's nicknaming scheme impressed Vinnie even more. "A real shame what happened to Slider. Alice and I gave up our season tickets."

But Ben's reaction maddened Vinnie because of his befriending the professors. "Fucking stupid to let more people know about you. You're in hiding."

With Ben's words, Vinnie felt that his isolation had become internment. He and Ben weren't a real family; he had no one.

Looking up from the park bench, Vinnie watched Slider with Ralph. *They are good together, just like Kaelin and Grace. Why can't people be honest? Wasn't that Kaelin's point?* Vinnie's mood darkened. He repeated Ralph's name like a mantra to rid thoughts of Kaelin and Grace's breakup—a breakup that would have consequences for him too. He dreaded being removed from the baby, not being part of his or her life. *Now I'm sounding weirder than Slider. What's my problem? Should I talk to Slider? What would I say? I'm lonely and miss having a family? Why?*

Leaning back, Vinnie stretched, his fitted designer jeans extending across half the path. The sunshine accentuated his model-perfect face, his emerald eyes, high cheekbones, and sculpted torso. He and Slider were weekend companions and friends.

Vinnie concentrated. *"Why" is the point, for Grace and for me, not "how."*

He recalled Slider's knee-slapping laugh when after a month he had said, "Slider, I've become your fuckin' weekend substitute Ralph." Vinnie stopped short of adding, "Except for Ben's visits, then I'm fucking him," which would have revealed too much.

For months Vinnie allowed Slider to believe Ben was only his landlord who stayed at the house for his business visits. Slider knew Ben before Vinnie. He knew he was a professional body-builder. "Doesn't take a bunch of cowboys chewing around a campfire to figure out that two-hundred-forty-five-pound steer sitting on next to you is his own rodeo." In Slider's lexicon, Vinnie became "Chime" to contrast with Ben's nickname of "Gong."

"Your landlord can move the San Andreas Fault," Slider had said.

Playing along, Vinnie answered, "Yeah, like he went to Barney's for biceps, matching triceps, and triple X thighs, and the store threw in a bowling ball ass that needs two hands to grab." *Had he said too much?*

Slider explained that Ben was Vinnie's landmark landlord, like London's landmark Big Ben. "He sways side to side when he walks, like the bell tower gong. Y'alls only a little chime."

"Makes sense," Vinnie said, but thought, *Nah, that's cuckoo.*

Vinnie saw in Slider's nicknaming his irrationality and intelligence. Kaelin's all-purple wardrobe resulted in her becoming "Plum." "Get it? *Nom de Plum.* Ha ha ha ha."

Nicknaming relaxed Slider, but only medication kept his mumbling, explosive laughing fits, grinning for no apparent reason, and his non sequitur thinking in check.

Vinnie told Ben, "Slider's not stupid. He lives on a park bench in a liberal neighborhood where nobody complains. His after-ballgame analysis is better than most media pundits."

Ben didn't care. "Be smart. Trust no one. The mob notices if you draw attention to yourself."

"Yeah, yeah. But I'm not Vinnie Briggs who had moved to Los Angeles, I'm fuckin' Vincent de Paul in San Francisco." Vinnie detested the alias on the leaseholder's contract. "Why a Catholic charity?"

"To make Google searches harder and to keep your first name so you don't get confused."

"Fuckin' fuck you, Ben." Vinnie cried leaving New York.

On first meeting Slider, Vinnie saw past his gritty clothing, unhygienic smell, unshaven face, and mangy hair. He saw a beautiful man, all six foot two inches that towered over him. Dirt didn't hide Slider's handsome face; nor did the filthy, baggy T-shirt disguise his fit, sculpted body.

Aside from physical attraction, Vinnie bonded with Slider, commiserating over their similar family backgrounds: the zero tolerance for gay sons.

Vinnie helped Slider. Insisted he shower; wear new clothes; shave; have a salon haircut. Vinnie paid all costs. *What a fuckin' hot body, so different to Ben's oversize bulges and nasty veins. Slider's GQ sexy—since I've cleaned him up.*

Ben's short visits every couple of months made New York seem even farther away, and the emotional distance increased. Vinnie's friendship with Slider took on a new context.

Stretched out in the sunlight, Vinnie concluded that the *how* he had become friends with Slider didn't matter. *It's the why, just like with Grace's pregnancy.*

Loneliness had brought nasty thoughts. *Ben says he loves me, so why remain three thousand miles away? Because he's surrounded by muscle-worshipping men. They say pumping iron is the best climax. He's getting off and I have bupkis.*

If Ben pumped iron, so too did Vinnie with Slider, his workout buddy. They trained half-naked, and Vinnie looked at Slider's rippling striations, wondering if he could be a possible friend with benefits. He thought Ben's daily phone calls sounded more like check-ups than romance. Vinnie realized he wanted a relationship with Slider.

His face sun-baked, Vinnie oscillated between past and present. *Had jealousy been his why for wanting Slider? Lack of sex? Can there be more than one why? Could that be true for Grace?*

Vinnie had played his own devil's advocate. Ben's excuses for infrequent visits had seemed lame; his "keep-a-low-profile-and-raise-no-alarms" sounded like bullshit.

Vinnie belittled his own worth as a sexual partner when Slider didn't respond to his touches—the workout massages; the rubbing of cramped calf muscles. *I got excited, not Slider.* Vinnie's self-esteem plummeted.

He had convinced himself that Ben's attachment had been nothing more than an inverted version of Stockholm syndrome in the months Ben had nursed him to back to life.

Then he wondered why Slider had not responded. *What's wrong with me?*

Mark gave Vinnie an alternative for Slider's disinterest.

"He has sublimated any form of gay sex as a form of psychological protection. It's not you."

Mark also explained Slider's hit-and-run accident that had smashed his kneecap and destroyed his baseball career. Newspapers made no connection to Slider's previous month's announcement that he was a gay baseball player on the San Francisco Giants' roster. No one explained the lack of witnesses in broad daylight. But Slider knew the reason. Mark too. And so did every gay fan.

The Giants' owners' and teammates' slow response had disgusted Mark and Alice, so they gave up their season tickets. The Giants had recruited Slider at twenty-two, an all-star University of Texas freshman. "The Texan Wonder" threw a breaking ball pitch like he was roping bulls at a rodeo. No one had seen anything like it before or since. Sportswriters called him "The Slider," which fans turned into the refrain, "Slider... Slider...

Slider," as he took the mound.

Gay friends had encouraged Slider to come out, explaining that he was safe in San Francisco; but not one of these friends was a ballplayer.

A tapping at his shoe interrupted Vinnie's thoughts. Slider stood grinning, his feet bobbing and voice giggling. Vinnie knew this was not the time to reveal his fascination with Grace's baby, nor his intention to investigate Grace's betrayal. He stood and handed Slider a fifty: their pretext of Vinnie's contribution to Ralph's upkeep, but meant for Slider's barber and snacks at the local café.

Vinnie turned away. Kaelin's harsh retort stuck in his head: "Really! You think there's a good explanation other than Grace cheated on me?" He should have been honest and said, "No, I don't fuckin' think so."

He renewed his unspoken vow of moments before. *Family means raising a child. Families stay together, grow together, stick with each other. If I'm ever to be part of a family, even indirectly as the "kind uncle" then I'll have to get involved and investigate. No more putzing around with missing pets, absentee landlords, and other bullshit jobs as favors to Mark and Alice's friends. It's time to get back to real P.I. work.*

Chapter 3

Stir Fried

Stir-fried beans sizzled as smoke filled the kitchen. NPR's *All Things Considered* finished minutes before Grace entered the room and placed a glass of Californian Pinot on the table. "I miss this. Something smells good."

Kaelin grunted, taking a quick sip from the wine glass before draining the noodles.

In under half an hour the women ate, cleaned up, and moved to the divan in the house's large, open-plan living room. Kaelin looked out of a side window and spied Vinnie's garbage barrels. Years before, Kaelin's father Curt had asked Ben to hide the unattractive barrels, saying, "Too bad the old city ordinance allowed houses so close." As an architect, Curt had designed a shed that Ben had built, but which Vinnie didn't use.

Turning from the window, Kaelin surveyed the room. She wouldn't admit to anyone but Grace that her father's house renovation validated his architectural firm's awards. Grace's face had lit up when she learned Curt had offered them the apartment at one-third market value. Kaelin had refused with lingering resentment. She never accepted her father's bullshit offer as a demonstration that he accepted her lesbian lifestyle. No, his offer was atonement for abandoning her and her mother in Minnesota for a twenty-two-year-old Californian trophy wife.

Grace begged Kaelin—they could never afford a house like

this, or indeed any house in this neighborhood. All they had found were dumps, or postage-stamp size, or in tough neighborhoods—all long commutes to their city jobs.

Examining Grace's eyes, Kaelin saw deception. Just like her father. All pretense. Both liars. It was her childhood revisited. Within two years the Californian bimbo had divorced her father, taking a sizable chunk of his assets that reduced her mother's alimony.

As if the Minnesota winter had entered the room, Kaelin shivered. The divan appeared to elongate to push Grace away. Kaelin stared into the space separating them. *For the sake of a beautiful house she brokered a reconciliation between me and my father, and then she betrays me.* Kaelin felt like spitting. Her mother's words wormed into her brain: "Never trust that bastard father of yours."

Grace touched Kaelin's leg. "You all right, honey?"

Kaelin brushed Grace's hand aside.

Grace leaned forward, a lilt in her voice, "What's a matter? You okay?"

"Maybe I prefer silence to lies."

Grace jolted backward, her mouth gaping as she took a deep breath. "What? Where did *that* come from?"

"Don't pretend. Did you really think I wouldn't find out?"

"I have no idea what you're talking about."

"Right. Like where did that come from?" Kaelin pointed at Grace's extended belly.

"Is this about me being the surrogate and not you? You know we had no choice."

"We agreed to choose a donor together, not for you to fuck a guy."

Grace's head rotated, her long hair swinging.

"You know exactly what I mean. Who was he? Who did you fuck?"

Rapid eye blinks held Grace's tears inside her lower lids. "I didn't want to tell you. It's not what you think. I... I... oh my God, this is so hard."

"Hard! Fuck hard." Kaelin's teeth snapped as if intending to bite Grace's tongue.

Grace rose from the divan to stand in the room's corner, her back to the front window. "I was raped." No amount of blinking held her tears. Water drowned her chin.

Kaelin catapulted from the divan, her arms outstretched, running to fold Grace to her; her hands took hold beneath Grace's chin, tugging her head upward. "What! When? Tell me." Kaelin's arms wrapped around Grace, pulling her upright, and their bosoms pressed together.

"It happened a month before our planned clinic visit." Grace wiped her cheek. Kaelin used her sleeve to dry Grace's moist skin. "You were away on a training course. I went with a work group after hours and… and…"

Kaelin felt Grace pull away and watched her walk back to the divan. She looked bloated, and waddled.

"I can't talk about it."

"Please. Let me help."

"It's awful. I considered an abortion. But we wanted this baby so much and… I'm pregnant, so, at first, it didn't seem to matter. Now it does."

"No, it doesn't. We'll have this baby. And we'll go after whoever did this. Do you know who he is? Did you make a police report?"

"He's married. I wanted to but… I know who drugged my drink but I can't remember details. If I accuse him, I could jeopardize everything. I'll never advance in the firm. They won't fire me but I'll be marginalized and forced to find a new job. A new employer won't be generous with extra time off—and who'd hire me looking like this?"

"Then fight. That bastard is the one that should lose his job. He should go to jail! We can get DNA to prove he's the father."

"No, I don't want my baby—our baby—to know her father is a rapist. Or give him paternity rights. We'll raise our amazing daughter."

Grace said no more and went to the bedroom to change into her nightgown. She slid into her bed before nine o'clock after a hot shower. Kaelin watched her from the bedroom doorway, her thoughts a cocktail of advice, rage, and sadness. She sat on the bed to smooth Grace's hair, then she switched off the bedside lamp as she left the room.

* * *

The garbage barrel scraped the sidewalk with its broken wheel.

"Need a hand with that?" Vinnie called out from his path, dragging his own two barrels behind him.

"No, I'm good—thanks." Kaelin aligned the barrel to the curb. The tree limbs blocked the streetlights, but not the full moon that illuminated her face and slumped body.

"Want to talk about it? Come on over." Vinnie motioned to his house.

"No, I'm okay, really." Kaelin didn't move.

"I'm a good listener. Come on. Don't hold back. Let me help. I'd do anything for you and Grace. You know I want to help with the baby." Vinnie moved closer. He leaned on Kaelin's garbage barrel and saw her violet cheeks and wondered if she was experimenting with purple face powder.

She sighed. "Maybe we should talk."

Vinnie leaned forward, looking into Kaelin's silver dollar pancake eyes as Grace's rape story was told. "Fuckin' scumbag. She can't let him get away with it."

"I agree but... she's right. We'll have an awesome daughter and why should she know about her rapist father?"

"Something's not right. Trust me, I know. I have a sixth sense for these things. I'm a professional private eye."

Kaelin chuckled.

"What! You don't believe me? It's true. I took an online course and have a certificate."

Kaelin's smile widened. "I believe you, Vinnie. It's just... umm... you don't strike me as a private detective kind of guy. You're sensitive and caring. What would happen if you met an angry husband?" Kaelin touched Vinnie's arm. "You're not Ben."

"For your information, being a P.I. is not all about brawn. It requires brains. I found the Datones' neighbor's cat, and one of their graduate students couldn't get a hold of his absentee landlord, who I tracked down out-of-state." Vinnie puckered his lips.

"I'm sorry, Vinnie, no offense." Grace stifled her smile. "We won't require your services. Grace isn't taking this further."

"If you change your mind, I'm available. And I'm strong too." Vinnie flexed his arm, but stopped short of saying that his one important private eye experience had put him in a coma and forced him to relocate to the other side of the country. With a strain, Vinnie kept his thoughts to himself. *Ben's not my landlord, he's my partner who I met investigating the fuckin' bastards who tried to screw my best friend Dan.*

Kaelin ran her finger across his bicep bubble. "I didn't mean to be rude. You've put on muscle these last few months."

Vinnie released his clenched fist and spread his fingers.

"What?"

"Can I attend the birth? I'm no stranger." Vinnie put his hands together as if praying.

Kaelin tilted her head. "We'll see."

"Please, let me help."

"Why is this baby so important to you?"

Vinnie had asked himself this same question many times. Why did Grace's pregnancy bring him joy? Did he have an obsession like Ginny's weird sthenolagnia, her fixation on muscular men? No—she admired muscular men in ways he didn't understand. Vinnie once considered bodybuilders freaks, nothing more than slabs with veins, until his first time in bed with Ben. But his kind of enjoyment wasn't Ginny's. And his baby obsession was nothing like hers.

"I don't know," said Vinnie, lifting his eyebrows.

"I'll ask Grace, see what she thinks."

Vinnie stood at the basement door next to the bespoke garbage shed. *What is it with me? Why do I want to be at the birth?* He paused turning the doorknob. Not only the birth, he wanted to help raise their child. *I fuckin' want my own baby that can never be taken from me.*

Vinnie closed the basement door behind him.

Chapter 4

Walk in the Park

The morning refuse collection clanked, but did not rouse Vinnie because he was already awake; his mind had been active and agitated for an hour. How to tell Ben? He had tossed and turned all night anticipating Ben's visit. He had tidied the basement gym; dusted tons of iron as if the few specks might strain Ben. Vinnie knew the idea ridiculous, for a man like Ben, built out of rocket fuel. Yeah, that's a good name for his performance-enhancing drugs.

The infrequency of Ben's visits gave them greater significance. Ben would have visited more often, but for prudence. The same precaution made trips outside the house to restaurants and movies rare. The less exposure, the less likely someone might notice. Everyone noticed Ben, which would connect him to Vinnie too easily. The more trips, the greater the chance someone might follow him from New York—the fickle mob could reinstate Vinnie's contract at any time. Or political pressures could spur the New York DA to attempt serving him a subpoena. Whether valid or paranoid, precaution limited Ben to short visits.

Cleanup completed, Vinnie swirled his glass of power protein drink at the kitchen table, one more change in his lifestyle after moving to California. Not that he had adopted the mythical healthy Californian lifestyle. No, this was in part to mollify Ben, so that he put on muscle. And Kaelin had stumbled on the other reason: in New York he would become a registered private investigator. Bulking up would impress potential clients and aid his job performance. If Kaelin had seen before-and-after pictures from three years ago she would have appreciated the forty-five pounds of muscle as testament to Ben's rocket-fuel mixture and Vinnie's dedicated lifting regime; well, drugs too, but Vinnie wouldn't tell her that.

The glass circled with each thought. How to broach the subject? Tell him he desperately wanted a child? How would Ben react? Vinnie raised the glass to his lips, the thick slush coating the inside of his mouth, while a few ounces trickled down his throat. *Something was wrong.* Vinnie rubbed his forehead. *What?* Leaving the half-full glass, Vinnie walked to the bus stop.

The *something* arrived as Ralph exited the bus and Vinnie attached the leash to the dog's collar. The feeling dragged Vinnie like Ralph. He had the same fuzzy sensation he had with Dan. He had figured that out talking to his co-worker Blanca. That's the way his brain worked; he talked out loud. He heard his words and watched the effect on someone he trusted. That was his method, and it worked. But Blanca wasn't here. Who could he confide in? His idea couldn't be blabbed around. He looked at Ralph. "You're a good pooch, but you lack fuckin' conversational skills."

In the park Vinnie sat on the bench with Slider, releasing Ralph's leash to let him roam, contradicting his frequent admonitions of his friend. Their conversation soon moved to Kaelin's revelation. Vinnie couldn't stop, so he told Slider of Grace's rape, not expecting him to jump up, flinging his arms around. He swiveled as if picking off a runner attempting to steal second base. Ralph trotted back over to the bench. Vinnie searched for Ralph's deposit and returned to Slider via the doggie refuse receptacle.

Both men stared into space. Both agreed that what had happened to Grace was tragic. Slider called her "Good'un" because she was the only good lawyer he knew.

Vinnie watched Slider rub his hands, mesmerized by his adroit movement.

"Why? I mean why accept anonymous spunk then want to know who gave it? Man, that's fucked up. Y'all know if they'd have gone and done ask me they's known soon enough who was the donor." Slider's vertical hand motion caused Vinnie to turn to see if anyone had noticed.

"You're missing the fuckin' point. Kaelin found out Grace never used the clinic's sperm bank because she didn't need to. She was raped."

"I mean I'd have done it no charge. I do it free all the time." Vinnie's hand rested on Slider's forearm to stop his gesturing.

"Shut up, Slider. I don't fuckin' want to hear about your jerking off. And never in the park. Use the spare key to my basement. You be fuckin' careful what you do in public, got it?"

With a shake of his head, Vinnie walked away. Slider was as much help as Ralph.

"If you'd have asked me, I'd have said Upper Deck is the father." Slider used the nickname he'd given Kaelin's father for his large stomach and architect profession.

As if on ice, Vinnie revolved on the ball of his foot. "What! Don't make random statements. Imagine if Kaelin had heard. That would push her over the edge. She'd fuckin' end up sharing the park bench with you." Vinnie put his hand over his mouth. He'd said too much, just like when he told two New York mobsters to fuck off. They obliged by beating him into a coma and shoving a dildo up his ass.

"I'm so sorry, Slider. I didn't mean that. Please forgive me."

"No problemo. The ump calls 'em the way he sees 'em. I'm fucked up, I know it. But I see things, y'all knows that? Anyway, we just having some locker talk, that's all. Like you said, not a word to anyone." Slider held a finger to his lips while looking down at Ralph.

"Fine. And, remember I'm here for you. Anything you need, anytime. And for God's sake, use the basement bathroom for all your needs. I've restocked the refrigerator." Vinnie hesitated. Holding his nose, he added, "And right now you need a shower. Drop this about Grace. She doesn't want to take this any further and neither should we."

They were startled to see Kaelin enter the park gate.

"Morning, Plum. How's things?" Slider's voice had a slight singsong quality.

"I'm good." Kaelin turned, closing in on Vinnie. "You said nothing about our talk last night, did you?"

"Me and Slider were just going over the extra provisions in my basement. I picked them up while shopping for Ben. You can't imagine how much food I need. He eats enough to cause panic at the butchers." Vinnie smiled and gave a hand signal behind his back, like a catcher calling for a slider on a three-two count.

"Did you want to talk?"

"Not now. I'm on my way to work. Maybe tonight. What time does Ben arrive?"

"Oh, shit, this afternoon. I gotta run or I'll be fucked."

"Isn't that what you're hoping for?" Slider smiled ear to ear.

"Fuck you too." Vinnie looked at his watch.

All three stared at the flowers, their concentration broken by Ralph barking at a squirrel.

Vinnie left the park and walked straight home with his mind wandering: *Let's see, steak or chicken to go as the secondo after the linguine con pesto for my man? Don't listen to Slider. Do surveillance on Grace in case the rapist is stalking her. Keep an eye on Curt too. Whoever it is, they picked on the wrong fuckin' person to mess with. I'm a better private eye now, and this time there's no mob involvement.*

Vinnie would later pin this as the moment he made this his case to solve.

With Vinnie and Kaelin gone, Slider walked around the park's periphery, trailed by Ralph. Despite wandering in body and mind, he reached conclusions similar to Vinnie but excluding Ben's meal preparation. He'd keep a closer eye on Upper Deck. No one would hurt Good'un or Plum. He'd protect both from ending up like him. "Ralph, y'all know this cheer's a new ballgame and I reckin' I need to warm up a mite in the bullpen." Slider walked to the middle of the park, stood in the center of the rose trellises and imitated throwing an imaginary baseball with the park gate home plate. "Stee... rike!"

Chapter 5

Dinner

The front door shut with a bang and Ben marched into a kitchen overpowered with the smell of sautéing garlic.

"So much for intimate kissing."

Vinnie widened a smile that had seeped out the minute he had heard the front door close. "Maybe for you. I find garlic a turn-on."

Ben lifted Vinnie off the floor to crush him into his chest. Vinnie's arms clung to Ben's neck, which was his pattern after his first attempt years before to embrace the sixty-eight-inch barrel chest. Vinnie had complained: "I need ape arms to hug you." After a few minutes of lashing tongues, Vinnie pushed away. Ben smiled and unbuckled his belt.

"Nice thought, but I've worked my ass off on this pesto with *pignoli* so if you think I'm going to let a quick blowjob ruin my masterpiece, then you should have used the oxygen mask on the flight." Vinnie gently nudged Ben's crotch with a wooden spoon. "You'll be pleased you waited when you find out what I have planned for dessert."

Dessert was their code to mean Ben had finished work and Vinnie was naked.

"Besides, I want all the news from back home." Ben grumbled and pointed out that Vinnie had lived in California for over two years. "If I wanted conversation, I'd have phoned."

Vinnie understood. Lust was not Ben's exclusive preoccupation, but his steroid-supercharged testosterone levels might have given him an edge. Vinnie thought, *He's so fuckin' hot. Did I really think his muscles were disgusting? Not now, knowing what he can do with them. I'm burning up.*

"I don't care how long I've been here, I'm still a New Yorker."

Vinnie ignored Ben's smirk to serve up the pasta while launching a volley of innocuous catch-up questions.

With forearms resting on the kitchen table, Ben relayed the New York gossip: family, friends from Vinnie's former employment at Del Vecchio & Neale, people at the condo, places, and events. Vinnie believed half the stories, knowing that New Yorkers embellished.

They had a real dessert of fresh fruit sorbet on the living room couch, sitting shoulder to shoulder. Ben finished first and pushed Vinnie off so he could lay flat, one arm behind his head, pulling off his shirt. Vinnie slurped the remaining strawberries and mounted Ben's naked torso, planting his ass over Ben's crotch. Rubbing cocks separated by soft fabric elevated their desire.

Before Vinnie's hands moved to increase the excitation, Ben grabbed Vinnie's forearm.

"What? You too tired?"

"No, don't worry on that score. But I do have something to tell you. I wanted to as soon as I arrived but you were too involved with cooking. Besides, this is a better time. Your father called."

"What! Is it about my mother? Is it really bad? Fuckin' spell it out!"

A large smile opened to expose Ben's teeth. "You always think the worst, don't you? Well, in this case you've got it completely wrong. Your father said the price of Sicilian olive oil has dropped, and there's no need to continue with Californian."

Vinnie froze atop Ben's chest, tears streaming. Ben sat up to smother Vinnie's crying, whispered words. The message was clear: Carmine "Cooler" Aquafreddo, the New York mobster, had reprieved Vinnie from hiding in California. Vinnie was no longer sought as a corroborating witness against Carmine for murder, including Vinnie's own near-death beating three years earlier. Carmine and his right-hand man, Sal "Chopin" Friscollo, were no longer being pursued by the New York prosecutorial office, not after their chief witness, Bill Barrington, DV&N's former executive vice president, had committed prison suicide by stabbing himself in the back multiple times.

"I love you so much. I can't believe this is true. I gave up on the idea of ever returning to New York."

"Do you know what this means?" asked Ben.

Nodding, Vinnie moved to Ben's side. He held his hand and rubbed his thigh. "It means we can walk around openly, no constant looking over our shoulders."

Tears flooded down Vinnie's cheeks, which Ben flicked aside with an index finger. Vinnie rested his head on Ben's chest, his hand continuing to rub his thigh.

"This will be our best time. Are you happy? I am." Ben's hold tightened.

A submerged voice bubbled, "I could melt." Vinnie straddled Ben's lap and Ben stood. He lifted Vinnie skyward, trophy style. On the descent, Vinnie took hold of Ben's neck, his head plunging forward. Vinnie kissed Ben as if diving. His legs wrapped around Ben's waist for leverage, driving his tongue deeper, his passion singeing their throats. Ben's fingers pressed Vinnie's ass, and sinewy biceps crushed Vinnie's sides. Hard penises shuffled until freed by clothes discarded in all directions. Legs tangled. Vinnie's shirt came off and he would have willingly shed skin to increase the intimacy.

Vinnie's bare chest sought refuge against Ben's flexing pectorals, a canvas of linear striations. This was prelude. *I'll eat him alive. I love him so much.*

A single hand polished Ben's hubcap shoulder, then a bicep, while the other explored Ben's rising excitation. Vinnie's hand nudged Ben's hard, near perfectly round, artificial testicle implants. Ben's soft exhale came with eyes half-closed. Vinnie saw. Ben wanted this. They both did. Their adrenaline pushed, knowing they had reached the end of a long, painful separation. They entwined, celebrating the best way they knew.

Yet Vinnie restrained himself. He stopped wiggling. He stopped sucking on Ben's famed man-tits. He stopped his mining of Ben's crevices. He remained still, butt naked on the wood floor, soaking up their heat that outperformed the fireplace's glowing embers. For all his desire, Vinnie needed comfort more. He needed Ben's reassuring embrace, a reassurance it was true—that he was free. "Vinnie, I didn't travel three thousand miles for cuddles." Ben lifted Vinnie and positioned him over his pelvis.

Vinnie wanted this too, a different kind of reassurance. He splayed his legs wide across Ben to assist entry. *I want him. I want to drain his balls dry.*

With each pump by Ben, Vinnie stroked his own erection. Ben's power thrust pressed on Vinnie's prostate, creating agony then pleasure. Herculean strength ensnared Vinnie. Caressing lips turned to near biting with Ben's scream; his pulsating scrotum followed muscles rippling upward.

Vinnie held. He waited for Ben's final pulse then quickened his own stroking until he busted, his outburst echoing Ben's. He spasmed violently, but was held in check by Ben's steeled arms.

"I love you," said Vinnie, to which Ben replied, "I want to be with you forever." Neither heard the banality of the overused words. Both thought they had never been said in the English language before. They believed in them.

Their communal shower became another opportunity to prove their love.

"Now we've got to fuckin' wash again."

Ben laughed while crushing the soap bar, flakes filling his hand. "I'll do you first."

In bed, Vinnie snuggled facing Ben. He didn't care that Ben's single leg overtop crushed him, or that his eyes were half-closed. He rubbed Ben's chest, a sailboat tacking in light wind. He loved their being naked.

"I need to tell you something… about our neighbors."

Ben's eyes opened.

"You know about Grace's pregnancy through artificial insemination, right? Never happened. Grace was raped by an office manager."

Ben sat bolt upright, nearly knocking Vinnie out of bed. "That's terrible. When did it happen?"

"Just before she became pregnant, when do you think?" Vinnie paused. "I'm sorry, I didn't mean to be sharp. I'm upset."

They talked and speculated over Grace's decision not to press charges, and meandering social implications. *No, not my point,* thought Vinnie. He reoriented the discussion, outlining Grace's rationale, hoping to get to his original intent.

Vinnie waved a hand at Ben's list of questions, then twitched. "Stop. I've something else to say, related to Grace but more about me… us."

Lines formed on Ben's forehead.

"I've been thinking, maybe we could help. We have plenty of money. I'd like to help with the baby. Then we'd have Anthony as our New York godchild and one in San Francisco. I can do it alone if you don't want to."

Ben's chin rose. "Wait! It's not the same. Ginny and Dan have been our best friends for a long time. They asked us to be godparents. Grace and Kaelin are friendly neighbors, no more. They didn't ask us. And you're coming back to New York—right?"

"I've been their friend for ten months. And I don't need to be a godparent to help. I can babysit, cover when Kaelin's away, or if Grace works overtime. We don't need to be in New York all the time. You talked of starting another gym here, remember?"

Ben threw off the bedcover, moved off the bed, and looked down at Vinnie's naked body with a scowl.

Fuckin' stupid. I didn't think this through. I've ruined our first night together.

"You've always said you wanted to return East. Their baby isn't your problem. Don't get involved. I'm happy to offer financial assistance if they ask for it. And what about Curt? He's sort of the grandfather, isn't he? Can't he help?"

Sitting up and pulling his legs to his chest, Vinnie talked into his knees. "Kaelin has hated her father for years. They've only just been reconciled and she has lingering resentment issues." Vinnie paused. "She's convinced her father is using Grace's pregnancy to get closer to her. She refuses to let him help."

"As I said, not our concern. Keep out."

"And the baby? Why should she suffer? It's a girl, by the way. I'd want to help raise her." Vinnie stopped to bury his head between his knees. He cursed his runaway mouth.

Ben moved to the foot of the bed, and with his enormous hands took a bracelet hold of Vinnie's ankles.

"What's going on?"

Vinnie muffled his words. "I meant to tell you after dinner, but you beat me with your news. I've been thinking... maybe we should have a child of our own."

Ben released Vinnie's ankles and jumped back. "What the fuck! Are you fucking kidding me! Don't you know how that would destroy me after losing Carl?"

The bedroom door slammed, and Ben's descent vibrated the staircase. He spent the night on the living room couch, considering all the guest bedrooms too close to the master. He had a decision to make, and this wasn't the time for sleep.

Chapter 6

Leftovers

The airport lounge could have been anywhere: generic chairs, themed wall coverings, tiled floors, and TV monitors tuned to CNN with scrolling subtitles. People flowed, some cruising the main corridor, others wandering, some rushing to catch a flight or retrieve luggage. Ben stared out the window waiting to board the JFK-bound flight, his visit cut short by a day. The previous night's tension had ruined his stay. Vinnie's involvement with his neighbors had worried him, but his request they raise a child had upset and angered him. How could he be so insensitive? Maybe he didn't know him after all.

The morning discussion had clinched Ben's decision to leave. Vinnie didn't just want to adopt, he wanted a surrogate mother, and one of them to be the donor. Vinnie did leave wiggle room on this, but Ben knew this was to temporarily placate him. Ben's outlet had been to go to the basement gym. Vinnie yammered while Ben pressed four hundred pounds twelve times, repeating it five times, then flung on more weights. He yelled at the iron bars the words he meant for Vinnie. He grabbed dumbbells the way he wanted to grab Vinnie's throat to stop him talking. Ben felt his anger and knew he had no choice but go back to New York on an afternoon flight.

* * *

Vinnie sat side by side with Slider. Ralph sniffed behind the bench, stretching his leash as far as possible.

"He didn't even hear my reasons. He cursed me for being insensitive. As if I didn't know he feels responsible for the accident that killed his four-year-old son. Of course I do! But that was years ago and he needs to understand my needs. Raising another child doesn't diminish his love for Carl. This could be the end for us. You know that, don't you?"

With his head tilted skyward, his arms stretched along the bench back, Slider appeared to be searching for a pop-up fly ball. His response came in the time the ball would have reached his glove.

"Don't know about being a daddy. My'un busted me like a ripe watermelon when I fessed up gay. He'd be dumb, but don't take no genius to spot a goat in a flock of sheep. Tossed me out. But if you want something, then time to stop painting your butt white and run with the antelope. You'll find another Gong. Might take some doin', that's for sure."

Vinnie turned to Slider. "I don't want another Ben. I love him. I want him to do this for me. I need to convince him, that's all, and if he won't talk about it then how do I do that?"

"I hear y'all. Same with Good'un, she needs to come clean to Plum."

It took Vinnie a moment to realize Slider had switched topics; his nicknames sometimes made conversation hard to follow. But Vinnie got it, a psychological remnant linking Slider to his glory days. *Fuckin' baseball homophobes.* "What do Grace and Kaelin have to do with me and Ben?"

"It's like the same. You need to tell Ben a kid's important to you—and why. Good'un needs to tell Plum that Curt's the baby's daddy."

Vinnie's eyebrows lowered, his cheeks moved up. He'd had

enough of Slider's outlandish, unfounded speculation on the baby's father. Vinnie hated when Slider didn't take his meds. He became stupid. Vinnie didn't need this bullshit, not today. Couldn't Slider stay focused on the problem with him and Ben, not some fantasy story? *Fuckin' stupid.*

"Okay, stop there. You sound crazy, you know that?"

Slider shrugged.

"If Curt's the father, then you're saying he raped Grace? If that were true, then why wouldn't Grace tell Kaelin?"

"Because he didn't rape her."

Vinnie's hands flew up as he jumped off the bench. Ralph barked and ran from behind to jump on the bench next to Vinnie. Two heads stared at Slider.

"Good'un likes him."

"You mean Grace likes Curt?"

Slider nodded slowly, his catcher's call agreement for the next pitch.

"What?! I'll grant Curt's nice to Grace, but so what? He's nice so she has sex with him?"

"Sure does."

The conversation had become too illogical; Vinnie swung his arm in an arc. "Has Grace told you this?"

"Doesn't need to. She always stands close to Upper Deck, or by his side. She pecks his cheek every time they meet."

Shaking his head, Vinnie argued that this didn't prove any-thing. Ralph lost interest and returned to the grass. Vinnie thought the whole scene would make more sense if he joined Ralph. Vinnie had worried that Slider's long days alone provided too much time to ruminate on wild notions, and now his worry proved justified. Slider needed more structure. In the meantime, Vinnie needed to understand. "And Kaelin? Has she said any-thing?"

"Nada. She dislikes her old man too much to notice anything. She'un just want to create a family feud."

"Then you have nothing. I don't think what you say would hold up in court." Vinnie had had enough and walked home, accompanied by Slider's conjecture.

* * *

With Ben gone, Vinnie was left alone in the basement. He thought working out would distract him from Slider, but the first few curls of the twenty-five-pound dumbbells had him peering down the rack to the forties, Ben's warm-up weight. If Ben had stayed, weights would have been off both ends of the rack. Why had he raised his wish so soon? He should have waited until Ben's last day.

Now Vinnie was alone, lifting weights according to a training routine Ben had hand-tailored for him. Vinnie had told Ben he thought lifting weights wouldn't be a good idea—but he stopped short of calling it "stupid," which was what was on his mind. But Ben countered that working out would keep Vinnie off the streets, and help him to be both physically and mentally fit. And it would also protect him from gay-bashing bullies, which existed even in San Francisco. Slider's case proved Ben correct. And the training program had worked, the results noticeable after six months. A muscular Vinnie projected strength.

About the same time Ben boarded his flight, Vinnie finished pumping iron. He stared at the cornucopia inside the refrigerator, the stockpile bought for Ben. Even with a hard workout, Vinnie couldn't match Ben's caloric intake. Digesting a half chicken, two cups of rice, and a large protein shake, Vinnie had a thought.

* * *

"Hi Vinnie. What's up? Come in." Kaelin stepped behind the door and Vinnie entered.

"Thanks. I have extra food and thought you and Grace might be able to use some of it, with her eating for two. Ben's returned to New York early, leaving me too much." Vinnie held out a large shopping bag.

Kaelin looked inside as she walked to the kitchen. "Would you like something to eat or drink? Looks like I have a full pantry." Kaelin giggled.

"No thanks. I just finished lunch. I'm puttin' on a little weight."

"You're looking good, Vinnie. Real good." Kaelin put her hand around Vinnie's arm and he flexed. "Wow, that's impressive. Very hard."

Vinnie relaxed his arm. Was this some kind of trick? Seduce him into a momentary hetero lapse to have her revenge on Grace? Not him. He didn't move in and out of gayness like a commuter, and certainly not over somebody feeling his muscles. He wasn't Ben. "How are things with you and Grace? Is the baby okay? How is Grace feeling?"

"Nothing's changed. Grace won't confront the man. She's stubborn but maybe she's right."

With a look around, Vinnie stared at the bottled water. "Do you mind if I have a glass?"

"Of course not." Kaelin moved past the center island and brought Vinnie a glass and one for herself. Vinnie drank half too fast, causing water to dribble, and he wiped his chin with the back of his hand.

"How's Curt?"

"What?"

"Well, I wondered if you'd told him. I mean, this is his grand-child too."

"It is not his grandchild." Kaelin slammed her glass on the island's ceramic surface.

Vinnie's eyes widened. "Technically not, but I mean the baby will be part of the family."

"Our family, not his. Curt's not going to raise our child." Grace stared into Vinnie's eyes, her lips stuck to her teeth.

"Has he said as much?"

"No, just the opposite in fact. He's told Grace he'd like to help us out and she thinks it's a wonderful idea. I've told her not to trust him. He's unreliable. He left me and my mother for a bimbo." Her index finger thrust to an imaginary person. "But you know Grace, she thinks everyone is as good as her."

Vinnie wondered if Kaelin would have also added "faithful" before. He raised his water glass and emptied it. "Mind if I have a little more? Probably the workout."

Kaelin handed Vinnie his refill. "Is something wrong?"

"No, I'm just exhausted and with Ben leaving early I'm a little lost."

Vinnie felt dejected; he had learned little, and only confirmed Kaelin's distrust of her father. Vinnie pondered a new approach. Maybe he should follow Slider's lead and observe how Grace behaved with Curt.

Chapter 7

Something Stirred

Depression arrived after dinner, as Vinnie knew it would—he had felt the onset during his afternoon workout. The weightlifting failed. He remained preoccupied with Ben's abrupt departure and Slider's ridiculous notion. Why had he bothered to lift at all? He only did it to please Ben. The entire weight training had been Ben's idea. Stupid. Who cares about flexing and hard bodies? *I do more for our relationship than he does.*

As he washed his dishes, Vinnie carried on a conversation with himself, a revival of his solitary teenage coping mechanism. "You're being fuckin' stupid," he said with his normal voice.

Vinnie's double replied in higher pitch. "No I'm not. I do everything."

The lower octave voice answered, "Bullshit. Look at how much Ben's given you. He saved your life. And don't say the sex isn't worth it, because it is."

Vinnie stopped talking. He looked out the window to spy his neighbor's living room, a clear view since a mere twenty feet separated the two houses. Grace's silhouette patted a beach-ball belly. Vinnie imagined he could stretch his arm and join in.

The round, perfect belly fascinated him. He imagined the baby sucking its thumb. He thought about the infant's future. The baby cries that would be soothed by cooing. Fingers pointing and silly words spoken with the infant's first picture book.

Bedtime reading to the small child—*Goodnight Moon; Frog and Toad; The Polar Express*. Vinnie cried as he imagined the future child's laughter.

* * *

The familiar ringtone came at eleven o'clock eastern time. Ben's thumbprint answered his smartphone.

"Hi."

"Is this too late? Can we talk? I need to talk."

A short silence followed from the long-distance relay delay.

"Oh, Vinnie. I miss you. I'm so sorry. I shouldn't have left like I did. I love you."

More delay but not caused by satellite transmission. Soft crying echoed on both ends of the line.

"Me too. I love you. I'm so sorry we fought. I wish you were here or I was there." Vinnie choked on his words.

"You will be. It's only a few months to July. I can grab a flight tomorrow. The contest is in three weeks and I'll find someone to take over for the guy I'm training."

"No, that's unfair. You need to stay. Go to the contest." Vinnie rubbed his eyes as he spoke.

"You're right. He shouldn't suffer for my idiotic behavior. As soon as it's over I'll return."

"I love to hear your voice. Talk to me. Tell me what you plan to do to me."

Phone sex wasn't Ben's thing, but Vinnie's exile meant it was unavoidable. He wasn't as good as Vinnie. Skype's visual helped but not much. Ben thought Vinnie's voice on speakerphone made him sound tinny. Ben never mastered a headset, like Vinnie. He felt stupid wearing it during sex.

The sexual release came after their crying had stopped. Ben laughed with Vinnie's smart-mouth comments after they had climaxed. "Pay-as-you-go would be cheaper if you climax that fast. I didn't have time to use my vibrator, and a middle finger fuck hardly merits being gay."

Ben had no retort and allowed Vinnie to pretend he was releasing himself a second time. "Oh yeah, now I'm there. Mind if I put you on hold while I call a cleanup service? I'm flooded in white gunk. Good thing I took swimming lessons."

Vinnie's tone turned serious. "I wish you were here."

"Me too. This sucks. I'm sorry, it's all my fault. But at least we got off."

A grunt came down the line. "You call this getting off? It's nothing like last night. Forget ATT, Verizon, and T-Mobile." Ben doubled over, his laughter more from emotion than humor.

Vinnie stood to wipe himself and caught sight of his neighbor's house. "I saw Kaelin today. She's definitely excluding her father from the baby's life. I don't think she trusts Curt."

"Neither do I... uh, and about the baby."

The silence lasted longer than any satellite relay delay. Ben changed the subject and mumbled the details of his return. His business class upgrade to get on to a full flight. The long security line.

Vinnie drummed his fingers, thinking *Who fuckin' cares about his trip or how much he paid for a ticket?*

With no response from Vinnie, Ben continued to explain about the solicitous flight attendant in business class. The way she handed him his orange juice and water, then brushed his arm, saying her husband was a weightlifter. Vinnie yawned loud enough for Ben to hear.

"Stay awake. This is important. She squeezed my bicep and said, 'I'll bet you swing your kids around for fun, like my husband. The kids love it.'"

Vinnie held his breadth. *Kids.*

"Uh... well, maybe I was too hasty. Maybe there's a possibility."

The shrill scream pierced Ben's ear.

"You okay, Vinnie?"

"I'm fuckin' great... do you mean it?!"

"Yes, but keep calm. I've been thinking about how it would work, like where does the baby come from."

"Well, a stork flies around looking for good homes to leave babies." Vinnie was laughing as he spoke.

"Very funny. I mean, since you said surrogate rather than adoption, I assume you want one of us to be the donor. But who's the mother?"

A small hiccup preceded Vinnie's rattled thoughts. "There are agencies. Or we find someone among our lesbian friends. There's lots of ways."

"I have a suggestion." Ben paused. The super masculine, alpha male couldn't speak. He hadn't been this tentative since he had asked Vinnie to be his boyfriend.

"Uh-huh?"

"What if we ask Ginny?"

"Are you crazy! Ginny? That's sick!"

"Wait, think about it. We'd know the mother's healthy. And the child would have a connection to its biological mother."

A long silence followed.

"Hello? Vinnie? You there?"

A hushed voice came out, almost as if Vinnie had a hand over his mouth. "And the father?"

"That's tricky. My feeling is that if—and it's a big if—*if* Ginny agrees, and don't forget Dan, then she'll want it to be me."

"You? What's wrong with me?"

"Nothing. But as Ginny's long-time friend and trainer, I know her. She'll want a special connection, which I have with her. You know about Ginny's sthenolagnia, right? Well, that's the connection and also how we convince her."

Throughout the entire flight and his short workout after arrival, Ben's mind had ruminated. Now he had to explain. He took a deep breath. "I know you would have liked it to be you, but I know Ginny."

...

"Vinnie? You there?"

40

...

"Vinnie?"

"And what about you? How will you react, psychologically?"

Ben didn't know how to answer Vinnie so he said, "Honestly, I don't know." How could he explain his mixed feelings and apprehension? The flight attendant's words reminded him how he missed having his son to toss around and love. Another baby wouldn't be Carl, but just the thought gave him solace. And he'd never forget Carl. This might even help keep Carl close.

In the pause, Ben felt his chest tighten, like the feeling he would get moments before stepping onstage, wishing he had worked harder. "Right now, I think it'll help."

Ben hated not being able to explain himself. He took pride in his clear explanations as a trainer. "Maybe it could make me feel I've done right by Carl. A second chance to prove to myself that I can be a good father. That I'm not a bad person."

Looking away from the cell phone as if Vinnie could see him, Ben grabbed his head. He couldn't stop himself and he knew it. He'd have to tell him. "Vinnie, if I'm fully honest, I want the love and joy only a child gives. I loved Carl so much."

Ben's cry reached San Francisco in seconds. His teeth ground together as he inhaled his voice. "This might be good—but only with Ginny as surrogate." The next pause became a short break. Neither hung up nor spoke.

The silence broke with Ben outlining a strategy to convince Ginny. They'd have to get into Ginny's head—use a psychological approach. And that meant manipulating Ginny's sthenolagnia, but how that could happen he wasn't sure.

"Sounds like voodoo," said Vinnie, which helped Ben to smile until Vinnie added, "And voodoo has risks."

Ben suggested he plan a special show. Vinnie said he'd work out harder. "I'll do a pre-show first, then you'll be the big-gun main attraction." Vinnie laughed at the double meaning of his word.

"Good. You may be small, but Ginny will admire your great proportions."

"Hey, who you calling small? Just today Kaelin said my biceps were hard as rocks."

Vinnie's silence told Ben that something was up. Ben reached for the phone but stopped. The Kaelin and Grace issue could wait.

They talked about the risks of a complete relapse of Ginny's obsession. Then came the second obstacle. Dan. Vinnie said he'd work on that—just like Ben's special connection to Ginny, Vinnie had his to Dan.

The next question Vinnie whispered. "What's Plan B if Ginny refuses?"

Silence was Ben's response.

Chapter 8

Gotta Go

The street lamps supplemented the house's automatic outdoor light that triggered as Slider approached. The extra light helped Slider to locate the hidden key compartment behind the garbage shed, not that he needed to see it. He'd done this so many times he could have found the key box blindfolded. For that matter, any amateur thief could locate the key, a place 95 percent of all homeowners hid their spares.

Vinnie worried about Slider and his antisocial behavior, as defined by ranting right-wing radio commentators. That's when the idea came for the hidden key to the basement bathroom facilities. Over time, the basement accumulated kitchen appliances: refrigerator, microwave, hot plate, coffee maker. A den-like space evolved with the addition of a small pull-out couch and flat-screen TV, cable connected. Slider had an indoor home within a few months of Vinnie's move to San Francisco. Still, Slider used it sporadically, other than the toilet and refrigerator. Ben didn't object, as long as nothing impinged on the workout area.

Tonight, Slider had a "cellulose obligation," one more area where he and Vinnie had similar values. "Slider, always care for your tush and you'll do yourself a big favor."

Cellulose aside, this was Slider's special night for two reasons. First, Vinnie's monthly routine of replenishing the bathroom reading material with new editions of *GQ, Flex, Sports Illustrated,* and a selection of men's porno magazines, plus Internet photos Vinnie hand-picked to match Slider's proclivity. Slider would do more than satisfy his cellulose need, and he would need extra time in the basement bathroom.

Slider wasn't alone. He had Ralph, extended dog-sitting since Professors Books and Ivy were at a weeklong conference in Hawaii. The professors had offered Slider their home, but he said he preferred Vinnie's—to make it a "boys' outing for me and Ralph."

Closing the bathroom door, both missions accomplished, Slider turned off the lights to the renovated basement. He had been duplicitous with Ralph's owners—he considered forty-five minutes inside met his indoor obligation. But he didn't plan on spending the night there, not when he and Ralph had a perfectly good bench in the park. If the temperature dropped or if it rained, he would return to the basement, otherwise some busybody, worried for the homeless man's safety, would call the police. Slider had been dragged too many times to a shelter, and twice to a local precinct holding cell when he had protested. Better to accept Vinnie's luxury basement on bad-weather nights, and even more with Ralph in his care. Luckily, the weather held.

In the dark, Slider moved like he had just retired the opposing team side as he mounted the five half-step basement stairs to reach the side-door exit. Tucked under his arm like a pitching glove was an unfinished magazine. He had lingered over Vinnie's glossy, high-quality, full-color Internet photos of two hunky men with more limbs than seemed possible that they had inserted into more orifices then Slider could count: a real turn-on.

Ready to exit, he stretched to turn the lock and doorknob simultaneously, and the magazine dropped to the bottom of the staircase. Walking backward and bending, Slider saw two pairs of legs through the narrow casement window. He recognized both from their footwear, and was surprised they were on Vinnie's property. Every word carried in the crisp night air.

"Come on Grace, telling Kaelin wouldn't do any good. You'll just upset her. She doesn't need to know. You'll be upset, too. And me. We know the truth, and that's all that matters. I told you I'll take care of the baby. We'll find a way to do it without Kaelin finding out I'm helping."

Voice recognition confirmed Slider's initial ID. Although softer, he heard every word of Good'un's response to Upper Deck.

"It's not fair to Kaelin. I feel bad enough that I've kept this from her. She'll hate me, I know it. But she has a right to know. She and I have based our relationship on honesty. I think we should do the same."

"If you had so much honesty, then why'd you fuck me?"

"I didn't. You fucked me. You took advantage of my being drunk."

"You could have said no and I would have stopped. You didn't. And as I recall, you didn't complain the next two times either, when you weren't drunk."

"Don't remind me. This whole thing has been a mistake. I was curious and exploring. It meant nothing."

"That bubble belly says otherwise."

Grace felt her abdomen. "I'm telling Kaelin. I've made up my mind. I only wanted to let you know ahead of time and in person."

"You tell her and you'll be out on the street, if not by Kaelin, then by me. I'll raise the rent so neither of you can afford to stay. It has taken me a long time to have any communication with my daughter. And I might lose contact with my first daughter, but you can't prevent me from being part of this baby's life. I can have legal visiting rights. Think about it. You don't want to go down that route."

Stepping back from the window, Slider covered his mouth. He looked down at his magazine and wished he had taken time for another round with Vinnie's photos. He didn't want to hear this. This would set him back, no matter how much medication he took. Slider emitted a nervous laugh, causing Ralph to give a short bark. "Shh. Quiet, Ralph. No barking."

"What was that?" said Curt.

"What?"

"That noise. Didn't you hear it?"

"All I heard was you threaten me and Kaelin. You're disgusting. I wish so much that this wasn't your baby."

Slider knelt and held Ralph. He'd been heard, or Ralph had. Slider's hand covered his grinning mouth. He waited until Grace and Curt walked past the window before he made his exit with Ralph, the magazine stuffed into his back pocket.

Standing in the small grassy lot kitty-corner from the home occupied by the two women, the skulking figure brooded. He waited until the front door opened and a brief burst of hallway light illuminated Grace as she entered. He remained lurking, his patience rewarded as a hooded man limped along the path of the bodybuilder's house, now rented by the gay New Yorker. He tracked like a nighthawk pursuing a field mouse, careful to stay covered by tree limb shadows cast by street lamps. The stalker approached the park's iron fence just as the hooded man and dog strolled through the entry gate that confirmed their identity. He glared as they settled on a rear bench secluded by large bushes, not their usual location.

Chapter 9

Plans Change

Vinnie's original two-year exile had seemed a long time, and now it was three years later. He thought the time had flown at about the speed of him in the window seat of the Boeing 757. For two months his anxiety had mounted. Why? He loved New York—bagels with attitude, pizza without smiles, and people that walked like they meant it. He hated the West Coast swishy, take-your-fuckin'-time-to-walk-a-block mentality. He had felt an outsider in San Francisco, even three years later. He had grumbled to Slider. "They call this place a fuckin' city? We have burbs outside the City that stay open later." Slider queried Vinnie's use of "City," so Vinnie explained that he meant Manhattan—the only real city in the USA. Slider replied, "Houston's a city," and Vinnie deferred further debate on urban centers and suggested they discuss religion.

Homesickness had stuck to Vinnie like his accent; he couldn't discard either. He had missed his friends. Ben, of course. Dan and Ginny, for sure. His friends at Del Vecchio & Neale. Not to mention his mom and her *spaghetti alle vongole*. He had missed not being able to see his godson Anthony grow; their last time together, and indeed their only time, had been when Anthony was just six months old. Dan and Ginny had made a visit to California, and even that had been at one of Ben's bodybuilder friends' Venice beach house to maintain the secrecy of Vinnie's

San Francisco location.

His exile was over, but not his anxiety. Vinnie knew why. His every move and interaction with Anthony would be a test, an evaluation of how he behaved with a child. Ben would be observing. Ginny, too, as a mother, and later she would recall his every interaction.

Vinnie had been lonely in San Francisco. Ben had stayed in New York to keep up appearances and manage his UltraFit Gym health club; to create a barrier between him and Vinnie's real location. His California trips, more than any other state, could easily be explained. Ben's competitive bodybuilding obligations were focused in California—organizing committees, advertisement photo shoots, sponsor promotions, and fitness magazine interviews, the majority Californian-based.

For every trumped-up excuse Vinnie spat out a small laugh. "Just say you have a fuckin' California boyfriend. Who'd guess it was me? Unless there is someone else—in which case I'll fuckin' strangle you." Vinnie's two hands had stretched around Ben's neck as if choking a twenty-one-inch tree, and Ben's lips had pursed, "Owwwww."

Vinnie loved Ben's puckered lips better than the pumped-up brawn, so he had shifted from choking to smothering, sealing his lips to Ben in hopes of an oxygen-deprived fantasy climax. At the end of each visit, Vinnie was cloaked in loneliness and endured bouts of homesickness.

Prudence was invoked before Vinnie's return, a delay to his New York homecoming. Both he and Ben felt the mob's pronouncement might well be tantamount to buying the Brooklyn Bridge. This delay reaped an unanticipated benefit—Ginny invited Ben and Vinnie to a summer's shebang on Martha's Vineyard for Anthony's third birthday, and to celebrate Vinnie's return. Vinnie cheered as Ben explained, in his posing suit, how he could use the hot summer beach to provide Ginny with a full-on muscle display without appearing contrived. Vinnie imitated bodybuilder poses, but recognized Ben's strained, fake smile. *Damn, I'm so fuckin' inconsiderate.* Vinnie knew Ben's sensitivity to bodybuilding mockery.

"Sorry. I'll use the extra time to build myself up and look like a Greek god."

Ben said he doubted the possibility, but agreed to revise Vinnie's training routine and increased his caloric intake.

"No way! I'll look like a blimp and spend all day eating. Is this to keep me housebound?"

Ben lost his smile. "Do you want a baby?"

Vinnie's reply was a grin. "Hey, let's make a new UltraFit poster." Vinnie mimicked writing on a page as he spoke: "Want a baby? Try UltraFit. Workout. Pump Iron. Eat a horse."

Ben gave a short snort, not exactly a laugh but enough to let Vinnie know he'd forgotten the minor slight from earlier. Vinnie promised he'd pump twenty-four-seven and eat everything on his plate.

"Just stick to the routine," Ben said with a flat voice as he raised his eyebrows.

Vinnie made his eastbound reservation six weeks in advance, which didn't resemble anything like his westbound journey three years before. That journey had been arranged in twenty-four hours from the mob's "get out of Dodge" advice.

He had high hopes to leave San Francisco within a month, right after he heard about Bill Barrington's prison "suicide." The mob had other ideas, wanting confirmation that the DA's office would drop all investigations into Carmine Aquafreddo as Barrington's co-conspirator to commit murder, a police officer murder, accessory to murders, and racketeering. "Bullshit," Vinnie said. "Anyone who watches *Law and Order* knows my testimony's bupkis without Bill." The DA knew, but Carmine—Cooler—took two years and nine months to be convinced.

What had galled Vinnie, more than his exile, was that he had accepted help from his father. Vinnie had confided in Slider, including his father's neighborhood nickname, Big John, due to his size. Slider said it didn't fit, not after Ben. "I'd have called him Disgrace. What kind of father kicks their son out of the house because he's gay?"

Vinnie pointed out to Slider that he had been disowned by his own father for the same reason.

"Seeing how Texans' and New Yorkers' daddies have a lot in common but y'alls came first, we best be goin' with Disgrace Uno and Disgrace Dos… better still, DU and D2."

Dan had attempted to broker a reconciliation of Vinnie with his father. He pointed out that both he and Vinnie owed their lives to Big John and Jack, Vinnie's older brother. Vinnie relented with his father, encouraged by his mother and Ben's opinions. As for his brother, Vinnie huffed.

* * *

The Kennedy runway approached fast, and Vinnie stepped on an imaginary brake under the seat in front. He twirled his still unfamiliar wedding ring, which he had worn infrequently in San Francisco to keep his identity secret. His stomach clenched as the plane descended, like it had on his wedding day. He and Ben had argued over nothing only hours before their allotted slot at the San Francisco registrar's office. Then the tires hit the ground, jolting Vinnie's memory like the pothole hit by the taxi to City Hall. Slider had turned from the front seat to check on him and Ben. "Gong and Chime going to the chapel lookin' like they're bottom of the league. Y'all need a change-up, now, ya hear!"

Vinnie sat on the plane, even after the fasten seat belt light went off. Ben's marriage proposal had been sudden, and not romantic. Vinnie wanted romance more than a wedding ring. Ben's proposal, six months into Vinnie's exile, was almost businesslike. He cited civil rights should anything happen to Vinnie in California or to him in New York. Neither predicted a future Supreme Court extending the rights across the US, which would have made Vinnie see the proposal as even more pragmatic and less romantic.

Ben's wedding gift was the San Francisco house. Vinnie had protested, then graciously accepted when gripped by Ben's near lung-crushing WWF wrestler's hold. San Francisco would be their getaway home, and Ben's condo in New York their permanent address.

And Vinnie sat, ready to disembark, as planned. *I should've told Ben. Pretty fuckin' stupid. Now what do I do?*

Vinnie's first change had been to delay his return. "Could be a trick by Carmine. Let's wait to see if my father hears any rumors." Vinnie used an entire weekend to convince Ben his concern wasn't cold feet on his part about living together.

The original May 1st return had one appeal for Vinnie: his joy at seeing Central Park's spring bloom, and the return of song-birds. He told Ben it would be like him, which Ben thought a non-sense metaphor.

Ginny's proposal for a summer celebration around Anthony's birthday caused Vinnie to burst. "Yes." He stuck out his tongue at Ben, saying, "Got a July Fourth metaphor for yourself—big bang?"

Ben argued over waiting two months. "Why the end of June and not the last week in May?"

Vinnie grinned throughout his convoluted excuse. He should have told Ben, but feared his angry response; telling him to not to interfere with Grace and Kaelin, to forget Slider's speculation over Curt.

Vinnie disembarked at JFK on the last day of June.

Walking the long terminal alley to baggage claim, Vinnie worried. *Was Big Sal at the luggage area? And what did Carmine mean by "Sicilian olive oil prices are better than Californian?"* Vinnie carried two fifty-five-pound suitcases with his carry-on bag slung over his shoulder. When he left New York he had a single carry-on.

He easily spotted Ben waving his arms, bigger than the shuttle bus behind him.

* * *

Vinnie had returned home.

A subway ride to Queens to visit his mother, followed by the return to Manhattan to DV&N headquarters to meet former co-workers and friends. Everyone had been impressed. "Vinnie, you look fantastic!" "Have you been working out?" People grabbed his arm and Vinnie flexed, smiling as their jaws dropped. He took it all in; he loved the praise. By the week's end he and Ben were prepared for their month on Martha's Vineyard.

Vinnie waited until the last day before the start of the holiday to tell Ben about his revised plan. He braced for his negative reaction. *I hope this doesn't fuckin' change everything. Better to tell him now than wait until we're on the island.*

At their kitchen table, Vinnie's voice quivered. "Honey, I have something to tell you and you're not going to like it."

Screw that, thought Vinnie, *who wants to hear they're not going to like what they are about to hear? I've fuckin' screwed this up already.* Vinnie saw Ben's face contort. "I'm going back to San Francisco from Martha's Vineyard."

Vinnie flinched as Ben rose, not a volcanic explosion but controlled anger. Ben's forearms piled his fists into the granite tabletop. Vinnie recognized Ben's methodical waddle-walk, legs spread by muscles too big for their bones. Vinnie knew. Ben was headed to UltraFit to crush iron into dust.

Vinnie cried in bed, laying on his side, making no attempt to sleep. He didn't know why he felt compelled to help Grace—he and Ben would have their own family.

In the dark, Ben's hot lava chest molded into Vinnie's back. Vinnie pushed his ass into Ben's crotch, an act of asking for forgiveness. He opened his legs, hoping Ben would pump into his cavity, hoping that desire might vanquish anger.

With a slow turn so as to not upset the equilibrium, Vinnie faced Ben. He needed this, his face crushed into Ben's chest. It was Ben's turn to spread his legs, allowing Vinnie to slide under. Vinnie willed himself to disappear inside Ben.

"I get it, but I don't like it. You need to do this. Just be careful."

Shocked by the words, Vinnie stretched his neck to look at Ben's face. "Why?"

"If this is going to work between us, then we can't control each other. We'll both do things the other doesn't like, but we have to accept we're different. Otherwise we lose our identity, and I married you for who you are."

And Ben proved his acceptance with grunts as he lifted Vinnie overhead like a light barbell; Vinnie took in his overhead view of the sweat-stained sheets, twirled his ring, and thought Ben's action the most unromantic romantic act he had known.

* * *

They stood on the top deck, with their luggage, logic, and muscles. From the boat deck Vinnie spied Martha's Vineyard and said to nobody in particular, "It all comes down to a wing and a fuckin' prayer, doesn't it?"

Chapter 10

Happened at Night

Walking around the park in the cool evening summer air, Slider believed the fog had descended on him and no one else. His companionship was gone the moment he had handed Ralph's leash to Ivy and Books. Slider acted as if the professors' return was happenstance more than a planned itinerary, a conspiracy with the weather directed against him. Ralph's week with Slider provided a strict routine for the entire day. Slider roamed the park, and moved away from the bench he used as a bed to cross the street to enter Vinnie's home. He convinced himself this was a favor to Vinnie, checking the unoccupied house on a dark, foggy night. Slider considered himself superior to Vinnie's installation of automatic light timers and state-of-the-art anti-burglary devices. *I'd totaled forty pickoffs in my career. How many burglar alarms could match that for thievery?* Slider's meds were wearing off.

Puffed by pride and with nothing else to do, Slider conducted a house safety check. Climbing the basement stairs, he entered the first floor, territory he had seen no more than six or seven times. He walked the space, touching furniture until he reached the kitchen refrigerator. "Looks like Chime keeps a hygienic ice box," muttered Slider to the back wall, fingering the few condiments in the door shelf.

At the front door mailbox Slider paused. Vinnie had placed mail on hold, so Slider gathered the items that were unstoppable: advertisements, flyers, and circulars, with some addressed to the deceased former owner, Davis McGregor III. Slider's eyes squinted. *Y'all mighta passed, but y'all still get mail.*

Entering the upstairs master bedroom, completely unknown territory, Slider walked to the window that faced the adjacent house. Grace stood in the downstairs living room window, peering out. Minutes later Slider pressed her doorbell.

"Uh, hi, Slider. What's up?" Grace's flat monotone dribbled out the opened door.

"Y'all gotta a minute? Something's buzzing my mind."

"Sure... come in."

"Plum here?"

"No, she's at an emergency delivery, which means she'll be gone a long time. You know Kaelin, she'll stay until both mother and child are settled."

Slider surveyed the living room, a place he'd seen twice passing through to the kitchen, but never to sit. Grace pointed to a two-seater divan.

"Want something to drink? Eat?"

"Nah, I'm at Chime's and he provisioned his fridge pretty darn good before heading to the Big Apple. I have his cell if I needs an online restock."

"I heard. What a surprise, too. I never knew Vinnie had been hiding out. Did you know?"

Slider glanced around the room for a long time. *Of course, I gone done figured it out on day one. A fella arrives out of nowhere, lives in a rich man's ranch, says stuff about Gong youse could only knows by being real close like. Then the fella spouts a BS working home yarn, and never takes hisself out... business sorts all needs road trips. I knows a bunch more, like the wedding, but I ain't tellin' shit till I know youse on the up and up.* Slider looked down to his feet, the entire conversation in his head.

"I've something to ask you. It's a little bit... uh... uh... shall we say delicate? Mmm hmm, delicate."

"Oh?"

"You see, last week I happens to hears youse with Upper Deck outside Chime's place. I was in the basement, doing... doing my stuff. I had Ralph with me. Anyways, I gone hear things that make no sense."

"You should stop now. That was a private conversation and it doesn't concern you."

Slider's head moved muppet-like, side to side. His grin lasted a few seconds. "That might as be, but I heard so I can't unhear."

"And what exactly did you hear?" Grace's arms braided as she moved them tight across her chest.

"I heard Upper Deck's the baby's daddy. I heard his threat. You ought go on tell Plum. Did Upper Deck violate you?"

Unfolding her arms, Grace rose from the couch. "It's none of your goddamn business. You should leave. And keep your nose out of my life. And Grace's. And Curt's!"

Slider felt his jaw drop, expecting it to hit the floor.

"Hey, Good'un!" Slider paused—it was a name he thought no longer fit—"I'm just saying, if y'all need help, I'm here. But I'm counseling you to tell Plum her father done raped you."

Grace sat down on the edge of the divan, her tears gushing. "He didn't rape me."

Slider sank back into the seat cushion as if it were quicksand. He wanted to put his hands over his ears and hum loudly. He wanted to walk backward to the front door and to the park bench. *Why couldn't things be undone? Unhear things none all his concern. Unannounce he was gay? Unleave Texas?*

"I'm not sure, but I felt something for him. I didn't know what I was doing." Grace sobbed, her fingers brushing aside tears. "I don't know what I want anymore."

Grace wiped each eye with a slow stoke. "I know I should tell Kaelin, but I'm afraid she'll get angry and leave me. I don't want to hurt her. Curt doesn't want me, not like I thought... I thought he loved me, but I'm not sure anymore. Maybe he used me, just like Kaelin says he does. I thought it was different with me. I'm confused about my sexuality, if I'm honest." Grace buried her face in her hands, her voice muffled.

This here's all wrong, thought Slider. *Not my doin's. Gone and done bad. Goin'a be messed up.* With short, slow steps Slider reached the front door. Looking back into the living room, he called out, "Tell Plum, she'll figure it out." He went out the door then returned before it had closed, and yelled, "I'll fix it with Upper Deck, y'all leave it to me."

* * *

The cell phone message was unclear. Not the sound or caller, only the message.

"Chime, y'all call me, ya hear. We need to jaw. Upper Deck planted in the garden and won't water the flower bed. Good'un needs advice on turning over the soil. Loads of junk flyers messing your front hallway, but I stored them on your kitchen table. Ralph's gone homestead."

After listening three times, Vinnie handed Ben the phone, but he had even less of an idea on how to decipher Slider's message.

"Sounds like a problem. I'll call." Vinnie saw Ben's grip tighten around the cell phone, about to pulverize it. He stroked Ben's forearm, tendons ridging the skin.

"Don't you think maybe Slider's off his meds? If you call, you'll change our plans. Leave it. No more listening to messages until after Anthony's party. This is our time. The perfect opportunity, if you're serious about what you want from Ginny."

Ben dropped the phone into Vinnie's open palm. Vinnie looked and turned it off. He knew Ben was right. Slider needed to take his fuckin' medication.

Both men finished packing, Vinnie's suitcases twice the size and weight of Ben's.

* * *

Ben had been thrilled to learn the summerhouse adjacent to Ginny's parents was available. He only wished his rent offer had been accepted.

Doctors Anna and James Swinburne had met Veronica and Harold on their first trip to Martha's Vineyard, predating the birth of both couples' children. Veronica had alerted Anna to the sale of the adjacent property, Barrow Cottage, which quickly became the Swinburne summer residence.

Barrow Cottage sat on a half-acre of land, stretching across a secluded spit of sandy beach shared with Veronica and Harold. Rachel and Ginny spent every summer of their youth at the cottage, with invited friends. Rachel had her share of wild teenage boyfriends, which Anna accepted and carefully controlled. But Ginny was persuaded not to invite boys on medical grounds—any boy faced with her in a dawn-to-dusk bikini of minimalist design would indulge in excess masturbation. Anna didn't know how she would explain a boy's penis skin infection to the parents. Ginny acted angrily at her mother's absurd logic, but was secretly pleased. A guest boyfriend would handicap her culling the island's summer stock of buff lifeguards.

A 1920s design, the original Barrow Cottage had been the quintessential summer beach cottage. Over the years, expansion resulted in three en suite bedrooms, a kitchen addition with a central granite six-burner stove, a two-car garage, a family room of a thousand square feet, a living room of fifteen-hundred square feet, and a study over the garage large enough for both Swinburne doctors. Barrow Cottage was anything but a summerhouse despite Anna's insistence.

Within minutes of learning that Anthony's godparents planned to stay an entire month, Anna called Veronica. "Are you and Harold still planning to be away this summer? Ginny's friends would like to rent your house for the whole of July. Is twenty thousand the going rate these days? Would you and Harold agree to rent to them?"

"Out of the question," said Veronica, and nearly caused Anna to drop the phone. Then she heard Veronica's deep-throated laughing. "It's free. We'd be so happy to help Ginny's friends."

Anna's delight over her friend's generosity dissipated in her return call to inform Ginny. "There's no need," Anna said on hearing Ginny announce she, Dan, and Anthony would also stay at Veronica's home. "Of course the men needed their own place, and Barrow Cottage would be cramped with them. But no problem for you, Dan, Anthony, Rachel, and her partner Ted."

"No, mother, we want to spend alone time with Vinnie and Ben. We want this and them too."

Ginny didn't mention Dan's refusal to spend a month cohabiting with his mother-in-law. A weekend was too long. Anna somehow always managed an "open" discussion of his sexual issues.

Anna agreed on condition that her grandson spend a few nights each week at Barrow Cottage. "After all, dear, won't that provide you and your gay couple more alone time? And isn't Ben the bodybuilder? Won't that be nice for you?"

Ginny restrained cursing at her mother, but yelled, "YES, MOTHER, it will be nice, very *exotic*."

Finishing the call, Ginny muttered to herself. *I'm like her. I made no sense. Why do I let my mother goad me? What possible exotic activity could a gay couple and a straight couple do? Especially when Dan's involved. He's done all the experimenting he's ever going to do.*

Ginny hand covered her face, laughing out loud recalling Dan's one-time unplanned experiment with Ben. No, nothing exotic.

Chapter 11

Ferry in Port

The two men had dressed for the worst summer heat wave on record. Ginny had warned them—authentic Martha's Vineyard summerhouses didn't have air conditioning. Only year-round resident islanders had AC: garage mechanics, plumbers, carpenters. And, of course, the nouveau riche, whose very survival depended on an ostentatious lifestyle. Ginny's parents, and their neighbors Harold and Veronica, were old-school. Ginny had summarized for Ben her mother's no AC rationale: "Why come to an island retreat to stay indoors? The whole point is to cool down at the beach. Besides, no heat wave lasts more than three or four days."

Along with a thousand-plus people on the Woods Hole ferry, a combination of foot passengers and those traveling in cars and campers, Ben and Vinnie's disembarkation took time. They strolled to one side of a pseudo gangplank with cars passing on the ramp. People stared, as Ben knew they would. He overheard a boy behind say, "Del, look at the muscles on that dude!" His friend answered, "I'll bet he's a bodybuilder." *Got that right*, thought Ben.

How could they not? He arrived in Santa Monica muscleman attire. His shorts cut up to his ass exposing redwood tree legs; his tank top's slim straps crossed over trapezii that touched his ears. His deltoids prepared for take-off. Vinnie had admonished Ben over the overexposed pecs: "You look like a two-bit hooker."

Ben ported two large suitcases like children's lunch boxes, swinging with his gait. The suitcase trolley wheels were as good as new. His triceps rippled with each sway. Ben raised his arms overhead to attract Ginny's attention, swelling his biceps, and giving the impression he had beach balls tucked under his arms.

"Del, look at those biceps!"

"Oh my God, Jordan, they're huge!"

If Del and Jordan had made Ben smile, his cheeks nearly cracked on seeing Ginny wave and her jaw drop. Seconds later, Dan's jaw joined Ginny's on the pavement. *A good start*, Ben thought.

Ben had stopped training Ginny for a few months, making an excuse, with some truth, about needing to concentrate on his upcoming competition. She had not seen him bulk up. For the last five weeks he had been in full prep mode, and he had arrived ripped. His new peak was unlike any time before, and he knew it. He had studied every surface ripple on his body in front of double mirrors; he had flexed and posed; he had adjusted lighting and changed his poser suits, and posed nude. To win a trophy he had to see what the judges would see and more. He was on first-name terms with his every muscle fiber.

If Ben anticipated the Livornos' awe for him, he could not have predicted their reaction to Vinnie as he emerged into view. Ben heard Ginny's yell: "Dan, is that Vinnie? Look at him!" She stared at the muscular dude with a pumpkin grin disembarking from the ferry.

"Uh, I think so," said Dan, tilting forward.

Vinnie's biceps swelled as his arms tightened, as much from anxiety as for show. Vinnie dressed with style, with only one concession: a body-fitted T-shirt that combined cotton with synthetic stretch. The elastic swelled with each arm movement. Vinnie had no conceit. "I'm not your size, Ben, but I'm no longer the wafer-thin pretzel of three years ago. Anyway, nothing looks good on someone as big as you." Vinnie came with one purpose only: to create a vision of strength and fashion for Ginny.

Ginny's hands clasped in front, her eyes focused on Vinnie as he walked across the tarmac. He looked at Ben and mouthed, "I was right." Hours before, dressing in their New York condo, Vinnie had predicted Ginny's reaction. "She'll take more notice of my trim masculinity and grace than your airbag muscles." Her expression proved his point.

Vinnie stopped and released the handles of his rolling suit-cases. The sun glinted off his soft blue shirt, his slightly fog-white shorts with contrasting blue border trim matching his top. He completed the look with blue canvas sneakers, sans socks. Ginny called out, "Hey, someone stuffed footballs into your calves!" Vinnie preened, running one hand through his hair, forcing his T-shirt to tighten, clinging to reveal his cascading steppe-muscled abdomen.

With two feet separating the couples, Ben dropped his luggage and marched over to Ginny. He picked her up, threw her into the air, and caught her on the descent. Before placing her on the ground, he kissed her cheek. Ben paused as he had rehearsed. With one foot behind, his teeth gritted, he flashed a double-bicep flex. Ginny yelped and clapped her hands. *Yes*, thought Ben.

Del added to his comment: "Jordan, look at the size of those fucking biceps!" Ben heard a hand connect to the back of Del's head and words that told of consequences to Del for such language. *Ah, someone's in trouble.* Ben faced Del, bent to one knee, tilted his head, and flexed an arm. He created a mountain that in another year would give the young man an erection. He shook his index finger at Del, and skimmed his bicep's vein, pressing on the top peak. Del's mother gasped. *I'll bet her tight vagina's wet now. Maybe she'll give Del a pass on being grounded.* Del's teeth glistened as he gave Ben a thumbs-up in solidarity. For an instant a shadow crossed Ben's face. Carl would have been about the same age as the youngster. *Maybe I could make a good father after all.*

Ben rose and Ginny kissed both his cheeks, continental style, and copped a feel of his arm. Ben's weak smile hid his guilt for his deceit.

Ignoring Ben's show, Vinnie had embraced Dan with a bear hug that did not stifle his friend's soft sobs. "I've missed you so much, Dan. I can't believe it's been two years. Fuckin' A, you're still gorgeous."

Of all Vinnie's expectations, he could not have predicted stoic Dan Livorno to have moist eyes. Dan sputtered as if he had sand in his mouth. Vinnie remembered only one occasion that words had failed Dan, a time Vinnie had hoped to forget. This was a moment he hoped to remember.

A squeal broke them apart. Dan turned to see Ginny holding Ben's arms. He knew this had nothing to do with Ben's hard body, because Ginny didn't squeal over muscle.

"Look at them. You'd think they were all alone," said Ginny with her million-dollar smile as she walked to Vinnie. "Look at you! What did you stuff into your sleeves?"

Vinnie smiled and raised his arm to flex. Dan's lips parted and Vinnie smiled.

"Not what you fu—fudging expected, huh?!"

Taking advantage of the surprise, Vinnie grabbed Dan's shirt and pulled him closer. He kissed Dan on both cheeks then on his lips.

"I've missed you so much."

Laughter erupted from behind Dan. "Hmm... looks like I might have to keep a close watch on Vinnie." Ben held his chin with his thumb and two fingers while Ginny walked over to Vinnie.

"Let me show you how it's done." She grabbed hold of both sides of Vinnie's head, her palms covering his ears. Leaning in, her lips parted and pressed on Vinnie's. They remained together so long he thought she had changed professions to become a dental hygienist. Before pulling back, she took hold of his arms. Their breasts crushed and he thought hers harder.

Vinnie couldn't remember the last time he'd been held this tight by a woman. Not like this, as if crushing juice from flesh. Blanca Santos, his best friend and co-worker at DV&N, had given him a teddy-bear hug a few days before. But she was definitely not Ginny—no one was. His chest sunk.

"Uh, Ginny…"

Ginny released, and Vinnie lowered his eyes. "Sorry, sometimes I forget about them," said Ginny, adjusting her halter top.

Vinnie peered over to Ben, laughing his words. "I've just gone fu—fudging straight! See ya." Vinnie would tell Ben later that Ginny's breasts crushing against him recalled Dan's words years before. He had confided that Ginny's secret weapon against male bosses was her breasts, confident they'd turn stupid when it came to a woman's tits.

As if they had nothing better to do, Ginny stood back, grabbing Vinnie's arm the way Dan had done, then felt the concrete layered under his T-shirt. Vinnie flexed, the bulge swelling, and Ginny's hand moved along.

"What have you to done to my Vinnie? Did he fall overboard?" Vinnie beamed, partly for the compliment, but also from knowing his part in the plan was working. Ginny took notice of him in a new way.

Arriving at Barrow Cottage after the short drive from the ferry, Vinnie was flush with compliments. No one had noticed he'd gone quiet. All the years away he had wallowed in misery, missing his friends, and believing he missed them more than they missed him. Their teasing was proof they loved and missed him too. For each joking chide he heard a declaration of love. His esophagus struggled for air. The engine stopped, the tires no longer crunching along the pebbled driveway. The silence emphasized Vinnie's wail. "I'm so happy. Nothing can go wrong now."

Chapter 12

Renewal

Before the car door opened, Dan turned from the front passenger seat to face Vinnie. "Anthony is so excited to meet his godfather, but—"

Vinnie's full-blown hysteria interrupted Dan. Using Ben's handkerchief, Vinnie wiped his eyes, taking a breath to say, "I'm such a fuckin' crybaby," until Ben nudged him and he changed his mantra to, "I'm such a fudgin' crybaby."

The front door of Barrow Cottage swung open and a small, unsteady creature tumbled forward, holding tight to Grandma Anna's hand. Ginny stepped out from behind the driver's side. "Hey, Anthony, your godfathers are here!"

Anthony recognized Ben as he opened the rear passenger door. "Toss me into the clouds, Unca En."

Ben held Anthony over his head, enjoying the acrobatic game as much as his godson. Anthony's squeal delighted him. Grandma Anna interrupted the display of strength. Ben had an inkling she could be an obstacle to their plans.

Although he had only met Anna a few times, at crowded events with not much time to converse alone, she had found an occasion to warn him about his strength display with Anthony. Ben recalled Ginny's gritting voice. "Mother, isn't this premature? Anthony's still in diapers."

"Nonsense, dear. Every age has vulnerability. Of course, Anthony needs maturity before we can provide him with a coping mechanism."

"Go ahead, say it: or he'll become just like me."

"When the time's right, dear, we'll know if there's a predilection to your condition. No need to set off a trigger before he's prepared."

Ben remembered Ginny's hardened tone telling her mother to stop implying a genetic link to a nonexistent problem, and denying that sthenolagnia was a real issue. Ben had smiled at Ginny's self-contradiction as she said, "Besides, I'm over that phase. All *my* son needs to know is that I enjoy bodybuilding competitions."

Ben had felt uncomfortable at this mother-daughter exchange, and hoped to avoid a repeat encounter, especially with what he and Vinnie had planned.

He knelt to place Anthony on the ground. Vinnie had emerged from the rear of the car but Ben's size blocked Anthony's view. Vinnie heard Anthony ask Unca En to make a muscle and, from Anthony's yelp, Vinnie knew that Ben had complied. He heard Ben's fake cry, "Ouch, you're hurting me. You're so strong!" Ben improvised a dramatic fall and rubbed his arm, repeating, "So strong! You're hurting me! Please stop!"

Anna stood over Ben, arms folded.

Anthony jumped on Ben's chest, a jump that would have caused serious pain to anyone else. Anna reached out and took Anthony's arm. "Now that's enough, Anthony. You mustn't jump on people. You could hurt them."

"I'm fine, Dr. Swinburne. We're only having fun." Ben's smile didn't last long, as Ginny's mother stepped closer, towering over him. *She's going to put her foot on my throat.*

"I'm going to say two things, Ben Hausen, so listen carefully. First, my name is Anna not Dr. Swinburne. Second, when I say enough is enough, that means enough is *enough.*"

"Yes, Anna, you're the boss," Ben replied in a lilt that imitated Anna's.

The elderly woman took a step closer, her sandals rubbing Ben's latissimus dorsi, her gaze drilling into his eyes.

Fuck, she is going to step on my throat! No sense of humor. I'm not messing with this woman.

"As for you, Anthony, jumping on people is not allowed. Not everyone is as strong as your Uncle Ben."

No sooner had Anna said her words than Vinnie stood beside her.

"My oh my, another one. Ginny, are all the men you know descendants of Hercules?"

Vinnie hugged Anna and pecked her cheeks. They had met only once, five years before at a party held by Dan and Ginny at their condo. Pulling back from Anna, Vinnie looked down at his godson clinging to his grandmother's leg. He squatted on his haunches. "Do you remember me, Anthony?"

Although they had talked via Skype, the toddler remained motionless, a confused look on his face. Anna patted his head. "It's okay, Anthony."

"You're Unca Ninny." Anthony's voice rose, suggesting that his reply was a query.

"Yes, I'm your Uncle Vinnie. Would it be all right if I give you a hug?"

The small head made a slight nod, enough for Vinnie to stretch out his arms and allow Anthony to walk into them. With Anthony making contact, Vinnie folded his arms. "I love you, Anthony. We're going to be best friends, aren't we?"

"Yes, Unca Ninny. I love you too."

A torrent gushed from Vinnie. His chest heaved and he lost his balance. Anna placed her hand on Vinnie's back as Dan moved forward to kneel between his son and Vinnie, and tightly took hold of both.

"Daddy, why is Unca Ninny crying?"

"He's happy to see you. He's missed you and wants to be your very best friend. Will you play with Uncle Vinnie?"

Vinnie crumbled. Anna tapped Dan's shoulders. "I think we

should go inside and have lemonade and sweets. Let's go, everyone."

Trooping into the house, Ben marveled at Anna's military-like
authority. Dan had told Ben, "No one contradicts il commandant." *This woman is something else. How does Dan manage family
visits?*

Anna prepared two snack trays in the kitchen, leaving Ginny's
father James to take over as host. As she meticulously arranged
items, she gathered her thoughts. Before meeting Ben for the
first time, a short while after Vinnie's exile, she had envisioned
that he would be an arrogant and egotistical person, based on her
experience of people that pushed themselves to the extreme and
to the top of their profession. She believed bodybuilders would
be among the worst kind of egotists, next to politicians. She
held this opinion despite her own experience when Ginny was
a little girl with the local ice cream truck vendor, a bodybuilder,
who was a kind and gentle person. In Anna's mind, their ice
cream man was the exception to the rule. Besides, he wasn't
Ben's supersize, nor did he have a shelf filled with first-place
trophies.

The snack preparation slowed as Anna paused to delve into
her thoughts. How could men like Ben be anything but egotistical? *He lives for his body. And he's wealthy.* Anna looked around
to see if she'd forgotten anything. *He's gracious and never acts
privileged. But I really don't know him. How he treats Vinnie during this month will tell me everything.* Anna was sure her MD in
psychiatry would uncover the truth about Ben.

In her plan, if Ben was as good as he seemed she'd have an
ally. Maybe two: Ben *and* Vinnie. With their help, she'd make
her case for Ginny and Dan to leave New York and move to Stamford. Be nearer to her and James. Her argument with Ginny had
fallen flat. "I only see Anthony every few weeks and for short
periods. There are too many strangers caring for him at the daycare. You and Dan would have more time to concentrate on your

careers." Ginny's rebuttal hurt, telling her mother to mind her own business in the crudest possible language.

Anna finished the trays and carried one of them through to her houseguests. *I have a month, so no need to panic.* But her stomach clenched. She had felt the panic the minute Ben stepped out of the car showing off his muscles, and she had caught Ginny's stare.

Swinging Anthony into the air, Ben's upper torso had swelled. Anna read Ginny's thoughts from her posture. She was assembling Ben's IKEA muscles, placing slot A into slot B, the way she had with He-Man figurines as a little girl. Anna felt unbearably tense. She feared a full-blown return of Ginny's sthenolagnia. A cloud crossed her mind. *If Ginny relapses, then she'll never leave New York. She'll cling to Ben's gym and the stable of men he trains. I'll have to ask Ben to dress conservatively—and no power displays. I have one month.*

Seeing Anna with the tray, Dan stood to help his mother-in-law. Ginny went to retrieve the second tray. Anthony and Vinnie were on the floor, unconcerned by the arrival of the snacks. They were playing with Vinnie's ice-breaker present to Anthony, a toy car that spoke—electronic words imitating car noises. On pressing the horn button, a beep was followed by "Look out. Coming through." Anthony and Vinnie giggled in unison.

Ben nudged Vinnie's leg as Anna bent down to hand him his glass of lemonade and a plate of treats.

"Oh, sorry, Anna. Can I help?" Vinnie leaped to his feet from his cross-legged position.

Anthony wheeled the car across the room: "Beep-beep. Look out. Coming through."

Grandpa James suggested he and Anthony go to another room while the adults talked. Vinnie almost screamed, "Can't I come?" James made no response, so Vinnie turned to Anna.

"Of course, dear. This is your first day with Anthony. You do as you please. No one will tell you what to do in this house."

Vinnie smiled until he noticed Ginny's head moving sideways, eyes rolling to the ceiling.

Anna told Ben she hoped he and Vinnie would be comfortable in the neighbor's house. "Although it won't be the luxury you're accustomed to..."

"Don't be silly, Anna. It will be great and I can't thank you enough. To tell the truth, I prefer simple. It's friends that count more than expensive stuff, don't you think?"

"Very astute. However, if you or Vinnie need anything, you let me know." Anna's lips barely moved as she maintained her smile.

"Likewise from us. We're here to help too. We want to pull our weight."

"An interesting phrase, Ben, very interesting."

With a turn to Ginny, Ben tilted his head. *Was he talking to Anna, Ginny's mother, or to Dr. Anna Swinburne, psychiatrist?* Ginny moved her index finger to her lip and whispered, "Wait."

Wait for what? Ben thought Ginny looked like someone about to be sick. *What's happening? This is our friendly get-to-know-you time, so what's Ginny's warning?*

Ginny removed her finger and clasped her hands into her lap, schoolgirl style.

"Tell me, Ben, is it the Californian air or because you and Vinnie are gay? In less than an hour I've been treated with courtesy and politeness and thanked for doing very little. Should I surround myself with gay men or Californians?" Anna chuckled.

Dan coughed.

"Oh, Dan, you're kind too. It's just that I've gotten used to you."

"Nice recovery, MIL." Dan used his acronym for mother-in-law whenever he wanted to score a point with Anna. "But no dice. I'm not gay, and I've only been to California on business. You can't amend a compliment."

"Shall I grovel? I'm sorry, SIL." Anna walked to Dan and patted her son-in-law on the shoulder. "I think you are courteous and helpfulness personified."

Ginny, looking exasperated, cleared her throat. "Okay, Mom, what's up?"

Anna shrugged.

Ginny unfolded her hands.

Ben's thoughts rushed forward. *What's happening? This is so unreal.*

"I have no idea what you mean. Can't I compliment my son-in-law?"

"I'm not buying it."

Dan stared at Ginny sitting opposite. "Let it go."

"Mother, you better not be trying something."

Ben crossed his legs. *What the hell is going on? What kind of family dynamics is this? I won't be able to take a month of this bullshit. I might not last until tomorrow.*

Anna's voice lilted. "I guess if I'm not wanted then you won't need me to sit for Anthony over the next month. Good luck with the afternoon sex."

"Checkmate," called out Ginny.

This knocked Ben back. Dan leaned over and whispered to Ben, "My advice: don't say anything." Dan's eyebrows raised. Ginny had noticed him confide in Ben.

"What, Dan, you don't think my mother knows we plan to have afternoon sex? Other times too. That's not the point."

This is so weird. How did we start talking about sex? Ben folded his arms, uncrossed his legs, then crossed them again. *This is a master class in psychological warfare.*

Dan stood, beginning to walk away, a tactic he had learned from his father-in-law.

Anna also stood and turned to Ginny. "I'm going to prepare dinner. We'll eat around six. Ben, you come with me. I'll need someone polite to help lift my cauldron."

Il commandant had spoken. Ben approached Anna, who patted his chest. "Actually, there's no need. I'll use witchcraft to levitate the pots. Dan, show Ben his accommodation and help him settle in. Vinnie can play with Anthony a little longer."

Ben followed Dan to the front door and glanced at the ticking hallway clock. Two hours. Weird, but on balance he and Vinnie had made a good start. Ginny had taken notice of their bodies. Anna seemed to like them. He had no idea what had just happened, but it didn't affect him and Vinnie. Nope, they had a good start. Mission on target. He'd just have to limit his time with Anna and Ginny in the same room.

Chapter 13

Birthday Surprise

The formal table contrasted with the cottage's rustic beach setting. Anna preserved her idea of informality by insisting that everyone sit wherever they liked, aside from her seat on one side of Anthony, and Vinnie flanking the other. She asked Ben to sit at one end, given his girth, placing James at the other for easy access to the barbecue. That only left Ginny and Dan to choose seats, not counting the family dog Foo Foo, a white bichon frise that roamed freely underneath the table.

In further recognition of Ben, Ginny had requested her father add additional protein to the menu. James said, "Ginny, it's a barbecue. There'll be steak, hamburger, and hot dogs." Ginny hugged him, and added four half-breast chickens. Her dad was lovable and naive. She had never been mad at him.

The first comment about Ben's plate came from Anthony. "Unca En, can you really eat all that?"

With everyone finished, apart from Ben and Anthony, Anna directed the conversation to Anthony's third birthday party the next afternoon. She spoke in code, which confused everyone. Anthony became bored and behaved like any three-year-old. Anna's next words were not coded.

"I think Anthony would like to play before his bath and bedtime story." Her single command initiated action. Vinnie lifted Anthony out of his high chair, saying he'd like to help. A frown creased Vinnie's face as Anthony blurted, "I want a horsey ride from Unca En."

"My pleasure," said Ben in a monotone. In Anthony's request he heard the words often spoken by Carl. A horsey ride from his father had been among Carl's favorite activities.

Walking around the table, Ben caught Vinnie's hunched body. "Let's ask Uncle Vinnie to be a spare horse, wouldn't that be fun?" Ben signaled to Vinnie.

"Yeah. Two horsies!"

Both men wished Vinnie had been first choice.

* * *

By noon the next day balloons were strung across the garden patio, the first of many decorations waiting to be hung. Anna and James had taken their grandson to Edgartown for a special treat, then deposited him with Ben and Vinnie at Veronica and Harold's house for his nap. The five o'clock party had been for Aunt Rachel and Uncle Ted's benefit, allowing them ample time to catch a noon Woods Hole ferry.

Rachel and Ted stumbled onto the sidewalk, a stark contrast to Vinnie and Ben. They had barely caught the boat even though they had started from their friend's in Plymouth, about an hour's drive.

Dark sunglasses hid the couple's drooping eyelids. Ginny had donned large tinted shades for fashion. The sisters pecked each other's cheeks without seeing each other's eyes.

"Hi, Ginny, how are the birthday plans going? I could've brought a band if you'd have wanted." Ted, forever ebullient, had removed his sunglasses and made a big fuss over Ginny.

"Thanks, Ted. It was a nice offer but a grunge band isn't really appropriate for a three-year-old," said Ginny in her motherly authoritarian voice.

Despite his immaturity, Ginny had grown to like Ted. On their first meeting, she had thought him odd but tolerable. She quickly learned much of his oddity was typical junkie behavior, but not all. Once he had cleaned up, Ginny thought Ted a perfect match for her sister. After Ted had helped save Dan and Vinnie during the DV&N troubles, he'd moved up in her esteem. And her sister had helped too, which Ginny hated to admit. But likable didn't mean Ted wasn't still weird, which was how she put it to Dan, who replied, "And how does that make him different from your sister?"

* * *

"Best birthday party ever," said Anthony. Vinnie agreed. "I've been to a lot of fu… I mean a lot of parties and this is the best."

And it was fun. Vinnie looked around. *This is a good party, especially for a three-year-old. Look at all the gifts! I love Anthony's squealing like a piglet. I love the way he jumps around, not worried about what anyone thinks. Was I ever free like that? I should have picked out better wrapping paper, something even more fun. Why would Ginny's mother say Anthony's reaction to the bright paper had been programmed by adults? She called his squeal a Pavlovian reaction. How dare she compare my godson to a trained dog? Ginny sure got a winner for a mother.*

A clap from Ginny announced it was time for Anthony to receive his godparents' present. She and her mother debated whose present should be last, the godparents or grandparents. Vinnie rose and heard Anthony's squeal again. After Anthony took possession of the package, Vinnie's arm remained outstretched. *Am I proving Anna's theory correct? I'm just as excited as Anthony. Does it make me Pavlov's dog? Why am I so insecure?*

Anthony looked at the packaging, unsure how to start. Ginny signaled her son to come to her, taking control from her mother who had been helping Anthony unwrap his presents. Ginny took hold of Anthony's finger as they traced over the battleships imprinted on the paper. She moved his finger across the bow that encased a toy airplane. Vinnie unfolded his arms, his little subterfuge around Ginny's rule of only one gift. Well, he had included two—actually three if you counted his welcoming gift. *Ha. Got you, Ginny.*

Ginny helped Anthony avoid ripping the paper, unlike her mother's brute force approach.

"Ginny, he's not going to be a professional unwrapper. Just rip it open."

Ginny glared at her mother.

Anthony loved his toy. He'd been primed by his grandmother to show appreciation—another Pavlovian response, thought Vinnie—and Anthony ran to Ben and leaped on him.

"Thank you, Unca En." Anthony's little boy arms couldn't stretch across Ben's chest but without a perch he could not kiss Ben's cheek.

Ben's eyes were closed, and the warmth of Anthony's small body entered his. He listened to the purring breaths that reminded him of Carl's. Ben had feared he'd be repulsed, but he wasn't. *I need this. If I can give this small child some happiness and security, then this has to be good. Why shouldn't I? I made one mistake; never again. I feel alive... even if...*

Lifting Anthony, Ben turned his head to speak sideways, holding back tears. "I... I... I hope you like your toy."

"I do. I do! Thank you, Unca En."

A tap on Anthony's shoulder from Anna reminded him there was someone else to thank. Anthony slowly moved to Vinnie, speaking in a flat tone, "And thank you, Unca Ninny."

Ben saw the hesitation in Anthony and Vinnie. He rose to lift Anthony on to Vinnie's lap. Vinnie kissed Anthony's forehead, and spoke with tears on his cheeks. "I hope you... you... uh..." Vinnie croaked his words: "I hope you like your toy, and you'll let me play with it too."

"Sure, Unca Ninny. You're the best at playing."

Vinnie gasped, as if suffocating from lack of oxygen.

"Are you very happy, Unca Ninny? I'm happy too, but I don't cry when I'm happy."

Placing Anthony down, Vinnie stood. He moved away and

heard Rachel say to no one in particular, "Fuck, the kid's got brains." Rachel's coarse language matched Vinnie's, which Ginny said explained the friendship between them. It had been Rachel who had wheedled an interview from Dan, which led to Vinnie being his assistant at DV&N.

"Rachel, I think we can do without the cursing," said Anna.

James looked to Ben. "Please excuse my daughter."

Dan roared, doubling over.

Everyone stared at Dan, but Vinnie knew. Dan had told Vinnie the inside scoop about Ginny's parents: "My mother-in-law admonishes, and my father-in-law apologizes."

Ginny took hold of Vinnie. "You okay?"

"Yeah, fine. Three years and I'm the same old crybaby. I love Anthony. I'd want a son just like him."

Ginny stepped back. Had he said too much? Did she understand? *I'm a goddamn idiot.*

"I mean anyone would love to have a son like Anthony." Vinnie pecked Ginny's cheek and Ben placed an arm around Vinnie, the veins running down his bicep holding Ginny's gaze. He squeezed Vinnie's shoulder, pulling him closer. "We both love Anthony, he's so adorable."

Ginny took Ben's arm and leaned forward to whisper, "I know this is tough for you. Carl is here too. You know that, don't you?"

Ben's closing eyes told Ginny she had erred. Ben, unlike Vinnie, held back rather than revealed his vulnerability. Ginny did what came naturally and squeezed his arm, whispering to him to flex. They understood each other. How could they not? Ben had been her personal trainer for years. Ben appreciated her diversionary tactic. He sunk his dark thoughts into his sinew.

No one had been watching except Anthony, who recognized competition for his mother's attention. "I have big muscles like Unca En!" Anthony reached for Ginny's hand. "See, I have big muscles too. Feel them?" Anthony raised both arms, imitating Ben's double-bi pose.

The posture made Ginny laugh and using her thumb and index finger she squeezed her son's arm, feigning a cry of astonishment. "Anthony, your muscles are so strong!"

Anna heard and glared at Ginny, the message as clear as a flashing neon sign. Ginny thought this time her mother might have a point.

"Anthony, you know I love you no matter how big and strong you are."

Anna thought an Oedipus complex was too soon for her grandson, if you believed that old stuff. She generally favored Kagan's position that emotional development derived from a complex blend of context, history, and biology. Anthony's display was something, but what she could not say, and this worried her. She believed early events influenced later adult life. She was certain Ginny's obsession began about Anthony's age, partly from a well-intentioned bodybuilding ice cream man.

And raising Anthony in New York City didn't help. She was sure the environment was wrong for her grandson, given Ginny's obsession and Dan's submersion into his start-up company. She thought Anthony spent too much time in daycare. In Stamford she would provide proper guidance and stability. Anna stared at Ginny beside Ben's galaxy-wide body.

Throughout the party, Dan had been recording, something he had started with Anthony's birth. Anthony had been the sole subject of his home videos, but today he recorded anybody and anything. Anna had told Dan, "Pull your head out of the camera and observe with your eyes and listen with your ears. What do you learn from videos?" Dan said a lot. He had seen things on a second and third viewing that he had missed the first time, and would never have recalled without a recording. He had watched Anthony grow. His recordings provided additional backdrop details: litter blowing in the wind; pigeons pecking in the park; shadows drifting across the condo wall.

On this day, Dan captured four adults telling his son about

virtues beyond the physical. No amount of reviewing the video would reveal the thoughts behind the faces. For that, he'd have to wait.

Chapter 14

Beach Walk

According to Anna, everyone needed respite the morning after the birthday party. She strongly suggested that Anthony stay with her after breakfast. "There's nothing left to plan, so take the time to do just that—nothing." The blatant lie burned her tongue, unaware that Vinnie and Ben felt the same.

Ginny paired with Ben and Vinnie with Dan. They had decided that strolling along the private beach outside Barrow Cottage suited them perfectly. The pairs headed in opposite directions, with the common goal of private conversation.

Ben and Ginny spread a beach blanket a few feet from the high tide line on Nantucket Sound. A perfect view of billowing white and multicolor sails passing by, contrasting with the crystal blue water. Ben suggested moving away from Barrow Cottage and prying eyes. He held back that Ginny's mother's observations made him uncomfortable, almost intimidated, which was unlike him. Ginny pointed out that on the blanket they were below the tall beach grass. "You have to stretch from the upper bedroom windows to see us."

He knew the time to act was now. He asked Ginny to apply additional suntan oil in places he couldn't reach. Ginny asked if he wore his stage posing costume to allow maximum sun tanning in preparation for the contest. Ben nodded yes, and hoped his quick answer didn't reveal the lie beneath the semi-truth. *This isn't me. I hate this. She must know it?* Ben wondered how a smart person like Ginny didn't see through his stupid request. *Wouldn't it be simpler to just be honest?*

The thoughts of betrayal caused Ben's stomach to knot. In fact, Vinnie had applied oil in their bedroom, a precaution to avoid him burning in case it took too long before he asked for Ginny's help.

Ginny's palm massaged the lotion, starting along his spine that bifurcated each side of the muscular prairie. Her hand stopped and Ben thought something was wrong. Her pause was too long. No longer applying lotion, he knew she was exploring his muscles with her eyes, staring at their form and strength. He started to hate the plan because it was working. *Anna's right. Ginny is more vulnerable than I had thought.*

With his anxiety growing, Ben's back knotted with tension. He heard Ginny's deep inhales. Her head moved closer, as if she wanted to place it on his flared latissimus dorsi, wide like the sails on a passing forty-foot yacht. He felt her cream-filled palms moving in a circular clockwise motion, stopping to sink fingers into the spinal crevice that supported his two hundred and sixty pounds. Ben was sure this was the end of her long-time sublimation.

Her elegant fingers cruised his back, marching from lats to deltoids, then down his spine, sliding oil as far as his ass crack, an area she had never touched before. Ben jolted.

"Err… Ginny, I don't think there's much sun exposure there. Vinnie usually takes care of that with a hand-held sun lamp."

"Shy? That's fine, but don't blame me if you lose because of a white patch."

The sun's warmth penetrated Ginny's exposed back. If Ben thought he had chosen his bathing costume with care, he was no match for Ginny.

Two thin-corded straps crisscrossed her back, held together by a small clasp to form a delicate bikini top. Her exposure would have exceeded the Island's public beach permissible limits. Dan said so, and Ginny argued she needed to accentuate her assets. Dan felt that a brown paper bag would have been enough to highlight her assets. He asked Vinnie and Ben their opinion, to which Ben said, "Well, I'm not a zombie. Ginny's gorgeous."

Vinnie said, "So, you're saying even a gay zombie can appreciate a body like that?"

Ginny showed them all her middle finger as she walked out.

Vinnie isn't wrong, Ben thought during the morning discussion, and he thought the same again now. He had tried not to stare, but did not hide his looking at Ginny as they walked the beach. *What the hell? Damn, she has a magnificent body. Her face is perfection. I'd hang her portraits around the house if it wasn't so creepy.* Ben smiled, thinking what Vinnie would say, but dropped his smile when picturing Dan's reaction. He looked down, confirming there was no erection, but that didn't exclude his admiring her beauty. *I'm with a goddess.*

The sun baked, and Ginny's fingers dug into Ben, the hardness of each muscle layer too tough for her to dent. With his hands on his hips, Ben flared his lats to expose his wide prairie landscape. As soon as Ginny's hands stopped rubbing, he knew he had miscalculated.

"As much as I am enjoying this, you could have done this before leaving the house. I'm sure Vinnie would have been more than pleased… and, as you pointed out, he can go places I can't. What's up? You and Vinnie having problems?"

Returning his arms to his sides, Ben swiveled to face Ginny, knees sinking into the sand as he rested on his grade-A Angus rump. "No, not really."

"That sounds more like yes then no. Care to expand on the *not really* part?"

"Can I stay with not really?"

With a snake's smile, Ginny answered, "Not really."

"Okay. Here goes. We're very much in love. Fantastic sex.

We want to do everything together, especially as we can now be together all the time. To please me, Vinnie has worked, developed his body, and before you think it—that I wanted a muscular spouse—let me say that my concern was for his protection."

Ginny frowned. "That's a story for another time."

"Agreed. We'll put it on the back burner."

"For now, stick to what's bothering you."

Ben stammered, yet Ginny remained quiet, unlike her usual impatience. He gave her the gist, as close to reality as he dared. Vinnie wanted a child and he did not, at least not at first, but he had reconsidered.

"I'm afraid. You saw my reaction to Anthony. I would have cried had you not intervened. And thanks. My tears are bittersweet... joy that Anthony is happy, yet..." Ben paused and lowered his head. "Yet sad. I miss Carl so much... it's as if it were only yesterday I held him."

Ben's index finger poked at his forehead. "He's still in here."

Several seconds of deep breaths expanded Ben's chest to whale size.

"Memory plays tricks. I'd found a place to separate out the pain, but I have never forgotten Carl." Ben's chest expanded, sucking in air like a turbine engine.

Ginny shuffled closer, silent, and dropped the suntan bottle to her side.

"You know," Ben continued, "I nearly hit someone for saying I needed to move on. Fuck them. Fuck all of them. You do not move on from the death of your child. The best you hope for is to go forward... if not, you just end it all."

With a high pitch, Ginny cried out, "No, Ben, you don't mean that. Please say you don't mean it!"

"Ginny, I'm still here. I have a man I love and married. So, no, I'm not about to commit suicide. I've managed by going on, not moving on. You know who move on? People who get divorced. People who go bankrupt. People who have been fired from their jobs. These are the kind of things you move on from. Moving on from the death of your child is bullshit. I am here, I am alive, and I miss my Carl very much."

Ben didn't stop himself. He cried, allowing his tears to remain on his cheeks. *What have I done? What's wrong with me?*

Ginny knelt between Ben's knees, her crying accompanying his. The empathy of a mother. Was this guilt, too? Her Anthony alive and healthy, and Ben's Carl dead.

Her breathing synched with Ben's. She clung to him, using his sinewy strength to secure her expectation—that Anthony would outlive her—and battle her fear—that he would not. She shivered in the warm sun, knowing this was when she needed Anna, her mother, as well as Anna the psychologist. Was this why she sought mountainous men, to save her?

As both their tears subsided, Ginny grabbed Ben's neck, leaning in to touch his forehead with hers. "I am so sorry, Ben. So sorry."

Perfect words. Perfect and the reason he liked her. No, loved her. Ginny didn't tell him how to feel or what to do. She never said that horrible phrase, "You need closure." Her simple words started him crying again, harder, maybe harder than he had for a long time. His last bawl had been four years ago with Ginny and Dan, but under very different circumstances. Or was it?

Ginny shuffled her body closer, her arms resting on Ben's chopping-block thighs, her head slipping to rest on a single pectoral bigger than her skull. Ben pulled her closer, as if she were a small child.

From a distance, they might easily be mistaken for lovers in a passionate embrace.

Chapter 15

Exposure

In contrast to Ben and Ginny, Dan's and Vinnie's beach suits seemed ultra conservative. Both men thought exposing their bodies pointless, and solar rays dangerous. They moseyed along the beach, content that they would not offend even the most conservative granny. Of course, the only granny they might encounter would be Anna, and her issues would not be bare flesh.

Just as Dan had suggested to Ginny she change her bathing costume, she had suggested he change into his Speedo. Dan argued his skimpy bathing suit was designed for speed in a pool—hence the name Speedo—not a stroll along the beach. Ginny liked to see his hard body, his long, well-defined legs; he did not. She would scoff as he quickly covered himself after completing pool laps. His fastidious routine to have two towels at the pool ladder, one to dry and one to cover, always made her smile.

"What's with the baggy pants?" asked Vinnie, his eyes rolling skywards.

"And what about those?" Dan said, his fingers pointing to Vinnie's boxers. Both their faces beamed, which masked the mutual loss of each other's company over the past three years.

"Mine's nothing like your tent. Planning to open a circus?"

"Screw you, Vinnie." It was harsh, too harsh for what he intended. Had he hurt him? It was no secret Vinnie would have willingly had sex with Dan, had he not been straight—'A fuckin' waste of a good man,' as Vinnie once put it to Ben. Dan wondered, did Vinnie know about his one-time experiment with Ben? Of course he did, even though nothing had been said.

After a few minutes walking along the beach, Dan stopped and held Vinnie's arm. "I'm sorry about my outburst. It was uncalled for. You know I'm very sensitive about too much flesh. It's my hang-up."

"Fu—I mean, I fudgin' understand. No need to apologize, Dan." Vinnie struggled to control his cursing, even knowing that Dan had abandoned his cursing prohibition stance of years before. But he knew Dan's aversion to foul language lingered. "Want to talk about it?"

They strolled as two friends without a care along the beach. Vinnie knew most of the story, but could tell Dan needed to talk about it and urged him on. Dan shook his head. He was fine. Drop it.

The hum of Vinnie's babbling relaxed Dan. With each step he went further back in his mind, to being an eleven-year-old boy at swimming camp.

Vinnie picked up shells long ago discarded by their inhabitants. He examined a crab carcass. Dan looked at the remains as if it had been him, the day he'd been humiliated many years ago. He wanted to force out that memory, but the distant squawk of gulls drove his mind further back. The climb from the pool ladder. The older boys, their flexing and taunting. The bullying, and his trunks resting at his ankles. Dan kicked the sand in an attempt to push out the memory of him naked, full erection, exposed to everyone.

Vinnie poked more shells as sand flew up from Dan's feet. "You okay?"

The words Dan heard came from inside: "Hey, we have a faggot here! You like this body, queer?"

"Earth to Dan. You okay? What's up?"

"Huh? Oh, just thinking, it's nothing."

86

"Yeah, I could tell you were thinking. Care to share?"

No, thought Dan. *I want to forget, not remember.* But he had remembered. He remembered it often, something that should have long been erased. Hell, it was twenty years ago. Why shouldn't he talk about it? Vinnie knew. He had told him the story when their friendship became close. Ginny and Vinnie were the only ones who knew the full story, although Dan was fairly certain Ginny told her mother and sister—that's what the Swinburne family did; they took secrets and broadcast them to each other.

Like Dan's action minutes before, Vinnie took his friend's arm. "C'mon, tell me."

Dan protested, but knew once Vinnie persisted he would not let go. So Dan told him of his returning memory of his awful day, the day his life changed.

"Get over it, Dan. Look at you. Handsome, hunky, a gorgeous wife and wonderful son. It's in the past."

The rebuke hurt because it was true. "I know. But you know that nakedness and my erection haunts me. My first times with women, even Ginny, I'd put the bedroom lights out. Ginny changed that. And I'm sorry to say I worried throughout my adolescence that I was a homosexual. I didn't want to be different. I didn't want to be called a queer. I'm sorry, Vinnie, but that's how I felt."

"Don't be. I know the feeling, because I had the same, but in my case it was also true. I still feel it. Sure, the discrimination is not as bad, but it's there. Ignorant people still populate the world."

Dan patted Vinnie's neck.

"So, Dan, boxers or Speedos?"

Dan sputtered his laughter. "You're crazy. I've missed you so much."

"Me too. Shall we get naked? You know, check if you're still straight?"

Dan's embrace came fast and tight. "I am so happy you're here."

Unlocking themselves, both men turned to see if anyone had noticed. Dan's mouth dropped and Vinnie jumped back as Dan yelled seaward, "What the hell! Is Ginny kissing Ben?"

Vinnie didn't think so, but maybe Ben's muscle show had gone too far. No, it couldn't be. "Don't jump to conclusions. Ben's not interested in women. He's had opportunities… many offers from women at the gym. Sometimes right in front of me. He's told me he refuses all offers, men and women, and I believe him."

Dan stance widened, his arms resting on his hips as he squinted into the distance. Vinnie moved to block Dan's view, but Dan took one step to Vinnie's left, and being taller he could see down the beach.

"Ben's a good guy, he'd never do anything," said Vinnie with a lilt evoking a question.

Dan chewed his lip, moved his jaw. Vinnie continued. "Ben and Ginny have too much respect for each other—and us."

"You so sure?" Dan shook his head. "I've never seen Ben so pumped. He seems to have more muscle and his definition is unreal. This is not good for Ginny's condition, you know that, don't you?"

Vinnie looked down as if counting grains of sand. His head snapped as Dan yelled, "What's that!" Dan was pointing.

Following Dan's finger, Vinnie saw Ginny's head snuggled into Ben's chest. Vinnie moved to Dan. "It's not what it looks like. Ginny's helping Ben."

"Helping him get off, is that what you mean?"

The anger in Dan's voice shocked Vinnie; the situation was out of control. "Dan, I have something to tell you that will help explain. Please, walk with me." A tug on Dan's arm had him moving.

"This better be good."

After ten minutes, Dan learned about the child issue between Vinnie and Ben, but not the idea for Ginny to be the surrogate mother. Vinnie could not go that far, not yet. They talked about

Carl. Dan's skin prickled with Vinnie's retelling of a story he knew well, but he didn't know Ben cried at night for no apparent reason. Vinnie told Dan that he believed Ben was telling Ginny, and she was consoling him.

"I'm sorry for Ben. I can't imagine what it's like." Dan's arms folded, pulling close to his chest as if the sea breeze had suddenly chilled the summer heat.

"What about me? I think Ben uses Carl as an excuse."

Dan stopped walking, his tongue blocking the words from leaving his mouth. His silence a chastisement.

"No, I didn't mean that. I didn't mean it like it sounded. But Ben needs to understand he wasn't the drunk driver that killed his son. Nor was I. Why should I have to bear the consequences?"

Dan kicked at the words, turning from Vinnie. "Vinnie, that is so unsympathetic. Something's up. What happened in San Francisco?" Dan slumped; he kicked more sand and looked to Barrow Cottage. *Was Anthony safe?* Dan's leg muscles tensed, preparing to sprint. "Poor Ben, the agony...I...I can't imagine—"

Whether from the way Dan's words slipped and stalled, or the way his head hung, Vinnie blurted out, "Dan, I shouldn't have fuckin' said what I said. I'm fuckin' selfish. It's just that I want a child and this will rip me and Ben apart."

The return to Vinnie's needs jolted Dan. Raising his leg to brush sand from his feet, Dan peered at Vinnie.

"How can you be so sure? Lots of couples, and I mean straight and gay, don't have children. It's a choice. Maybe a good choice too. Aren't you overreacting?"

"Nuh-uh," replied Vinnie, reverting to Brooklynese. "Not-for-nutin' but youse wrong."

"Vinnie, English, please." Dan disliked Vinnie's vernacular to hide shame or a mistake, a ploy he'd applied many times in the office at DV&N.

"Ya gonna be a putz, fine. My point is this, if one person wants a baby and the other doesn't, then it leads to divorce or years of resentment. I've seen a shrink, so I know what I'm talking about. This will be crucial for us."

"Is Ben telling all this to Ginny? That you want a child and he doesn't? Or he does?" Dan squatted for a final brush of sand then his fist formed, which he placed under his chin.

* * *

From the back deck of Barrow Cottage, holding her grandson's hand, Anna surveyed the beach. Looking over her left shoulder there was a high dune stretching across her line of sight. In front of her the dune tapered until looking over her right shoulder it fused with the beach. To her immediate left the wooden erosion fence bolstered by high beach grass prevented her from seeing the beach. On her right neither fence nor grass prevented her from seeing to the horizon. Her unobstructed view allowed her to watch her son-in-law, bent forward, marching double pace, and Vinnie trailing.

If beach grass blocked her sight, it did not impede her imagination. She took hold of Anthony's hand as they walked into the house.

Chapter 16

Hushed Secrets

The basement door latch clicked, which confirmed to Slider that Vinnie's house was secure. He'd been checking the property for nearly two weeks. Ralph wasn't due for another hour. Slider patrolled the side path for windblown litter in the bushes that separated Vinnie's property from Plum and Good'un's. Voices carried through the shrubbery.

"I'll come back tomorrow. Don't say anything until I return."

Curt's eye caught Slider as he turned. Grace had closed her door. "Oh, it's you."

"The one and only."

"Well, fuck off."

"And a nice day to you, too. How can you dare show your face to Good'un after what you did?" Slider walked with a steady stride down the path and closed the chain-link gate. He was across the street heading for his daytime residence in the park before he realized Curt had followed.

"I don't know what you know or what you think you know, but I've warned you before. Stay out of our lives."

Slider turned on the grin he used to signal to a catcher he'd pick off the runner at first attempting to steal second. The smile unnerved Curt.

"Fuck you, queer."

"Ain't that pokin' in my business. Y'all need to know any

hurtin' you do to Good'un and Plum is my bullpen."

"Huh. Listen, faggot—"

"You won't be getttin' too many innings, you know. Good'un will tell Plum."

"Their names are Grace and Kaelin. And tell them what, exactly?"

"We both know what you gone done to Good'un."

Curt moved forward, his finger pointing. "You know nothing. You're a loser. That's why you're not on the team anymore. Fucking queer loser."

Barking caused both men to turn. Ralph had entered the park and ran to Slider, then gave a few sniffs of Curt's leg before running to the back corner for his business.

"Fucking stupid dog." Curt's hand flung upward. "It needs to be on a leash, like you." Curt's hand swirled in the air. "Keep out of things that don't concern you."

"Fuck y'all too, philandering hog. And my dog's none of your'uns concern."

"I'll say this one more time. You interfere in my life and you'll be sorry. You can count on it."

By the time Ralph had returned to Slider, Curt was out of sight. Slider settled into thought, knowing he had a period without distraction or observation; he once estimated that someone walked by every ten minutes after the morning rush of moms and dads with school drop-offs. Slider hunched, his head hung between his spread legs, and he stared at the ground. After several minutes of grunting, he felt an urge to talk. Slider and Ralph crossed the street.

"Oh, hi, Slider. How are you?" Grace blinked rapidly.

"Y'all have a moment to talk?"

"Sure. Come in. There's a chill in the air, so no use standing outside. Besides, Ralph looks like he could use a treat." Ralph's ears pricked up and he was inside the doorway before Slider could move.

In the kitchen, Grace tossed Ralph two treats, something she and Kaelin began to keep on hand for their visits to Slider and Ralph in the park. She placed a water bowl on the floor and offered Slider a freshly brewed coffee. Kaelin preferred the Keurig pod system, as she was always in a hurry, but Grace liked the smell of a steaming pot.

"Mighty fine brew. Been hankerin' for some, since Vinnie's gone."

"Come over anytime you want. You're always welcome. Have you heard from Vinnie? We had a postcard from New York."

"Gotta buzz when he put down. Sent a postcard, I've put it somewhere at the house. Yankee Stadium. Can you believe it?" Slider didn't mention the other cards in an envelope with men in various sexual positions.

Looking around the kitchen, Slider took a few sips of his coffee. He had expected the decor to match the underlying turmoil, but as he surveyed the room it all seemed normal.

"Here's the thing, Good'un. I got a gander of Upper Deck parting this morning and he crawled over to my range, lost like—" Slider saw Grace's head tilt. "The park." He waited for her to blink. "We got to exchanging some words."

Slider paused as he gave a small laugh.

"I let him know that I know what he did to y'all. He be botherin' you? I fear you bein' with him when Plum is away an all."

Grace showed no change in facial expression. She didn't move.

A few seconds passed, and Slider continued. "Y'all might want to tell Plum about her daddy being a rapist and all. She'un needs to know."

"What!" Grace's chair moved away from the table, screeching across the tiled floor. Her word was flung with hurricane force, ripping into Slider. Ralph barked. Slider's head shot back, a fastball to the face kind of snap.

"You don't understand. You have no idea."

"I'm hearin' y'all. Go on."

"I can't."

"Sure can. Y'all want, I'd be on the mound when you go tell Plum. Y'all can't hide forever."

Grace moved her chair back to the table, pushing her coffee to one side, and resting her elbows on the tabletop. "It's much more complicated than you know."

"Ain't so complicated. Upper Deck gone raped you. Y'all tell Plum then the authorities." Slider felt the heat rising inside him. People not being honest meant trouble. He knew from personal experience that the devastation is greater the longer the truth remains hidden. He started to explain but Grace shook her head.

"No, it's not that simple or easy. Please, Slider, let me handle this my way." Grace began to cry, and her elbows slid off the table as she wiped her eyes.

Slider knew about letting people do things their way. He had been assured his sexual preference wouldn't matter. His gay friends told him so. Said the world had changed; no hiding necessary. And he was a well-liked star pitcher. The Giants wouldn't dare act against him, and they had not. But some teammates shunned him, while other players jeered. Not every fan supported him. Bigots hated his homosexuality more than they prized a pennant.

* * *

Vinnie's cell rang five times before going to messages. Slider hung up. He tried an hour later, and again heard Vinnie's canned voice exhorting him to leave a message. This time he obliged.

"Yo, Chime. I've been having a spell with Good'un. She's upset, needs a bit of tenderness. Met Upper Deck in my office. He's stubborn like a billy goat. Ain't goin' take responsibility. Thrown me a few threats too. I fear him being with Good'un when Plum's away. Situation seems bad to me. Good'un says I don't understand, but y'all know I do. Talks about complications with Upper Deck. I can feel the dung on my boots. Best you give her a call. Me too when y'all get this."

94

It was nearly time for Ralph to go home. Slider cancelled the prearranged taxi and rode with Ralph on the number 31 bus. The nine-minute ride and two-minute walk had Slider pressing the professors' doorbell ahead of the taxi schedule. Alice Datone was surprised to see him.

"Hey, Ivy."

"Slider, what a surprise. I hope you didn't mind my leaving Ralph at the park entrance. I was in a hurry and didn't have time to come over. Was someone with you?" Alice paused. "Look at me going on. How rude. Please, come in."

"S'okay. I need to be gettin' back, things to do, like y'all this morning."

"Sure. But, please come in for a minute since you've made the journey."

Twenty minutes later, Slider was walking out the front door. They'd gone over Ralph's arrangements for the coming week. Slider would have the dog full-time while she and Mark attended a three-day conference in Vancouver, and a short break for themselves. The extra cash pleased Slider, but he mostly looked forward to Ralph's company. He again refused Alice's offer to stay at her home, citing his familiarity with Vinnie's place, but he would stop by every day just to keep an eye out for intruders.

* * *

Alice puzzled over Slider's comment, "Got myself some office politics that needs lookin' after." She asked if Ralph was too much, and would he prefer he go to a kennel. He adamantly objected, almost shaking. She repeated her concern to Mark over supper. They convinced themselves Ralph wasn't the problem, so it must be something else. Ralph and Vinnie were Slider's only companions.

She and Mark had been astounded by Vinnie's past life and his entanglement with the mob. His plans to return to New York caused them to worry over Slider's welfare. She saw the effect on Slider the day Vinnie left for New York. His permanent absence would be the end for Slider unless he received more social service support. Alice was saddened by the certainty that Slider would not get more help and he would break. Had it started? What could she and Mark do?

Alice shouted to Mark in his office, suggesting they call Vinnie.

Rummaging in his desktop for a conference folder, Mark shouted back, "Why worry him over probably nothing? What could possibly happen to Slider that would be worse than what has already happened?" Mark resumed his frantic search for his notes.

Chapter 17

Foggy Truth

Fog encased San Francisco, and cool air had the locals digging out their sweaters. Kaelin watched Grace finish the meal preparations in her light cardigan, a birthday present she had given her. She loved Grace's efficiency, the balanced meals of protein, vegetable, and fruit so perfectly arranged on the plate. Grace organized the household meals the way she conducted herself at work. Grocery shopping came from an online list. Every ingredient for each meal was listed.

"Too bad you can't join me with this chardonnay." Kaelin's lips smacked.

Without looking up, Grace continued to chop. She pouted. "Thanks for rubbing it in." She giggled as Kaelin continued her exaggerated lip smacking.

"Oh, sorry, pumpkin. Do you feel bad? I wanted you to know you made a good wine purchase last week."

"Good for you. I already knew that."

"Touchy tonight, aren't we?"

Both women enjoyed their jesting. But this evening Grace didn't smile. She planned her talk to Kaelin, a talk forced by Curt and Slider. Not exactly forced, but pushed to the top of the agenda. It had to be done and her procrastination had to stop. Curt wanted her to wait until the baby was born, but she worried Slider might preempt that time. She had called Curt earlier that night to let him know—she was going to tell Kaelin because it would be better she heard it from her rather than Slider.

The two women stayed in the kitchen after their meal. Kaelin poured herself a third glass of wine. Grace removed the plates, waiting for her herbal tea to steep. Dishes were piled in the sink to be placed in the dishwasher later.

In her seat, Grace carefully removed the tea bag from the pot and put it on a small saucer.

"Is everything okay?" Kaelin's voice was soft.

Raising her mug, Grace blew across it and took a small sip. "Hot."

She paused, blew again, then took another sip.

"There's something I need to tell you."

"Oh?"

"I… I don't know how to say it."

"What? Just say it. Now I'm worried. Is it the baby?"

"No. The baby's fine. She's been kicking throughout dinner."

"Then…"

"In a way, it is about the baby." Grace blew again. Another sip.

"And…?"

"I'm sorry Kaelin. So sorry. I didn't know how to tell you. I've wanted to tell you."

Kaelin stood, and walked to kneel beside Grace who was sobbing.

"It's okay, whatever it is. Just tell me."

"It's not okay. I lied about the baby's father."

Kaelin stood up, stepped back from Grace, and waited.

"Curt's the father."

The shouting accompanied Kaelin's hand banging on the table. "My father! He's our baby's father too? This can't be true!"

A range of emotions passed between the women. Grace went into full-blown crying. Kaelin cursed, banged the table several more times, and swung at other furniture in the room until her clenched fists circled in the air like a symphony conductor.

The recriminations, cries, and shouts went on forever, or so it seemed to Grace. She waited until Kaelin was spent. Grace held her belly, crying at the justified cruel words that had been flung at her.

Kaelin took a deep breath then spoke in her normal tone, the shrill of the last half-hour gone. "So, you drank too much with my father here while I was away on my course. You were inebriated and he raped you. Is that the gist of it?"

"He didn't rape me. I had drunk too much, but I consented. I don't know what came over me. I missed you. I felt lonely. Your father has always been kind to me."

Kaelin barked out a laugh. "That fucking bastard is not kind. He left me and my mother for a slut twenty years younger, a twenty-two-year-old just ten years older than me. Don't tell me he's kind."

Grace looked up, then to the window. "He didn't rape me. I agreed. Yes, I had a little too much to drink or I might not have consented at the time."

"And that constitutes rape. You acted in a way you would not have under normal circumstances. You need to go to the police and report him."

Grace covered her face with her hands, and peered out through her fingers. Tears formed again. "I can't. It would be a lie. Curt did not put a drug in my drink. I knew what I was doing. I consented, and now I regret it."

"Then report him. We'll make him pay. We'll make him pay for what he did to my mother."

Grace's chair scratched the wood floor as she pushed back to stand.

"We can't use this to make amends for what he did to your mother and you. Besides, hasn't he been generous to you over the last few years? Hasn't he tried to atone for his actions?"

"And so he should. I've never trusted him and this proves I've been right all along. He's a bastard. You need to go to the police or you're complicit in his treatment of me."

"That's not fair. I can't be responsible for his past behavior. Besides, he'll help us with the baby. If I accuse him of rape, he'll not give us a cent. He'll kick us out of this place. I can't lie under oath."

"Fuck you, Grace. You can and you will. This is my chance to get even. We can't lose. No matter what, he'll be forced to pay for childcare, and we can take the house too as part of the deal."

"Kaelin, stop. This is too much."

"You'll do as I say, you understand! This is my chance for payback. I'll be raising *his* child, so I deserve this."

The words stunned Grace and she moved back, observing Kaelin's contorted lips, her eyes sinking into her skull.

"I need time to think. I knew you'd react badly. Curt told me as much."

"What! You told him that you planned to talk to me? You stupid cunt!" Kaelin slapped Grace's face, who began to cry heavily again. "I'm so sorry. I didn't mean that. Please forgive me. I'm sorry I hit you."

Grace backed away. "I've asked for time off from work, a few days' rest. I'm going away tomorrow after work, and I'll return Monday night."

This news provoked a new argument. Kaelin didn't want Grace to leave. She needed to stay and plan the rape story for the police.

In the bedroom, Grace slowly packed the bags she would take with her to work in the morning. She moved to the downstairs couch to attempt sleep.

* * *

Slider was placing the key in the side door lock to Vinnie's house when he heard the shouting next door. Slider didn't own a sweater, and the cold foggy air wasn't good for his sleeping outside. Besides, he had Ralph. Now he wished he and Ralph could have spent the night in the park. Shouts and arguments stressed

him. He didn't need to know about the argument. He should not
have become involved with Good'un and Plum. Upper Deck was
right.

Chapter 18

Pots and Beds

"Mommy, mommy, I did a poo all by myself in the potty!"

Anthony ran into the kitchen from the downstairs bathroom. He pointed, shouting his words like breaking news on CNN. Dan puffed up, fell to his knees, and hugged his son. Vinnie cheered with two celebratory fists held high.

Anna explained to Ben and Vinnie, as if they needed to know, that Anthony's potty training had been erratic. In her opinion, her grandson's New York City daycare had been inconsistent. She reflected that if her daughter and son-in-law moved to Stamford she'd be available to assist with these kind of problems.

"You know, Dan's start-up venture requires overtime and Ginny's work isn't flexible either."

Everyone saw Ginny scrunch her lips. Everyone knew this bout between Ginny and her mother had gone way past ten rounds. Yet Ginny didn't say anything, because she had conflicting thoughts this time. Ben's beach revelation was still on her mind. Maybe her mother might be right—again—like with Ginny's sthenolagnia diagnosis.

Anna took advantage of Ginny's slow response. She turned to Dan, explaining her position on consistency in potty training.

"You'll have to go easy, try not to become anxious. Feces is easily cleaned up; emotion not so readily. It's best to have Anthony well trained on the potty before kindergarten. He'll have enough to deal with if he has your endowment, which seems likely."

The spinning of the high-velocity fan could not have matched Dan's turn as he left the room.

Ginny shouted, "*Mother!* Don't you know when to stop?"

"What? Dan has nothing to be ashamed of and neither should Anthony. I should have thought you'd be pleased to have two big men in the family."

"Pleased? The size of my son's dick has nothing to do with my upset. I mean you just totally embarrassed my husband."

"Well, dear, maybe you shouldn't have mentioned Dan's penis length to me in the first place."

"Fuck you."

Vinnie ran to put his hands over Anthony's ears. "Let's go play with your train set."

"What's a pen… enth, Unca Ninny?"

Ben didn't move, even as Vinnie shuffled Anthony out the back door. He watched Ginny and her mother argue until the words meant nothing. He returned to the cottage next door and placed his hand on Dan's shoulder.

"You told me about Ginny's mother but your descriptions don't even come close. Does she always just say whatever's on her mind? Does she ever show any self-censorship?"

"Nope. What you've seen is about it. I have been mortified more times than I can count. She's a corker. Of course, the only way she could know about my penis, my sex life, my hang-ups is because Ginny tells her everything. By the end of this vacation she'll know more about you than you do yourself. Be prepared, your turn will come."

Dan grabbed two beers, handing one to Ben, who refused. Training didn't take vacations.

* * *

By late afternoon the big poo was history, or as Vinnie put it,

"Seems we're hung on penis."

"Nice choice of words, Vinnie," said Ginny with no smile at all.

The couples retreated to their respective bedrooms and engaged in afternoon sex, exactly as Anna had predicted.

"What did Ginny say on the beach?" Vinnie asked while rolling on his side and playing with Ben's nipples.

Ben grunted, saying Vinnie was depriving him of his after-sex recuperation sleep. Vinnie acknowledged Ben's exertion had been high, but countered that he weighed nothing compared to Ben's usual barbell weight. "You don't fall asleep after pumping a gadzillion tons of iron, do you? So, what happened with Ginny?"

"Nothing. She was sympathetic and wonderful. Everything you could want in a friend. She knew exactly what to say, not the usual inane bullshit. I love her." Ben eyes focused on the ceiling, with Vinnie circling his hard pectoral muscles with his fingers.

"We saw you two. Dan almost blew his stack, especially when Ginny knelt in front of you. He was convinced she was kissing you. She wasn't, right? I mean you haven't gone hetero on me, have you?"

"Not on your ass, which by the way I was minutes ago, if you hadn't noticed. You know I mean platonic love not sexual, right? Do you really need reminding?"

"That's what I told Dan, ass action aside. So, what did Ginny say about our proposal?"

Ben's eyes closed.

Vinnie lifted up to rest his chin on Ben's chest.

"You didn't say a word, did you? You said you would. What happened?"

Ben's eyes remained shut.

"I couldn't. I was too emotional. We talked about Carl, me, my fears, and mental anxiety..."

A few seconds passed, Vinnie's head rising with Ben's deep breathing.

"What about Dan? What did he say?" Ben's eyes opened.

Rolling off Ben's chest, Vinnie claimed he felt tired and needed sleep.

"You didn't ask, did you...? You chickened out, like me."

With a half-smile, Vinnie yawned and turned on his side. "Let's sleep."

Ben cuddled Vinnie like a tumbling rockslide.

* * *

Down the hallway, Ginny lay on top of Dan, carefully lifting herself off as he gave a low groan.

"Careful, honey, I'm feeling sore. You rode me pretty hard." Dan spoke without hesitation. He'd overcome his shyness of bedroom sex talk, nothing like their first year together. Ginny's commentary and language during sex had shocked him. He'd learned that Ginny was very much her mother's daughter.

"I'm trying. Let me lift up. Can I put my hands on your chest or will it hurt you?"

"No problem. You know I have pecs like Ben. Feel these hard ones." Dan made an attempt to jiggle his pecs the way bodybuilders show off, but he lacked the mass and he had not practiced.

Ginny knew not to avoid comparison. She understood a man's ego was easily deflated if he came in second to another—muscle, intelligence, number of electronic toys; didn't matter what. And Dan was not second place to Ben, not for Ginny. He was her man and she no longer obsessed about strong, muscular men—well, not like before.

"You are big enough for me. Look at these puppies. Big as mine." Ginny went to safe territory for her comparison. And the effect was as she anticipated. Dan's hand flung out. He took hold and moved his head forward for another quick nuzzle.

"You up for another round?"

Dan grinned. They'd just finished their second time after his requisite fifteen-minute recharge.

"Can I take a rain check, unless you're looking to cash in the life insurance?"

"Sure, sweetie. Let me know when you think it's pouring."

Ginny moved off Dan, with his final groan as he was released from between Ginny's legs. She snuggled into his side.

"Ben told me the most incredible thing today. Did you know that Vinnie wants to have a child?"

"Yes. Vinnie told me. I want to ask you about your talk. I saw you kissing him. What was that about?" Dan's voice was strained with the barest hint of his former unpleasant jealous tone.

"I didn't kiss Ben. What are you talking about?"

"Well, it looked like it. Vinnie and I weren't that far away. Your hands were around Ben and you were between his legs with your head on his chest then your head moved up to touch his. I'd say you were kissing. I'm not saying it was passionate or anything like that."

"We need to make an appointment for you to see an optometrist. Yes, I was kneeling in front of Ben but our foreheads touched, that's all. Let me tell you what happened."

Tears flowed again from Ginny with the retelling of Ben's story.

Dan choked on his words. "If we ever lost our Anthony I don't know what I would do. I think about Ben and Carl all the time, especially when our Anthony runs up to him. The poor man. Do you think we should move to Stamford?"

. . .

"I'm sorry, Ginny, I shouldn't have said that. And I'm sorry for seeing something that didn't happen. You know that my old jealousy is gone, don't you? Sure, every now and again it comes back, but I know you love me, and our son."

Past obsession was like a faded stain on a tie: in the right light it became visible. They both knew neither of them was completely free, and both had pledged to maintain control to celebrate their mutual success in the best way they knew how.

Ginny rolled on her side. Dan spooned into her, a replicate picture of the bedroom forty feet away. Sleep brought dreams of friends, family, and unbridled sex.

The downstairs ticking grandfather clock soothed Ginny and Dan, while jarring Vinnie and Ben.

Chapter 19

Showtime

Dinner cleanup fell to Vinnie and Dan. Ginny and Ben were on the back porch, their conversation blended into the sound of waves breaking on the sand. Anna entered with Anthony, bathed and ready for bed. She had volunteered to take charge of the bedtime routine—another perk for the couples and for her. Anthony protested, but there would be no bedtime reprieve. He went for a final goodnight kiss.

"Goo nye, mommy. I love you." More delay.

"I love you too, pumpkin," said Ginny as she embraced and held him a few seconds longer than usual. More delay.

Moving to Ben in a hardback chair, the boy straddled his foot, the cue for a see-saw ride. With no effort, Ben moved Anthony up and down as if counting reps. On the final rise, Anthony crawled up Ben's leg like he was scaling a felled oak, and sat on his lap.

"Make a muscle, Unca Ben."

Ben's arm ballooned, blocking Anthony's beach view. Anthony grabbed to encircle Ben's arm, but failed. Ben placed his free hand underneath Anthony to lift him. They both knew this well-practiced acrobatic stunt. With his tiny hands clasped together, each flex swelled the mountainous bicep and lifted Anthony up and down.

"Ooh, an airplane ride. More."

A stern voice rung out from across the deck. "I think that's enough for tonight." Anna, with book in hand, glanced at Ginny, who understood the unspoken words: *stop this strength play now or Anthony might develop your fetish.* Anna didn't worry or care if her grandson was gay, but she did worry that he might develop his mother's sthenolagnia. And it was too soon to tell about either.

Anna's concerns mattered little to Ginny, and she had told Dan as much. "I know how to protect my son, whether gay, fetish, or both. I'm not moving to Stamford to give my mother free rein over Anthony's upbringing. Not in a million years am I going to be in the same state as my mother, let alone the same town."

Anna crossed the decking and the two women glared at each other, determined to have the final word at the end of the vacation. Each knew the other had been plotting, and each was convinced victory was theirs.

"Can we read about Billy Gruff, Gaama?"

"Yes, I have it here. Then straight to sleep. Grandpa's waiting for my help."

"I can help Gaapla too."

Anna's stretched hand took Anthony's and guided him off Ben. "Nice try, dear, but you know Grandpa needs quiet at night. You can seem him tomorrow."

Fifteen minutes later, Anna entered the kitchen to tell Dan his son was fast asleep, and she'd be at Barrow Cottage. "Ginny and Ben have moved to the living room. It's sprinkling, which means a summer shower's on the way—it'll pass in about ten minutes."

Dan and Vinnie entered the living room with three wine glasses.

"Can we interrupt, or do you two need privacy?" Dan's tone was petulant.

"No, we're fine. Nothing intimate here." No one smiled at Ginny's reply.

From behind Vinnie, Dan stretched to hand Ginny her glass, then froze as Ben extended a hand, not expecting him to break his training diet. He handed Ben a glass, then retreated to the kitchen. On his return, he thought Ben staring at Vinnie seemed odd.

Ginny's teeth showed.

"Ginny, what's up?" said Dan, sipping his wine while placing a full bottle on a side table.

"You have noticed Vinnie's changed, right? I think Ben's 'light workout' plan includes Vinnie."

Ben looked away. *I'm not up for this discussion.*

Vinnie sensed Ginny's amenable mood so suggested a demonstration, moving ahead of his and Ben's original plan—his decision aided by three bottles of Newcastle Brown Ale and after-dinner wine, plus a couple of upper pills. *Maybe the two pills were a mistake,* thought Vinnie, *but this was to be an early bed night.*

The pills were sex-enhancing, a concoction better than Viagra. Vinnie bought them in New York from a weightlifter at Ben's UltraFit gym. He had laughed and asked the dude if he was a fuckin' Merck rep when he saw inside his gym bag, and received a gorilla scowl as reply. Right now they were in full effect—Vinnie's head had started to hum and energy flowed through his body. He didn't tell Ben he had purchased booster supplements to offset his reduced erections from his steroid use.

Ginny accepted Vinnie's proposal for everyone. Ben's twisted lips showed his disapproval. Not of the show, but the timing. Vinnie's unilateral decision. But he couldn't object now, or he'd rouse Ginny's suspicions.

Ben moved a chair next to the sofa and nudged a corner stand lamp forward. If they were going to do this, they might as well do it right.

"Move over with the light behind you. And Vinnie, just your shirt off to start."

"Wait," said Dan. "Let me get my video recorder. This will make a good memory for Ginny... and me." Dan hesitated. "If that's okay with you?"

Creases crossed Vinnie's face. He wasn't an exhibitionist, but isn't that what was happening? Vinnie felt self-conscious. He wasn't like Ben. He had never exhibited his near-naked body in front of a thousand cheering fans. Even three friends seemed like a packed auditorium. He finished his wine, refilled, and swallowed most of it in one go.

"Yeah, just a little show. Shouldn't take long."

Ginny rubbed Vinnie's shoulder. "Calm down. Do as much or as little as you want. This is for fun, right? A look at the new you. Think of it as being on a catwalk, only your body is the clothing." Ginny swung her arm around Dan.

"Just like when I'm evaluating a new Hugo Boss line." She meant her prestigious position as a senior Bloomingdale's buyer.

"Valentino," Vinnie shouted, losing control of his voice.

"Fine, Valentino."

From his chair, Ben thought this was turning out better than they had planned. *Ginny thinks this is her idea, her show.*

Dan moved a large double-size hassock into the middle of the room, pushing aside a coffee table. He placed a gooseneck halogen lamp behind the couch, aiming the light to bounce off-center. He motioned for Vinnie to sit sideways on the hassock.

"Ginny, move to the other side." Dan set the tripod behind the couch with a direct view across the space vacated by Ginny.

"Are you ready, Mr. Fellini? Or should we call for make-up?" Vinnie relaxed. He enjoyed acting. He'd think of this performance as an act, like Ben said he did when posing at contests.

Dan stood and adjusted the camera's settings. "We might as well do this right. Give me a second. I only received this gift from Anna when we arrived."

Vinnie unbuttoned his shirt, but before he could take it off Dan called out for him to stop, and whispered something in Ginny's ear that produced a giggle in response. They left the room, with Vinnie and Ben shrugging shoulders.

Dan returned with an i-Deck, while Ginny inserted her iPod

and cued up some music. Ben recognized 'Un Bel Di' from *Madama Butterfly*; she had made this playlist years before for one of Ben's winning performances at a contest.

With the music playing, Vinnie threw off his shirt, but before his first pose Ginny walked over to him. He stopped.

Ginny's hand took Vinnie's left arm and squeezed, digging her fingers into the tight sinew, rubbing the striations. No fat.

"This is amazing. How much change?"

"I've put on forty-five pounds in three years."

"That's not possible." She looked to Ben.

"It wasn't easy with Vinnie being a vegetarian. I invented some serious protein mixtures, and not all vegetarian-friendly."

Ginny hummed. "I'll accept the diet, but what about steroids? Growth enhancements?"

Ben shook his head. "No injections or pills. None. Besides, Vinnie wouldn't try. He stops at raw chicken."

To cover Ben's lie, Vinnie blurted out, his words slurring more, "Hold on, the chicken's raw? You bastard."

Ginny put her hands up. "Vinnie, give me the stats. Start with your arms."

"Before, about twelve inches pully lumped," which Ginny understood meant fully pumped. "Now I'm sixteen on a good day."

"Impressive. Now let's see it."

Vinnie flexed his left arm. Ben signaled to slow down. Madame Butterfly's sobbing voice climbed as Ginny's hands reached, but she stopped at Ben's booming, "Wait, you have to see this."

With his face grinning, contorting, Vinnie squeezed to produce a near-perfect round bulb higher than his shoulder. He squeezed harder, flushed red, and two veins surfaced on top. Dan's lighting glistened on Vinnie's sweating body in the humid air; shadows highlighted the sinewy crevices.

"Now feel," said Ben, leaning back in his chair.

With her index finger running over the top of Vinnie's bicep, it was like riding on HO train track rails. Ginny's mouth gaped. Vinnie's arm was nowhere near the size of Ben's, but it had perfect shape, hardness, and texture.

"Magnificent. Dan, get a close-up. No, come and feel for yourself."

Dan shook his head and stayed behind his camera.

"Come over and leave the damn camera on auto-record."

Ginny's verbal knuckle-rapping sounded to Dan like her mother. With pursed lips he put down the camera and marched to touch Vinnie's little mountaintop, giving an obligatory squeeze. His eyes widened and his lips parted.

"Not what you expected, is it?" said Ginny.

"He's perfect. He'd win welterweight, but he won't enter," Ben added.

"Got that right. This is ridiculous. It's just muscle." Vinnie swayed; his flesh felt like it was burning. *Maybe I shouldn't have taken two pills.* Madame Butterfly had finished and her sighs subsided. The iPod stopped.

Ginny gave Ben a hard look. "Diet? In three years? Pure BS." She was squeezing Vinnie's arm.

"Yup. Also great genetics and hard work." Ben enjoyed talking about bodybuilding. He knew Ginny did too. This was better than he had hoped. *She's hooked. She's into it like old times.*

Ben launched into his new training routine for mesomorphs like Vinnie with good genetics; he hoped to persuade Ginny that steroids or other substances had not been used.

"Vinnie's around 8 percent body fat naturally and now under 4 percent, which is why he's so cut." Ben hissed out the last word, using bodybuilders' jargon to mean Vinnie's muscular definition. He waited for Ginny to absorb the sound. He kept the rest of his explanation private—*and a diet mixed with drugs you never heard of, the occasional steroid injection, and water-loss pills over the last four days.* Everything he had denied moments before.

"You are touching pure muscle."

Ginny's eyebrows raised as she pulled at the skin while Ben continued.

"He couldn't sustain this low fat level. He's lucky with his natural metabolic rate. His percentage is always low, something many bodybuilders would die for—some do."

Letting go of Vinnie's arm, Ginny's smile vanished.

"I have the same problem with runway models who try for 3 or 4 percent, which they achieve by starving themselves or throwing up after meals. Some use the same water-loss pills as bodybuilders. Anyone under 12 percent is off my payroll. And the clothes hang better."

Ginny didn't notice Ben's bowed head as she took Vinnie's hands and said, "You're incredible. This is a real turn-on."

Vinnie beamed. *This is working. I'm doing it.* His buzz spread from head to spine. He stepped off the hassock, using Ginny's hand for stability.

Dan stayed behind his camera, scanning Vinnie's body, and only a half-smile belied his unease. He didn't understand the fascination, so he opted for banality. "Don't worry, Vinnie. Ginny's mother will have you plump before you return to New York." He smiled like a cartoon character.

With a quick glance at Ben, Vinnie knew they shared the same thought: *Dan will be a problem.*

"Good. I don't like being emaciated."

"I know where there's a stash of Reese's Pieces." Dan's grin pushed his nose upward and he raised his arms overhead in victory sign.

It's like walking a tightrope between Ginny and Dan, thought Vinnie. But he wasn't a trapeze artist, certainly not in his current condition. He said, to no one in particular, "I'm fuckin' wasting away. I'm nothing but a muscle bubble." He continued with nonsense statements and Ben wagged a finger sternly.

Vinnie tightened his abdomen into a cascade of stepping stones, which regained Ginny's attention. She touched his taut skin, onion-layered over hard muscle, and said, "This is not wasting away. Show me more."

Dan barked, "Wait, not so fast." He adjusted the camera angle, then waved his hand.

Ben called to Vinnie. "Get back on the hassock. Remember what's next?" *Oh, shit.*

"What!" Ginny looked at Ben. "Is this rehearsed? You slick bastards."

"Did you really think I would allow Vinnie to come unprepared?" *It's the truth, if not the whole truth,* thought Ben.

Vinnie grinned, his head turning side to side. Ben didn't understand Vinnie's behavior.

Ginny turned to Dan. "Did you know?"

The sheepish grin gave Dan away and he pointed to Vinnie.

"Please, don't blame Dan. We don't have secrets." Vinnie's words continued to slur, his speech slowing. *But we do. Dan doesn't know everything. He'll be furious.*

Vinnie's head lowered. "I wanted Dan to be okay... with... me... you know... showing my bod..." Vinnie took a deep breath. "Dan...ny's shly, I mean shy, about the human body, don't you know? Or maybe not." Vinnie giggled then bent his head further, losing his train of thought.

Dan went to Ginny and whispered, although everyone heard except for Vinnie, "I thought you'd be pleased with the surprise." He paused, thinking of a time when he would have objected to this display. A time of intense marital discord because he had not understood Ginny's sthenolagnia obsession, her need to see strong men.

Ginny touched Dan's head and he returned to the camera.

Nudging Vinnie, Ben asked if he was sporting his peek-a-boo thong underwear, to which Vinnie murmured, "No, should I go get them?"

Ben gave Vinnie a disapproving look, and helped him remount the hassock. *He's wasted. Too much wine? So unlike Vinnie.*

Ben asked Ginny to help unbuckle Vinnie's belt.

A large O-shape formed across Ginny's face at Ben's request. "What!" When she saw Ben's sign that Vinnie was maybe a bit too drunk, she understood.

Ginny looked at Dan, who approved with a half-smile and quick nod.

Stepping to Vinnie, Ginny removed the belt and pulled down one pant leg. Vinnie shook his leg, then stiffened it the way a crane locks position. A striated dewdrop formed, constructed by channels and veins. *It's show... uh... showsomething... time, Ginny.* Vinnie's head spun.

As Vinnie relaxed, Ginny lowered the other pant leg, and Vinnie repeated his previous flex to yield another muscle layering. He kicked his pants to the floor, standing barefoot.

Dan gave a short giggle on seeing Vinnie in Versace low-rise Medusa briefs. He had only ever seen them displayed on mannequins, and never thought anyone actually wore them. Ben noticed the material bunching at Vinnie's crack so tugged to smooth them.

Vinnie stood on his toes, ass tightening, striations marching upward. He relaxed, reforming his perfectly round twin half-moon ass.

"Feel the shape," Ben instructed Ginny, seeing her concentration, directing her to the large, muscled legs and glutes.

Her hand rested on one cheek of Vinnie's backside. Vinnie shifted his right leg.

"Feel the curve. Run your fingers along the lines downward." Ben smiled, knowing he sounded like an art curator.

Ben suggested Vinnie tighten his buttocks again and that Ginny should follow a groove. She didn't move. Ben took her hand and guided it up and down Vinnie's striations. Vinnie relaxed, his perfect half-moons reappearing. Ginny squeezed one and Ben the other.

Fuckin' hell. The rise came as suddenly as the outside downpour. Vinnie's posing trunks tented, and his hands moved to cover his erection.

"Vinnie, it's all right. I have seen one before." Her head tilted to Dan.

"Again with my penis. Isn't your mother enough?" Dan's voice was on edge. Ginny and Ben doubled over.

Vinnie barked out, "I'm with Dan. Care to stand up here with your dongle up and running?" Vinnie's head cleared a little, and he felt excited after ass clenching. His penis throbbed. The laughter echoed the distant thunder.

"We girls don't have a dongle."

Vinnie stuck his tongue out.

Ben patted Vinnie's face and Vinnie bent to touch his forehead to Ben's. He spoke more harshly than he intended, strong alcohol breath carrying his slurred speech. "Let me finish the fuckin' show." Vinnie readjusted his tented posing trunks.

"Don't be mad, we're just having fun," said Ginny, running her hands along Vinnie's legs down to his calves.

"Maybe fun for you, but I'm the me… eat on the… the hook."

Ginny and Ben laughed. "I'm sorry for laughing," said Ginny, "Please stop if this is too embarrassing for you."

Vinnie lowered his eyes as his mind focused, his brain buzzing from the wine and erection hardened from the sex-enhancing pills. *Uh-oh. Not what I want.*

Like telling secrets, Ben mouthed in Vinnie's ear, close enough to chew it off. "Finish or get dressed."

Vinnie looked into Ben's eyes. *Screw all of you. I came to get Ginny's attention, but this is turning into something different. Ginny wants fun.* "Okay, it's fuckin' show time. Roll the camera, Mr. Director. You ain't seen nothing yet."

Ginny looked past Ben to Dan, then to Vinnie, hands on hips, his speech slightly less slurred.

The change in attitude stuck out, much like Vinnie's erection.

Chapter 20

Flying High

The odds of predicting Vinnie's next move were less than four fruits lining up on a one-armed bandit in a Los Vegas casino. Ginny hated uncertainty. "Move the camera to the front of the couch," she said, "for a better view of Vinnie. Ben will go to one side and I'll be on the other."

With chin raised, Vinnie looked like an ancient mariner stargazing, except for the hard-on. Dan refocused the camera and filled two wine glasses, handing one to Vinnie, who finished it in one gulp.

Ginny's neck moved back like a crane. "Are you sure you want to go ahead?" Her voice was pitched somewhere between a question and a concern.

I'm sure, but let's see about the rest of you, thought Vinnie, but answered, "I'm fine, just give me a sec." He felt less woolly, more horny.

Touching Vinnie's forearm, Ginny said, "If you'd rather not then—" In response, Vinnie made her smile by sticking up his middle finger. She tried to reassure him, to let him know that they all differed in likes and dislikes. She and Ben were into bodybuilding. Didn't Vinnie like fashion as much as her? And Dan—she looked across, well a brainiac into computer stuff; "except, of course, his big thing." Dan moaned and asked her to give it a rest.

Vinnie flared his fingers and his eyes moved upward. *I know exactly what I'm doing.* His lips quivered as he swayed.

Rushing blood turned Vinnie's skin pink. *All this touching makes me want to bust. There might be something to this bodybuilding shit after all. You're all going to blush so hard you'll need ice water to cool down.*

The wind rattled the screens, and the summer thundershower began as Anna had predicted. Vinnie's skin glistened in the saturated air. *When I'm done, she'll be begging to be a surrogate mother. Forget Ben's size, this is pure style.* Vinnie's smile grew until there was no space left on his face.

Tapping Ben's shoulder, Vinnie leaned in to hug him. He would have toppled if not for Ginny grabbing hold of him. With Vinnie's equilibrium restored, Ginny went to confer with Dan.

"Start your engines," Vinnie said with almost no slurring. His stance widened, his feet angled.

Dan's hand rolled to suggest action, director style, and he pressed the record button. Generic music played on the iPod. Ginny returned to Vinnie, and with Ben they caged him. Dan motioned for Ben to cover Vinnie's stretched pouch, hiding the visible outline of his penis.

Ginny clapped as Vinnie mimicked Ben's trademark opening routine. Vinnie knew all of Ben's championship moves, but Vinnie's goal was a baby not a trophy—well, it had been. Now he was into getting excited. He strained like Ben had taught, announcing each muscle as if they were musicians in a rock band. Vinnie caught Ginny's eyes as they raked across him. *I'm tight. I'm shredded. I'm popping veins. She can't help herself. She wants me.*

A shift of pose brought about the stretching of pectoral fibers. Ginny reached to touch, her hand skating across Vinnie's lower back and cool fingers cutting into his latissimi dorsi ridges, stopping at his hardened perfect planetarium-round ass. *"What the fu—"* The music drowned out Vinnie's voice. He froze. Without looking he knew his pouch had stretched further. *You wanted to see it all, well here it is.* He later blamed too much wine—and not the sex pills, which he didn't mention—to explain why he had pulled down the sides of his Versace briefs, hinging the front underneath his balls to exposed them and his fully erect penis.

Ben slammed his forehead with his palm, growling at Vinnie.

What have I done? His throbbing, elongated penis made adjusting his briefs and posing at the same time too difficult in his state. He heard Ben swear, which he took as a posing instruction. *Bam.* A most muscular pose. *Bam.* Hands on sides to press outward his pectorals. *See these, Ginny, a baby could milk off them.* Vinnie stood on his toes. *Bam.* The moon's out tonight. Two indented dimples formed on his butt, increasing the pressure on his prostate. *Bam.* His penis pulsated.

From behind, Ginny missed Vinnie's unusual front underwear adjustment, mistaking the bunching material in Vinnie's crack for a ploy bodybuilders use to get around judging rules. She concentrated on the increased striated ass exposure, followed by her hands traveling up and down Vinnie's back like a Long Island commuter.

Ben froze, then in a soft voice said, "Start the finale and I'll help fix the wardrobe malfunction."

"Finale? I'm just starting." Vinnie's hyena grin matched his howl. He moved to a side pose flex, turning away from Ginny, who stayed focused on his back and upper arms. She took hold of his upper deltoids as if hanging clothes on a rack. Vinnie crouched into his abdominal pose to reveal eight bricks.

"That's it. Side to side." Ben's anxiety mounted. He had to distract Ginny from Vinnie's actual posing. "Pinch his skin to understand low body fat." He expected her to grab Vinnie's tricep, but she peeled abdomen skin from Vinnie's rib cage like it was shrink-wrapped plastic.

"No, like this." Vinnie pulled the skin, separating the interstices along the abdominal sheaths. He giggled as his skin snapped back. Vinnie tensed his buttocks and his penis jiggled.

He became uncomfortable with the tightening pouch underneath his testicles and moved to adjust it. Ginny saw. Ben saw. Dan saw. Vinnie's penis moved with the rhythm of the music and his flexing.

"Nice one. Does Ben treat it right?" Ginny giggled and Ben thought, *she's her mother's daughter.*

Like a magician's stage trick, Vinnie's Versace briefs fell to his ankles, and he kicked them aside. Fully nude, his hard penis hanging over the hassock like a rower's oar, he flicked. Ben pinched the base, and deflated the erection.

"Hesh… whys youse fuuu… nn dos that?" said Vinnie, his words barely decipherable.

"No one's interested in your *stiffy,*" Ben said, pointing to Ginny. He then spoke as if addressing a medical conference audience: "Vinnie's lower muscle sheaths interconnect with the upper layer."

Following Ben's cue, Ginny tapped Vinnie's shoulder and said, "Relax a sec so I can see the movement."

Vinnie pouted as he replied, "I am re…relax… ed, seee." Vinnie's chin dipped to his flagging penis.

"I can get that back for you anytime, even if I'm not on your menu."

Vinnie's pout disappeared, a silly grin muffling his words as he stared down Ginny's blouse. "Yeah, you got shum pretty nice ashetts too, better than what Ben's got fo shure."

Ben bounced his pectorals and rolled his platelets.

Ginny mocked Ben by placing her hands underneath her breasts and pushing them upward, her version of Twin Peaks.

Vinnie's abdominals went hard, then harder still. Each brick curved around and subdivided into wards. Vinnie swayed and lost his balance, but Ben's arm was flung out to stop him toppling. Ginny reacted too, her one hand taking Vinnie's, her other grabbing his buttocks, and she said, "Amazing."

With four hands on him, Vinnie smiled. Blood filled his penis to full erection again. His head spun. *I'm going full out.* But then he stopped and called out, "Daa… n, youse K with this?"

"Yeah, it's fine. I'll blur it during the edit."

Vinnie grinned. *Fuckin' A, Dan has changed. A few years ago he'd have gone ballistic.*

With a slow turn, Vinnie transitioned between muscular poses. He held each pose for a few seconds, exposing every fiber before changing to a new position. He had never linked flexing and excitement before. That was Ben's thing, but now he knew.

Ginny admired, her rafting fingers reinforcing her words. Ben cheered. Vinnie felt the rush. He gritted, groaned, and spat cherry pits to build a muscle-mass unit. He reached out and held onto Ben's trapezoid like a shower rail as he concentrated on a single-arm flex. And his penis seeped pre-cum. His chest became a balcony, and his ass tightened as if cracking Brazil nuts.

"These glutes are magnificent. Can you make them harder?" Ginny's eyes were all over him.

Vinnie smile was smeared across his face. *You want hard?* He relaxed, spread his legs until his ass divided, then tensed like a closing bank vault door—airtight and impenetrable. Pressure made his prostate release more pre-cum.

Ben moved Ginny's hand from Vinnie's ass to his shoulder. She slid one hand under Vinnie's armpits to squeeze his pectorals from behind. Ben's hands returned to Vinnie's ass to prevent him toppling.

I've got her attention, thought Vinnie. He tightened his chest, which meant unclenching his rear. *How do you like my tits? Cleavage as good as yours?* Vinnie was into himself. He imagined Ginny's thoughts, unconcerned with Dan's.

The gentle warmth of Ginny's rubbing his nipples excited Vinnie further. He worked his single-bicep pose until a textbook split appeared. *My veins would make the Red Cross cream. Look at my baseball bicep.* Vinnie held hard while Ginny's fingertips explored every fiber. He grunted and swayed. He'd never felt like this before. Blood surged. Muscles popped. Four hands massaged him.

Ben became mesmerized by Vinnie's nude body. He loved this man. He had not anticipated his mounting desire. He whispered to Vinnie to spread his legs to the edge of the hassock. Vinnie used this new posture to flex his triceps into stallion-size horseshoes. Ginny examined him with her fingers but was not quick enough as he flashed into a double-bicep flex. His head turned side to side, acting like he had never seen his ballooning arms.

Ginny pulled the balled-up muscle, tightening her grip. *Yeah, ride your fingers on them.* Vinnie didn't look. He heard humming inside his head. He knew what to do.

Vinnie nudged Ginny's hand aside to feel his bicep. His arousal intensified. He had never been this excited over his own muscles, even more than Ben's. He cried out, "Fuckin' rocket blasters."

Ginny's laughter burst like the recent summer thunderstorm.

Unlike Ginny, Ben's interest was on Vinnie's seeping pre-cum. With the back of his hand, he toweled the glistening fluid and stepped back, exposing Vinnie to the camera. Dan whistled, and Ben quickly returned to sublimate Vinnie's stiff penis.

Dan panned to Vinnie's upper body, while Ben moved to subdue Vinnie's throbbing member. Vinnie wagged his cock from side to side as if saying, "Leave it alone."

"Have it your way." Ben's voice changed, knowing Vinnie had abandoned the bodybuilding show. He'd follow Vinnie's lead. This turned to pure enjoyment—his. Ben had no inhibition, not about bodies. He scooped Vinnie's pre-cum onto an index and middle finger, then with a hand on his shoulder pushed him into a partial squat to spread Vinnie's ass.

Vinnie's smirk receded, his eyebrows rising as Ben's fingers moved deeper into his anus. *What's he doing? This won't get Ginny's attention. Oh, that feels good.* He had no doubt this was going to be a classic Ben finger fuck.

With his refrigerator size, Ben's sideways position blocked Ginny's view, but not the camera on the other side. Vinnie lowered further in his muscular crab pose, allowing Ginny to examine shoulders separated from trapezoids.

Inside Vinnie's rectum, Ben's fingers probed. Vinnie could not relax his sphincter and flex at the same time. Ben's strength pushed Vinnie lower until he had breached the rectal cavity. The prostate massage paused all posing. Vinnie gave a muffled cry. He tried to flex, which only clamped his anus tighter around Ben's fingers. Ginny's hand massaged Vinnie's pectorals. Endorphins shut down Vinnie's inebriated brain; the sex drugs pulsated his penis at racecar speeds.

Pleasure took over. Red blood cells carried oxygen along pipeline veins to contracting muscle fibers. Vinnie's eyes shut, vision unnecessary. He screamed at his exploding ejaculate. The hassock elevation, his perch, and arcing spurt caused his jism to pass across the room, over a chair opposite the sofa, and land on the repositioned coffee table. The camera recorded all.

A second round shot out, hitting the table's edge. A third followed. Vinnie became an erupting Kalashnikov. His ribbon of cum filled the end table surface. His fourth and fifth spurts splattered a magazine strewn on the floor.

Fascinated by Vinnie's bifurcated bicep, Ginny had missed the build-up, but not his cry. She saw yet didn't believe. Dan saw and didn't believe. Ben saw and didn't believe. Vinnie saw and believed—he'd achieved stardom.

Taking Vinnie by his armpits, Ben lifted him high like a trophy, placing him on the floor, with his penis poking Vinnie's ass. Vinnie whispered something about a broom handle, happy to see him.

They held each other, unsure of how wrong their plan had gone.

Chapter 21

Director's Cut

Shock drove Vinnie's giddiness. He felt the way he had as a teenager, the guilty pleasure of committing some minor, tawdry act, like his masturbation under the bedsheets watching his nude brother after a shower, or imagining sex with a high school football player. He'd gotten away with it. He knew Ben would not have felt awkward or self-conscious about exposing his body for one reason—*alpha males never are*. He felt sure the same could be said of Ginny, as self-assured as Ben, forever exhibiting her perfect body and beautiful face around the city.

Vinnie felt exhilarated by his bold act, and not like he had committed a crime. He had exposed himself in the most intimate way to his closest friends. He thought, *I've taken back my life*, then looked down at his nude body. *No, I've taken control of my life.* He had never lived openly; not just gay openness, but freedom to pursue what he wanted to do. And his San Francisco confinement had changed all that. *I'm going to live my life as I want. I'll be an alpha male.*

Lifting his head, Vinnie looked at Dan, quiet, with half-closed eyes. What did this mean? Dan should have been easy for him to understand, but Dan's unsmiling silence left Vinnie wondering. *Embarrassed? Upset?*

As the others moved around with giddy laughter, Dan felt stifled. Not shamed by Vinnie's nudity or sex release, not *per se.* His suppressed words contrasted with his tented shorts. He knew himself to be a 100 percent heterosexual, apart from some experimental testing of the waters, and yet he had an erection. *How could this be?* By the time his penis was fully stiff his memory had recalled himself at thirteen, with his coach explaining to his mother the circumstances of her son's fear: an older, bigger teenager had bullied her son, inducing his exposed member to stiffen. This wasn't unusual in adolescent boys flushed with hormones. It didn't mean he was a homosexual, but her son was afraid it did. Afraid he would become subject to school jokes and ridicule.

But his adolescent hormone days were long gone. Vinnie's action was not that of a bully. Dan clung to his video camera, relieved as Ben said, "I'll take Vinnie upstairs and clean him up."

"Good idea. You do that," said Dan, conscious his response was too loud, too quick. He nearly panicked with Ginny's query that maybe he too would like a cleanup. He smiled as if cramped, worried his thoughts were readable. *She knows.* His shoulders slumped as Ginny continued, "Do you want a quick turn on the hassock first, or shall we go upstairs?"

Heat bathed Dan's face and his hand fluttered the air. *Did she know he had a hard-on?* "Give me a minute," he said, bending to lower the video tripod, taking a second to adjust his shorts. He saw Ginny move closer, so Dan crawled behind the couch. "Go ahead, I'll be right up. I just have to find the…" His voice trailed off.

No one returned downstairs after Ben's announcement of a cleanup break, and no one packed away the brand new video equipment.

The room remained empty until Anna arrived at six o'clock the next morning to fetch her grandson for breakfast at Barrow Cottage. Her routine never wavered, her commitment to strict routines to regiment children. She was brash in pointing out the bonus to Ginny and Dan of extra sleep and the opportunity for morning sex. Anna's message was obvious—these summer benefits could easily continue following a permanent move to Connecticut.

Anna returned to Barrow Cottage holding Anthony with one hand, the video camera in the other.

* * *

"What just happened?" Ben said, sitting on the beach late morning. He disbelieved his own recollection of events. It all had started with Anna's invitation to the men—he, Dan, Vinnie, and Ted—for morning coffee.

With the summer heat wave broken, the temperatures hovered in the low eighties, warm enough for all four men to arrive in shorts. Anna had choreographed the seating in the family room, placing Ted next to Ben on a two-seater sofa. "You're the only one who can fit, and it still might be snug."

Two adjacent single chairs faced the sofa. Leaning over his armchair, Dan whispered to Vinnie, "Brace yourself."

"What's that, dear?" said Anna's trilling voice.

Dan felt like a child in the principal's office after school.

Anna turned on the fifty-two-inch HDTV, with Dan's video camera attached by its cable. She fiddled with an oversized remote control until Vinnie appeared on screen atop a hassock in his Versace briefs. Ted spoke with glee: "Hey, cool man."

More remote fiddling caused a garbled hash on-screen until Anna managed to stop the advance. The image zoomed to Vinnie standing naked. "These things are so finicky. Never mind, this is a good starting point." Anna pressed play, waiting a few seconds before she pressed pause. Only Ted did not know what was about to happen. The image froze with Vinnie center screen, Ginny's hand wrapped around his arm, and Ben behind to one side.

Facing Ted, Anna spoke in her lecturer's tone. "Notice the angle of Vinnie's penis. Male erections have different positions. His nearly ninety-degree is common. However, the angle has no

127

effect on the ability to ejaculate, nor any effect on reproduction. Some women and some men find a penis in this position highly erotic."

Anna turned to Ben. "Is this true for you?"

Ben froze.

"What about you, Ted?"

Silence.

"Let me ask you this. Ted, in general, does Vinnie's erect penis arouse you? Or maybe you're excited a little by Ginny's hands around Vinnie's strong, sinuous arms?"

Silence.

"Come on, Ted, you must know how you feel."

"No," stammered Ted, his tongue slipping, unable to pronounce "cool."

"No idea? No excitement?"

Silence.

"Ted, an erotic arousal aids sperm motility. Let's look at this differently. Grab hold of Ben's arm."

Ted didn't move, so Anna moved across to place Ted's hand on Ben's bicep.

"Come on, Ben, don't act like you don't know what to do," barked Anna.

Ben's flexing pushed Ted's hand upward, his wide-eyed gaze fixed on Anna.

Crossing the room, Anna retrieved a hiker's walking pole from behind a curtain and returned to the television. She pointed to Vinnie's erection, then swung the pole like a saber and Ted squawked like a passing gull as the tip of the pole came toward his groin.

"Is your penis enlarging? It isn't only gays that react to another man's physique, especially a young man like you."

Dan looked down to his feet, his hand cupping his lips as he muttered an inaudible sound.

Anna turned. "What's that, Dan?"

128

Getting no response, Anna turned back to Ted. "Anything?" She rested both palms on the handle of the walking stick planted into the floorboard, as if she was surveying an open field.

"Ted, men of your age faced by someone of Ben's size can have a natural response to his obvious superior strength. One response comes through your penis. Another is mockery, but I wouldn't advocate that." Anna chuckled. "Listen, Ted. The good news is, assuming you became somewhat excited by Vinnie's on-screen ejaculate and Ben's hard muscle, your sperm flow will increase."

Tittering by Vinnie and Dan prompted Anna to face them, and both simultaneously raised index fingers to their lips.

"I've made a copy of this video for you to watch during sex with Rachel. Too bad there is only a single camera angle." Anna looked at Dan. "Not that this isn't good, but you're not a professional, even if this is new equipment. Over time, you'll improve to make higher quality videos." Dan's confusion increased—was his mother-in-law really suggesting that he could eventually produce quality porn films?

Anna continued her lecture. "Visual stimuli improve your chance to impregnate Rachel. The Romans and Greeks had rooms filled with priapic mosaics and homoerotic marble phalluses to enhance sex and reproduction."

Depressing the play button again, the screen images sprang into live. "Look again at Vinnie's penis angle." Anna pointed with the pole. "This penis's steepness occurs in about 25 percent of men. You should try different masturbation methods with your own particular angle. When you find the strokes that increase the ejaculation trajectory, teach Rachel. The goal is to improve the chances for pregnancy. A complete discussion of male masturbation would take too much time now, but I'd be happy to see you later. Perhaps Vinnie or Ben can talk to you about it, as I'm sure this is a topic they know far more about than me from a practical standpoint."

The video advanced to Ginny steadying Vinnie's sway, while

he rippled his abdominal muscles. Ben looked across to Dan. His on-screen thrusting hand in Vinnie's anus was obvious; Ben realized Dan had not worked out what was going on at the time. As the video played, Ginny and Rachel entered with trays of refreshments. The TV speakers groaned. Rachel smiled, lowering her tray onto an end table behind Dan. Ginny held her tray and faced the television.

Looking at Ted, Anna continued, "Vinnie has a well-proportioned rear end, probably bigger than yours." Anna touched Vinnie's TV screen ass with her pole. "Ben's glutes would make this easier to see, but too exaggerated to be helpful. No offense, Ben."

Anna rewound the tape, but not before commenting on the added stimuli of both Ginny and Ben's hands on Vinnie's body. She again took Dan to task for the poor camera angle, missing the way Ben's index fingers massaged Vinnie's scrotum. "Isn't that right, Ben? You are scraping Vinnie's perineum. I wish Dan had moved the camera."

Looking to Rachel, Anna said, "Ted's perineum may be further along than Vinnie's, depending on the shape of his buttocks." Anna dexterously hovered the pole over the screen as she traced Vinnie's rear end while fast advancing the video.

"See here, Ben's massage goes deeper. Again, the poor camera angle doesn't help. But I'm sure Ben's finger extends well into Vinnie's rectum."

The room was silent. Anna froze the screen, which seemed to have the same effect on the people in the room. She faced Ted. "Most homosexual men appreciate rectal massage. I assume Vinnie can relax his sphincter muscles fairly easily, but you'll need to practice." Anna turned to her youngest daughter. "Try helping Ted. If you succeed in entering all the way, you'll increase scrotum pressure and Ted's ejaculatory force. Really put some effort into stimulating that prostate gland. Watch."

The tape played and Vinnie's jet stream pulsated, the

surround-sound screams crashing into the room's silence.

"Really, Dan, couldn't you have moved the camera?" Anna replayed twice, the last in slow motion, her version of the Zapruder scene in Oliver Stone's *JFK* movie.

As the video moved forward, Anna said, "I know that living room like the back of my hand, so if Vinnie's description is accurate and he hit the table..."—Vinnie's nod confirmed Anna's statement—"...then his ejaculate went about twelve feet. With that emission, Vinnie would have no trouble producing babies. Same goes for you, Ted, assuming you have sufficient sperm motility and volume of semen." Ted sat aghast, his mouth hanging open, and his glassy eyes fixed on Anna.

Grumbles came from all corners. Dan marched out first, followed by Vinnie, then Ted. Ben sat, eyes fixated on the TV, until he heard Ginny's cursing. Rachel joined the choir. Ben thought this an unprecedented moment of sisterly solidarity.

The video continued, Vinnie's voice loud, but slurred: "Loosssh howse far... messshure it. My longissh ssshott ever."

Ginny lunged for the remote, yanking it from her mother to stop the play.

Anna's spoke with steady cadence. "You did clean up, didn't you? Veronica is very house-proud."

Ben took this as his cue to leave. He walked past Anna as she adjusted the tight ribbon knotted around her braided silver hair.

"What!" yelled Ginny, her face puffed with as much glamour as a blowfish. "Showing a private video causes you no concern, yet the possibility we didn't clean Vinnie's goo appalls you?" Spittle flew from Ginny's lips. "Don't worry, mother. If I can apply adequate pressure to a man's prostate, be assured I can apply cleaning fluid to a table."

"I'm simply pointing out that Veronica might wonder about a strange stain on her table. She wouldn't know it was Vinnie's personal best, even though I'm sure it surpasses Harold's capability."

Ben stumbled out of the room at Anna's last remark, waiting until he was through the back door before releasing a thunderous laugh across Nantucket Sound. On the beach, he bent to tap Vinnie's shoulder, as he was sitting with Dan, Anthony sandwiched between them. Ted was nowhere to be seen. James, eyes closed, reclined in a beach chair.

Vinnie and Dan rose to walk with Ben a short distance out of earshot of both young and old. Dan grumbled, taking to heart his mother-in-law's critique of his video methods. Everyone smiled at Ben's rephrasing Anna's comment on him: "She basically said I have a big ass."

With spirits improved, Dan said to Vinnie, "I guess you can impregnate a woman with your long-distance shots." He chuckled while Ben and Vinnie laughed hard. They enjoyed their male friendship, each conjecturing over the conversation between the two sisters and their mother.

Ben added, "Did you know your personal best outdoes Harold?" Neither Dan nor Vinnie understood, so he repeated the parting words he heard from Anna, causing them to fall to their knees laughing.

Dan returned to his son and father-in-law. Vinnie punched Ben's arm. "You forgot about my unbelievable sphincter control. Want a reminder?"

The two men held hands, happy smiles pushing them forward, their pace increasing on nearing Veronica's spotless cottage.

Chapter 22

Broken Parts

For the third consecutive day a cool fog seeped across the park. Slider rubbed Ralph's back. "Y'all and me sharing our locker room *agin*. Books and Ivy needin' their time and you wouldn't take to Vancouver."

Ralph's head tilted sideways, as if questioning Slider's excuse. Suddenly, the dog's ears pricked up as if he was hearing the National Anthem played before a game. He barked.

A tall man walked toward them from the gateway path. "Hush, it's only Upper Deck."

Curt stood over Slider and stared at Ralph. "I'd recognize that yap anywhere. You ought to keep your dog quiet when you're eavesdropping on conversations that don't concern you."

"This *cheer* bench's occupied. *Git* and find your own saddle."

"I'll be gone in a minute. I just wanted to tell you again, so there's no misunderstanding—keep your nose out of other people's affairs."

"Affairs is right." Slider's strange guffaw caused Ralph to yelp.

Curt moved closer, bent over, and hissed, "You fucking stay away from my daughter, got it?"

Ralph barked.

"And shut your fucking dog up."

"It's a free country. He can speaks his mind anytimes he

wants. Right, Ralph?"

"You're crazy. No one would believe anything you say."

Uncrossing his legs, Slider scuffed his sneakers on the ground. "Then won't matter none all me speakin' to Plum."

Curt's fingers balled into a fist.

"What, you planning on beating me like a redheaded stepchild? Bet you'd done that to Good'un, too."

"Fuck you, and her name's Grace, asshole." Curt stood still.

Slider gave his best shit-eating smile.

"Stay away." With one hand Curt smoothed his hair. "You don't know jack, got it?"

Mimicking Curt, Slider raised his arm, hand running through his hair. He looked around the park to see a woman pushing a stroller.

"You'un a bad man and a bad daddy. Fess up and tell your daughter. I've not shared but sure as flies find stink I will."

"Tell what?"

"You'un raped Good'un and have yourselves a baby."

Curt's laugh was raucous and unkind, enough to cause the woman to turn and leave the park.

Curt paused, spat on the ground, spun, and walked away. From over his shoulder he yelled, "Keep away from Kaelin and Grace."

Slider shouted back, "Y'all hat with no cattle."

Ralph barked.

* * *

Slider speed-dialed Vinnie, who at that moment was putting Ben's protein shake on a tray. Vinnie fished his cell out of his pocket.

"Hi Slider. Sorry I haven't returned your call. What's up?" Vinnie didn't like to lie but he hadn't wanted to waste time untangling Slider's garbled message.

"S'okay. You and Gong being immoral? Ha ha."

Vinnie waited, not wanting to get into sex talk with Slider.

"You have neighbor issues."

Vinnie removed the phone from his ear to stare at the screen for a second, uncertain if he heard correctly. "How so? Anything to do with Curt?"

"Could be. Don't know whether to scratch my watch or wind my ass," Slider mumbled. "Good'un's downstairs."

"Lover's quarrel?"

A long pause. "Don't think so." Slider digressed about his basement activity the night before, evaluated the men he thought most desirable in the new magazines, and mentioned Ralph's activities, including his bark. That led him to explain the conversation he had heard outside the basement door. Slider stopped talking and breathed into the phone.

Vinnie waved his forearm like a New York traffic cop hurrying cars through an intersection. He waited a few seconds.

"Did you tell Kaelin any of this?"

"No, but I gave an opinion to Good'un. Suggested she talk to Plum. I think she did." Slider had stopped mumbling.

"Oh. Well, you stay out of it, got it?" Vinnie began to shout, as he heard no response from Slider. "Let me handle this, please."

"Uh-huh." Slider hung up, deciding not to bring up his park conversation with Curt.

Unnerved by the abrupt end to the call, Vinnie left the protein drinks in the kitchen and walked onto the side porch. He speed-dialed Grace, who answered on the fourth ring.

"Hi Vinnie. How's Martha's Vineyard?"

Vinnie wasn't in the mood for chit-chat, not after Slider. But he knew better than to launch into his concern. *Start with gossip or you'll alarm her. She would have said something if it was important.*

He gave an abridged version of events on the island, but nothing of the video viewing. He questioned Grace about her work, then on her pregnancy.

As he listened to descriptions of the baby's kicking, her indigestion, and her uncomfortable sleep, he commiserated in his trademark staccato style. Yet he thought, *she's said nothing about sleeping on the couch. Something's up. She's too matter of fact. Slider's right, this is all wrong.*

"So, basically everything's fine," said Vinnie to Grace's final sentence. He paused, thinking, *what a stupid thing to say.* Taking a deep breath in of the sea-salt air, Vinnie forced out his words. "Grace, I know this is going to sound… well, I don't know how it will sound. Slider called me. He says there was shouting from your place, and he's worried something might have happened. Is everything really okay?"

Grace's non-verbal response unmasked her soft sobbing.

"Tell me. Tell me fuckin' everything." Vinnie heard himself. "I'm sorry, I didn't mean to curse. Please, tell me what's wrong."

"Vinnie, I screwed up. I told Grace about me and Curt."

In the following minutes, Vinnie received a rundown of events, including that Kaelin had struck Grace across the face. *Fuckin' bad. Fuckin' worse than bad.* Vinnie's thumb and index finger pinched his eyes shut, an attempt to help him decide what he should suggest next: *Have Slider talk to Grace? No, he'll only make it worse.*

"Vinnie, I'm okay. The baby's fine. We just need time."

"Okay. And Grace—don't do anything until I return next week. I'll be there to help you and the baby. It will all work out."

Returning the cell back into his pocket, Vinnie wanted to punch himself. *What a stupid thing to say. How do I know it will work out? I'm so fuckin' stupid.*

* * *

The day after he and Grace had talked, Vinnie called Kaelin at eleven in the morning Pacific time. He had woken her, which would not have been unusual if Kaelin had crawled into bed in the wee morning hours after an evening of midwifery. But Grace

136

had told him Kaelin was off work for the week. *She probably stayed up drinking to wash away her guilt.* Vinnie squinted at the sun's rays bouncing off the sea as he strolled along the beach. "Sorry, did I wake you? Should I call back later?"

"No, just stayed up too late; too much wine. I need to get up, anyway. How are you?" Kaelin reviewed in detail the East and West Coast weather, as if a meteorologist.

Her quick-fire commentary surprised Vinnie. *Is this her morning persona? Who talks so much when waking up? And the weather? I'd wear earmuffs at breakfast if Ben was like this.*

"It's not the heat, but the humidity," said Vinnie, and whacked his palm against his head. "How you doing?" Vinnie lowered his chin. "I talked to Grace a few days ago." Vinnie slapped his head again. *I'm lying all the time.*

"Oh?" Kaelin's voice went high.

"Okay, this is awkward. Slider called me yesterday. He's worried about you two." Vinnie paused. "He thinks something might have happened at your place. I tried to call Grace this morning but she's not answering. Is everything okay?"

"We're fine. Don't concern yourself about us."

The cool response unnerved Vinnie. He heard Kaelin breathing. *She's lying, just like me.* He remembered his P.I. training course said sometimes waiting revealed more than questioning. So he remained silent.

Kaelin cleared her throat. "Grace has a busy schedule today and she's taking the weekend for herself. She probably turned her cell off."

Vinnie stopped strolling to make a circle in the sand with his toes. *Grace never said she was going away.* "Good idea. Do you know where she might have gone? Is she okay alone?"

"She didn't tell me. Just that she wanted to prepare herself mentally for the baby's arrival. You know Grace, into her meditation mode. She's fine."

This sounded right, yet something nagged at Vinnie. *Sure,*

Grace is an independent woman, but her partner is a midwife so why go away? And why didn't Kaelin mention the argument? Or that Curt had raped Grace? That's what Slider said happened. Maybe she figured it wasn't a topic for long-distance discussion. Vinnie wasn't convinced. He made some excuses and ended the call.

He needed another conversation with Slider. As he was about to speed-dial him he heard Anthony yell out, "Unca Ninny, can we make a castle together? A really big one." A tiny arm wrapped around Vinnie's leg.

"Sure can. Shall we make a moat too?"

"Yes, a *moke.*"

Vinnie's cell went into his pocket as he knelt in the sand beside his godson.

* * *

Slider had waited for Ralph to complete his park meandering before he leashed him to cross the street. Entering Vinnie's side path, he glanced over his shoulder, catching Curt's stare as he opened his car door.

"You again?" Curt said with both forearms resting on the top of the car door, keys in hand. He walked to the front of the car onto the sidewalk a few feet from Slider. "I told you to stay away."

"Y'all's trespassing on my field." Slider looked at Curt's feet on the sidewalk. "Besides, you need to 'splain all to Plum, like the lowdown on you being a daddy after you raped her partner?"

Curt curled his lips. "Yeah, the baby's mine, but I didn't rape Grace. She willingly had sex with me. We've done it several times, not that it's any of your business. She's not a lesbo. It's a pretense and that's Kaelin's fault." Curt's finger wagged.

"That's just a cat covering crap on a marble floor. Y'all fucked the chicken, I'm just holding the wings."

Curt spun around, returned to the open car door, and drove away leaving Slider fumbling with his cell phone—dead battery.

Chapter 23

In the Flesh

Twenty-four hours later and dinners were still eaten in separate cottages. Ginny and Dan dined with Vinnie and Ben; Rachel and Ted went to a local fish shack. James barbecued for his grandson and Anna. The sticky heat wave had broken and a light ocean breeze cooled the evening air.

After dinner, the four friends sat in the living room like they had two nights before, minus the video recorder. Ginny asked Vinnie what had changed so that he started bodybuilding.

The reply came with Ben hugging Vinnie. "Long story." Ben squeezed Vinnie again. "In our little San Francisco house we had a guest…"

A hand went up from Vinnie, "Little house! It's fu—fudging three thousand square feet with a backyard stretching five hundred."

Ben laughed. "The front yard's twenty feet and twelve feet separate us from our neighbors."

Vinnie punched Ben's shoulder.

"Fine. In our humongous house we had a guest from Seattle. Freddie, a guy Vinnie met on his first trip outside San Francisco. It was—" Vinnie tugged at Ben's shirt. "Yeah, another story. Anyway, Freddie told us a story about something that happened once."

In ten minutes Ben told them about Vinnie's Seattle mugging

and Freddie's background: a fit gay man in his early sixties who saved Vinnie from a severe mugging. He single-handedly railed against three teenage homophobic punks. Freddie and Ben convinced Vinnie that with more substance he could avoid hassles. Like Vinnie, Freddie in his youth had been skinny and miserable from constant physical beatings. That stopped after a few years working out and lots of muscle.

With a crow's cackle, Ben said, "It took a virtual stranger to change Vinnie's mind."

A punch similar to before but harder landed on Ben's shoulder.

He explained the renovations to the San Francisco house with a small workout gym in the basement for Vinnie, rather than joining a gym. "Precautions over his whereabouts."

"And Ben's small workout gym is a goddamn bodybuilder's gym with two thousand pounds of weights, ceiling hooks, machines, a rack of dumbbells, floor padding, and wall-to-wall mirrors."

Ginny and Dan had already guessed the gym was also for Ben's extended stays, which never happened. However, Vinnie did gain a workout partner in Slider.

Ben finished by pointing to Vinnie. "You've seen the results."

Everyone went silent, a reminder of the video recording. Vinnie huffed and puffed his cheeks and folded his arms. "Yeah, yeah, I'm a fucking He-Man. Heard it all before."

The tension eased. Ben said, "At least he knows that regular weightlifting is not enough to become my size. Right, Ginny? You know that?"

Vinnie approved of Ben's subtle shift to Ginny, to body size and strength, and seeking her opinion. *This is how we should have started. What was I thinking? Ben's muscle talk will get her going.*

Ginny's head nodded as Ben explained that size came from dedication. He expanded his chest.

Looking to Dan, Vinnie said, "And maybe it's not so disgusting

140

as I once thought." He laughed out loud, before adding, "Still creepy, that's for sure." Dan joined Vinnie's laughter, but Ben's frown stopped him dead.

"I'm just screwing with you, my love. How could I be disgusted with those hard bulges that lift me in such fantastic ways?" Vinnie said this facing Ginny. *Say something, Ben.* Vinnie believed in his unproven telepathic power, but even he was surprised when Ben spoke.

"Sure, but most people thought me a perverted macho narcissist along with every other bodybuilder. Admit it, Vinnie, and you too, Dan, you both took a long time to see my dedication as sport. Ginny knows what I mean. She knows how to look, right?"

Ben stared at his flexed arm. Vinnie thought it a little too contrived and coughed. Ben spoke out: "Ginny's like an art connoisseur choosing a Matisse, while you two bought reproductions of dogs playing poker. Watch the video; you'll see that Ginny's touch and look at Vinnie is different."

Vinnie froze. Referring to the video was a mistake.

"Come on, Vinnie, admit that you could tell Ginny's touch was different? She wasn't groping, despite what her mother implied."

Vinnie shook his head no, vigorously. *Get off the video.*

Ben was watching Ginny and missed Dan's movement. "Yes, the video showed that her touch is exploratory, she examines the fiber structure."

With her smile gone, Ben stopped. He squeezed Vinnie's shoulders.

We're losing both of them. This is wrong. Vinnie began with a series of short stabs at affirmation. "I admit it… she's not sexual… she's sensual, but definitely not sexual. Clinical. Yes, *clinical.*"

Ginny interrupted with a barking voice. "I'm right here. And though I agree, even if I might have phrased it differently, please don't talk about me in the third person."

"Point taken," said Ben as he held Vinnie's hand. "And my

point is that Vinnie learned that lifting weights is not enough to make him super large." Ben's air quotations resulted in another tap from Vinnie.

"He's like Freddie, enough to cause homo-hating punks to take a pause."

Vinnie flexed and Ben pulled his arm down. "And he knows that on stage I receive admiration, which is not the same as street leering. Most people don't accept what I do as sport. That's fine. But what I do is for people who know how to evaluate. People like Ginny."

Ben turned to Dan. "It took you time, didn't it? Can you tell the difference in the stares Ginny receives? You know, when she's being admired, and when it's… the other thing."

Dan didn't answer, so Vinnie affirmed it for him.

After a short pause, Ben said, "When you dated Ginny—and I'm not saying anything you both haven't told me—her body did attract you. Now admit it. And Ginny, I'm not speaking in the third person here. My agreeing to be Ginny's personal trainer was for her to develop her knowledge about bodybuilding, nothing else. She kept me from going insane with the constant inane babble by muscle heads."

Vinnie bent over, "Fu—fudging corn's growing under my feet. Let's get back to me. I'm big and strong." Vinnie stood to flex.

With tag team precision, Ben stood and said, "Maybe, but not as strong as others in the room. Dan, get your video camera."

The room went quiet. Vinnie burst out laughing. "It's okay, Ben's done this too many times to be affected. He's nothing like me. And, Dan, keep the camera locked away from Ginny's mother."

Ten minutes later and with the room's lights adjusted, Dan un-characteristically placed the camera on auto-record as he moved away from the lens. Vinnie smirked, saying "Hey, Anna said you needed to change angles."

Dan glared at Vinnie, who was laughing, but harder when

Dan gave him the finger. Then Dan moved to the front of the camera, pulled his short sleeve above his shoulder, and flexed one arm, using the index finger of his other hand to point to his bulge.

Vinnie jumped in front of Dan, pushed him off-center, and mimicked Dan's pose. Despite smaller arms, his ketogenic diet created near-perfect exposed biceps that appeared bigger.

Ginny said, "Boys love size. Go ahead, Ben, join in."

Perfect, thought Vinnie. *She's playing along.*

Unlike Dan and Vinnie, Ben removed his entire knit-top shirt and shorts, standing in tiny brief posers. Vinnie had a shit-eating grin. *Fuckin' A, do they think that's his normal undergarment attire?*

Ben's two-hundred-sixty pounds cascaded, all grade-A, steroid-fed beef atop a five-foot ten-inch frame. His bulges had bulges. He was in near contest-ready ripped form. Dan and Vinnie stepped away as if Ben was a continental drift and might take them under.

With slowly craned arms, Ben's veins filled with Cherry Coke. As he had done a thousand times before, he lowered his arms a few degrees, then raised, and the mountain reformed. All eyes waited to see Vesuvius explode. Ben stopped and lowered one arm.

Now, a single bicep took center stage. Ben watched his own rising mass as his forearm moved to the perpendicular. He watched the split, a second bulge, as if it was an uninvited guest. His quick glance at Ginny could not find her eyes.

Ben lowered his forearm. Using his high-intensity vacuum-sucking lungs, air rushed through his windpipe, squeezing past gritted teeth and his expanding universe. Ben repeated, this time his forearm lowered to forty-five degrees from vertical, spread-ing rice-paper skin over muscle. His strain creased his forehead with lines, formed like a rake pulled across a sandpit. His eyes narrowed into slits, soaked by dew falling from his hairline. His contorted face turned grotesque. No one cared; no one was looking at his gritted face.

Ginny walked into Ben's galaxy. As if taking notes, she observed the details of his forearm, touched his bicep, and followed his index finger skimming the peak. His was self-admiration with purpose.

With slight movement, Ben's middle finger joined his index pushing into his bicep. He lowered his forearm to elongate the hard mass. Both fingers separated the two-headed bicep tendons anchored at the glenoid shoulder socket, the short head to the shoulder blade. The fingers moved to indent the small distal elbow tendons, and Ben winced at the self-inflicted pain.

His chest exploded as the forearm crept to vertical, now fifteen degrees from perpendicular. All breathing stopped except for Ben's, as if they might deprive him of oxygen. Ben's clenched teeth became a deceptive mask. This was not carefree happiness; this was work. He forced more growth: the lower bicep-base birthed another ridge, itself bigger than Vinnie's entire arm. Ben's eyes sunk, his vision clouded. He had withdrawn into himself, the murmurs of the room a distant prattle.

Ginny's hand stretched out but withdrew, startled by Ben's bark, "Wait for it."

The color of his face changed from red to purple. His eyebrows touched the bridge of his nose. The second bicep creaked, creating another bubble—a third mound? Awe expressed as hush. A room unbelieving, not knowing what would happen next.

Chapter 24

Show-Off

Ben strained to shorten muscle sheaths anchored from shoulder to elbow. Simple physics applied: no two objects could occupy the same space. Layers moved. Ben knew his third mound to be an illusion and not the only one.

Bushes swayed outdoors by the wind broke the cottage silence. Ben turned to spy Ginny's crystalline eyes. In their shimmer, he knew that damage had been done. He and Vinnie had miscalculated. They had betrayed a friendship. Ben recoiled, believing he had become complicit in Vinnie's selfishness. To satisfy their need, they risked this hurt.

Ben continued.

* * *

Ginny had seen this many times on many men: amateurs and pros; small and big; on the ice cream man. None compared to this. She felt engulfed in a nonexistent world. All that existed was the strength. Her desire rose like Ben's arm. She felt solidarity with each tugging fiber. Her fingers skipped, crisscrossed the power-grid veins. Ginny accepted illusion as fact. She believed in the third mound, overruling common sense that this was impossible. Her index finger plowed the furrow until it was swallowed. She thought herself immune, that her history would not repeat. *I can manage. I don't need this. Once it's over I will stop thinking about Ben's massive power. I won't need to see it again. I can control my feelings.*

Anguish disguised as grunts, using his own strength against himself, Ben stood in glory. He held, letting Ginny explore. Soon other hands joined hers. This was for everyone, or so she believed. Dan and Vinnie knew themselves to be a different species to the alpha.

Was this a game? Ginny lashed onto Ben's arm, and wondered if Vinnie explored every night. She didn't believe him when he said this provided no thrill. Had he not said he loved what Ben's strength could do during sex? Did he not marvel? She needed to know.

"Vinnie, you must find this thrilling."

"Yeah, unbelievable," Vinnie said, trying hard not to use his telephone survey tone. *Did Ginny hear my ruse? Had the entrapment in her obsession worked? Look at the gaze and her touch. Look at Ben. He is magnificent.*

Yet Vinnie did not know Ben's absence of joy in their success. Ben knew Vinnie lied. He did not enjoy a muscular display in bed. He was not a muscle worshipper, but played the part for Ben's sake. Ginny was not playing. *What have we done?*

As if he needed to participate, Dan said, "This is unbelievable. How big?"

Ginny was quick to scold. "Dan, it's not just about size. Feel the power. Look at the definition. See how the layers separate and shred."

Ah, thought Vinnie, *she doesn't get it. Dan doesn't really care so much about Ben as for her interest in him.*

Swimming was Dan's athletic interest. Sure, Dan valued endurance and dedication, and would give Ben his due. But size and sinews were not the point. Vinnie and Dan felt the same. Ben's sculpted body was a mere tourist attraction; his winged lats a curiosity. Ben trained with dedication, but for what purpose? Vinnie understood Dan. They were small boys next to

Ben. Vinnie paused in thought. Would this be a problem when the time came to ask Ginny to be surrogate? *And Dan, is it okay for muscle-bound Ben to be the donor?*

The little conversation dwindled further. Only one question hung, and Ginny asked it. "How did you train to do this? When did it happen?"

To everyone's surprise, including Vinnie, Ben glanced at his split peak, seemingly unimpressed, yet with a rising tone said, "First time I've seen it." He didn't add that besides normal contest training he had done extra for this occasion. He didn't reveal the extra doses of steroid enhancements for the previous five weeks, unconcerned for one reason. His biggest danger came with his increased diuretics to show Ginny something she had never seen. He had been on an extreme diet for two weeks, and excess water-loss pills for a few days. Had he gone too far? Ben worried about death induced by ketoacidosis, which was statistically more likely than heart failure caused by steroid abuse. Mortality had not really been Ben's concern for years, not since Carl. Vinnie had changed that. And for Vinnie he had taken this risk. In his mind, his preparation was to win the "Ginny contest." He had calculated the risk, and the fact that he was still alive proved that the gamble had been worth it.

And Ginny's rising cheekbones, smile, and the grip on his arm proved he had calculated correctly. His one miscalculation seemed to be Ginny's looming full-blown return of sthenolagnia.

Dan vied with Ginny to feel Ben's split peak. Vinnie lost interest and stepped back. Ginny's hand moved to Ben's relaxed, dangling arm as he continued to flex the other. She massaged it, tooling the central vein as if to draw blood. With Ben's groan, Ginny looked at his cragged face, teary eye sockets, flattened nose, and lips barely covering his teeth. She knew. Ben was about to enter a permanently flexed priapic bicep.

"Enough. Relax now." Ginny took charge and lowered Ben's

arm. She massaged, and said, "You're incredible." A short pause, and then she followed with, "All of you."

Dan took hold of Ginny's waist. "Nice try. We know who's the biggest and strongest in the room."

Vinnie confirmed Dan's view, and Dan continued. "But I agree with Ginny. You are fantastic, Ben. As a non-gay male I say you are a turn-on." Dan stopped, believing Anna had made him say this. *I didn't tell anyone about the other night, but Ginny noticed, I'm sure.* Dan continued, "I can't imagine how you feel but I understand your dedication. What a privilege to know you and call you my friend. You are a champion in all senses of the word. Thank you for sharing tonight..." Dan's voice cracked.

Tears formed in Vinnie's eyes and he smiled to himself.

Ginny took over. "I think what Dan wants to say is we love you for your integrity."

Ben bent to pick up his shirt, his face red. He turned to the rear wall while he dressed. Everyone heard his soft sobs, but only Vinnie knew Ben's shame, because he shared it. The integrity Ginny attributed to Ben was false. They both knew it. So Ben cried before Vinnie, which was a first.

Ben's eyes wiped, he turned to Ginny. "I'm sorry. I'll bet I wouldn't be able to scare off those Seattle punks if they saw me now. I'm such a wimp."

Laughter echoed off the walls. Dan's words barely escaped. "If you're a wimp, then I'm a French fry."

"What? That makes no sense." Vinnie made more comments to lighten the mood.

They gathered for a group hug, but instead of joining them Ben waited and lowered himself to wrap his arms around the three pair of legs above the knees. From a squat, Ben knotted them into one and hoisted the collective group into the air. From their lofty position Ben heard a cackle from Vinnie: "Yeah, what a wimp." This time the laughter bounced off the ceiling.

Ben held the group, which he hoped reminded Ginny and Dan

of AFF—Air-Fuck Friday, the Friday three years and nine months before when Ben had held Ginny and Dan above their bed as they copulated to produce Anthony. Today's lift wasn't subtle, but Ben's size and competitive attitude never suited subtle.

"Would the crybaby wimp mind putting us down? I'm getting dizzy." Vinnie touched Ben's shoulder.

As they took their seats, Ben cleared his throat to say, "Could we get serious for a moment?"

Dan spread his hands like catching a basketball as he said, "Excuse me, but W… T… F? Wasn't what just happened serious, aside from Vinnie's wisecracks?"

Dan creased his arm, unaware Ginny had put a hand to her face. She had her father's foreboding. Something was about to happen. She took Dan's hand and put one finger to her lips, then touched his.

"I'll bring us some refreshment," said Vinnie as he walked to the kitchen. As he loaded the tray with drinks, his cell phone rang.

"Oh, hi, Slider. What's up?"

After ten minutes, Ben went to the kitchen, returned with the tray, and handed Ginny and Dan their beers. Grasping his protein shake he said, "Looks like Vinnie has decided to take a walk. We'll have to postpone our discussion."

Chapter 25

Advice Given

The late-morning sun entered the side window of the bedroom. Vinnie watched Ben put on his workout gear and head for a local gym, not expecting to see him until noon. He didn't get how Ben had any energy left, especially as he did most of the heavy work in bed. Is this what people meant by getting away from it all? Vinnie didn't think about it for long, as he had his own day planned. A playdate with his godson on the beach; a video game with Dan after lunch; and a replay of the morning bed scene with Ben in the afternoon before supper. With Ginny, the play became more serious: review of current fashion, fabrics, Broadway shows, and novels. He didn't go out of his way to avoid Anna, but didn't seek her out either. Rachel and Ted spun around the island on bicycles on their last day before returning to New York.

Relaxation didn't come easy to Vinnie. He returned to the bedroom before lunch, ahead of Ben. Vinnie secluded himself for some alone time and to check his phone messages. This was another way to avoid a chance encounter with Anna. Even a half-hour alone with her and she would divine his every secret. Rachel had called Vinnie a "fucking pussy, afraid of an old lady." Vinnie made a rude gesture, saying, "Fuckin' right. You'd have to be out of your mind not to be terrified of her."

His answering service informed Vinnie that he had four new

messages. "Probably all Slider and his ramblings," Vinnie said out loud. He waited for the first message: Slider's from the previous night, but they had spoken after that so he deleted it.

"Hi, Vinnie," began the second message, and he was surprised to hear Grace's voice. "I'm sorry to bother you. I had wanted to tell you in person or at least speak with you by phone. I guess you're occupied with your friends and family. Anyway, things have moved quickly here. I didn't want you to hear this second-hand, so... uh, I've decided to leave Kaelin and move in with Curt. I know that sounds stupid but honestly it's not. Kaelin and I can't manage the baby... besides, after last night... well, trust me, it's better this way and I feel more secure with Curt looking after me and the baby... I'll catch you when you get back, but I guess that won't be for a while."

The message clicked off.

The third message was another from Slider. He provided his version of an update. He'd seen Upper Deck at Plum's house. Some three minutes later he was just reaching the point with Good'un having left early in the morning. The long message stopped abruptly. The fourth message was Slider continuing as if there had been no break.

"Me and Good'un jawed before she went. She had good reason to leave. Said she'd inform you herself, give you the low-down. Y'all be out in right field waiting for the pop-up from her. She got into it with Upper Deck. He's one real angry cracker who needs to be sent to the showers. He's like a rabid stud in a field of bitches in heat." There was a long pause that made Vinnie think Slider had finished until he heard a cough, then Slider's voice resumed. "Vinnie, this here's a big problem. Call."

Vinnie nearly dropped the phone. If Grace's message had surprised him, then Slider's stunned. He had not heard Slider call him by his real name since the day they met. This was big.

Confusion set in and Vinnie grabbed a beer before heading to the back porch. He stared at Nantucket Sound, filled with small sailboats crisscrossing in the mild breeze. Vinnie hit replay on the message service and made up his mind he'd call later, adjusting for the time-zone difference.

* * *

Anthony was fully rested due to his grandmother's diligence with his afternoon nap routine. Anna had kept her word and allowed the two couples their afternoon sex, but no one had used the opportunity today. Ginny and Dan strolled Edgartown's trendy shops and indulged in ice cream sold as "gelato," which seemed to justify the small fortune it cost. Vinnie told Ben he was too distracted, and begged off for alone time. Ben worried but knew Vinnie had his moods. He was also glad. His leg workout routine had been strenuous and he wanted to nap.

Ben arrived on the beach after his solo nap. He wore an acceptable, non-revealing bathing costume, avoiding his skimpier poser suit when with his godson. Vinnie was already with Anthony as Ben strolled over and, despite modest bathing attire, Ben burst out in all directions, pumped from his workout. The two men and Anthony built a large sandcastle and hauled buckets of water from the sea. Unca Ninny was buried as treasure in the sand by two notorious pirates.

By early evening, Vinnie had asked Ginny and Dan if they would mind him and Ben having dinner alone. They approved, maybe a little too agreeably, but Vinnie didn't care.

While walking the same Edgartown streets that Ginny and Dan had explored in the afternoon, Ben thought his baggy shirt sufficient to prevent stares, which Vinnie called a "fuckin' fashion nightmare." Ben hadn't expected Vinnie to don a tight-knit top with loose weave revealing his shimmering skin and accenting his buff torso. Two guys whistled as Vinnie walked by, then froze at Ben's menacing glare. Ben relaxed, flashed a smile and formed an O-shape with thumb and index finger. The men replied with index and middle finger forming downward Vs and started to ap-

152

proach until Ben wagged his finger. With a fake irritated tone, Vinnie said, "Hey, they were good-looking and well dressed, better than some people I know."

On their return to the beach house, Vinnie retrieved his cell phone from its charger: three new messages. The first was Rachel to confirm a goodbye party for her and Ted's final night. The second was Anna reconfirming Rachel's message. Ben and Vinnie found it incomprehensible that after a major blow-up less then forty-eight hours earlier, all had been dismissed and defused.

The last message was from Slider.

"Yo, Chime. Something's up. There's more to Upper Deck being the father to Good'un's child. It's a change-up pitch. I'm waiting to hear from Good'un… I might try Plum too, tell her everything. There's a yellow jacket in the outhouse, thought you ought to know… I'm still hanging at your place, this fog's hog-killing weather and no good for Ralph… he goes back to Books and Ivy's tomorrow… new reading material in your mail… I'll be in the bullpen, give some thought to it. I'm spectin' y'all be doing something similar with Gong. Gotta run. Oh, did I tell y'all of Good'un's change-up pitch. Upper Deck threatened to beat scc… scc… scc… like a rented mule."

Vinnie's grinning had lasted until Slider mentioned Curt's threat. The message broke up, but it seemed like Curt was going to get into a fight with someone. Who? And Slider left things hanging—what was Grace's change-up pitch? On the plus side, Vinnie thought Slider seemed less agitated, and he had returned to calling him Chime.

Placing his paperback book on the bedside nightstand, Vinnie kicked his shoes under the bed and mumbled, "Don't mess things up, Slider." He held his phone, fingers hovering over Slider's speed-dial number. From the window, he could see the balloons at Barrow Cottage. He had wanted to bring something special for Rachel, his first friend out of college, and the person who had introduced him to Dan many years ago. Vinnie placed his cell phone in the charger cradle. *Hell, Slider will be in the middle of jerking off with the new magazines. I'll call tomorrow.*

Anna called from downstairs, and Vinnie felt like a small rodent caught by a notorious mouser.

Chapter 26

A Promise

Before his bedtime story with Unca Ninny, a large scoop of ice cream with sprinkles was carried to Anthony, a candle on top. "A candle, another birthyday for me?"

Anna smiled at her grandson. "No, Anthony, you have to wait a year. This is a special decoration. Why don't you blow out the candle and wish that Aunt Rachel and Uncle Ted make you a baby cousin to play with?"

Heads shuffled, and all three couples grabbed their partner's arm. Rachel broke into a huge laugh, and whispered to Vinnie, loud enough for Ben and Dan to overhear. "That's my mother, telling everyone when her daughter's going to fuck her boyfriend. I can text you the exact moment we start if you like."

Only Vinnie laughed, being Rachel's soul mate. Dan turned to Ben and said, "I told you this vacation would be different, didn't I?" Ben shifted slightly while making small lip movements, neither smile nor frown.

Vinnie insisted he read Anthony his bedtime story, which James had been doing most nights, but he quickly agreed. Ginny understood—her father conspiring with his two daughters to encourage Anna to retire to bed early, leaving the room to the younger people. "I guess it has been a long day, maybe an early night makes sense." Anna yawned like a stage actress. Ginny turned to Rachel, and the two sisters raised their eyes in unison.

By the time Anna and James had entered their bedroom down the long hallway, Rachel said in her stage bellow, "I'll bet mom's found a way around menopause and we'll have ourselves a sibling next year."

The words caught Vinnie descending the stairs, but he didn't laugh, nor did anyone else. Vinnie produced a quiz he had prepared and teams formed. Soon the room became a real party, with laughs, hugs, and typical squabbles, mostly by the two sisters disagreeing over correct answers. Two hours later the party broke up.

Vinnie entered the bedroom intoxicated, while Ben managed to maintain his pre-contest diet except for a small Prosecco to toast Rachel and Ted. Vinnie felt Ben's fingers running across his chest. Vinnie turned on his side, and Ben nestled, covering Vinnie the way a big top covers a small meadow. Ben's breath warmed the nook of Vinnie's neck, a tingling excitement racing along his spine.

Keeping his eyes closed, Vinnie anticipated Ben's touch, the moment his big arm would cross his shoulder to pull him closer. Ben's fingers flicked Vinnie's nipples, and the adventure started. Ben pushed hard into Vinnie's back, making himself known as though Vinnie hadn't noticed. The light sheet covering them was flung to the floor. The open window filled the room with the slightly chilled summer air of Nantucket Sound. Ben's broad back shielded Vinnie until with one hand Ben lifted and opened Vinnie's legs, holding his knee up. Vinnie banished his thought of sleep. He waited for Ben's body to lower, for his head to move under. Vinnie's body rose, lifting his buttocks to allow him to turn on his stomach, spread wide his legs. Ben helped him up, and then the giant mountain avalanche descended.

Throughout the next twenty minutes, groans escaped the open window. For each anticipated thrust, Vinnie grabbed the pillowcase, feeling a warmth that did not stop until he imagined Ben had reached into his lungs. Although spent, Ben used his

156

remaining energy to lift off, or else suffocate Vinnie. He rolled to his side of the bed, and with one more exertion pulled Vinnie on top. Their kisses were more than lips and tongue. Grasping behind Vinnie's neck, Ben pulled him in. Vinnie took hold of Ben's handlebar traps, large enough for a team of mountain climbers. He waited for the next surge, Ben lifting his pelvis, Vinnie sliding along Ben's chest, their embrace and kiss creating a photographic pose.

Both men released once more. Vinnie did not want to talk, not now, not tonight, not ever. He remained silent until he heard Anthony's cry from the bedroom down the hallway. The child's soft voice brought the night to an end, this night, these summer weeks that Vinnie would never have thought possible. All was coming to an end. And maybe not just the summer, but everything. Permanently.

"I love you Ben, you know that?"

"Me too. I never thought I would have this again. I want you now and forever."

Vinnie moved off Ben, lying on his side.

"Vinnie, you okay?"

"Yeah… it's just that I've been thinking. Things have happened in San Francisco that I need to look after."

Ben sat up, his back against the headboard. "Like what?"

"I've heard from Slider. Something is happening with Grace and Curt. I'm worried about the baby."

"Vinnie, I know you are. But you can't be involved in other people's lives, not to this extent." Ben took Vinnie's hand. "I've agreed to talk to Ginny. I said I'd have a child with you, even though I have had second thoughts. But I promised you, and I will keep my promise."

"That's the point. Will you resent the baby? Will it drive you away?"

"I don't think so. I'm going to make it work for us."

"And I wonder if I'm asking too much of you. I love you.

I don't want to lose you. And Grace is having a baby that I can help with."

Ben let go of Vinnie's hand. "It's not your child. Not your business."

Vinnie sat up. "I know that. But she's a friend. Kaelin too. They need my help. Slider said some things that have me worried."

In an abrupt move, Ben got out of bed.

"Please, Ben, you have to understand how I feel."

"I don't. I said I'd talk to Ginny. What more do you want?"

A long silence passed. Ben walked to the window, his naked body filling the entire frame. No one would be up this late. No one was looking out the windows of Barrow Cottage. If they did, Ben didn't care.

Vinnie interrupted Ben's gaze, walking behind him and placing a hand on his shoulder. "I'm going back."

"What?" Ben turned halfway around to face Vinnie.

"I'm going back to San Francisco. I'll take a flight from Boston."

Ben turned to face Vinnie full-on. "What about our plans? You and me, together in New York?"

"I'll join you later. Besides, you'll be busy with the contest. You hardly take notice of me or anything else in the weeks before your performance. You'll be concentrating on your diet even more than you do now. I won't see much of you and you'll be too self-absorbed." Vinnie stopped talking.

"Me? Self-absorbed? What about you and your crazy involvement with other people's lives? Didn't you learn your lesson last time when you were doing your investigative work?"

Vinnie's lower lip covered the upper; he returned to the bed and turned to face the wall. Ben left the room nude, and walked on to the beach until his feet touched the high tide mark. At one-thirty in the morning he sought solitude, the salt air filling his nostrils, the pungent smell absorbing his fury.

A few minutes passed before he heard Anna calling to him from across the sand. He put his hands in front of his crotch as she approached.

"Ben, I'm a doctor. I've probably seen more men's genitals than you, which must be saying a lot."

With a nod, Ben removed his hand.

"Do you know what time it is? What's bothering you?"

"Nothing. I just felt I needed a little night air."

"Ben Hausen, you're a liar. No one steps out at this hour on to the beach naked, unless planning a skinny dip, which you are not. I don't mind you being naked but it bothers me that you're lying."

With his head lowered, Ben mumbled, "Vinnie and I had a disagreement."

"I figured that much. What about?"

"He's obsessed with a problem in San Francisco. He wants to return to help our neighbors, two women. He's already started an investigation. I'm not completely sure of the issue but Vinnie feels responsible for these women. One's pregnant. He said he doesn't want to come back to New York with me."

"Does it involve the mob again?"

"No, I don't think so. It's a personal matter between one woman, her pregnant lover, and her estranged father. The two women are having a baby together. Vinnie thinks the father raped the woman. That's all I know."

Anna moved closer to Ben, grabbing his hand, tapping his arm. "Such enormous physical strength yet inside such fear, such fragile inner emotion. You're vulnerable for reasons I don't know, but you are."

"Why do you think that?"

"First, you're out here in the nude. Second, you just said Vinnie doesn't want to go back to New York with you. But I heard he's concerned for his friends, one of whom may have been raped. You perceive his desire to help his friends as a rejection of you."

Hunching down, Ben folded slightly. "There's more than that. I can't go into it."

"Like I said, I've only made a quick analysis. There's an obsession here too, that I can tell. I know about obsessions... Ginny's, for example."

A smile came over Ben. He straightened up, looking into Anna's eyes. "Me too."

"Then why did Vinnie and you perform for her? Do you know the risk of a setback?"

Ben's smile disappeared. Was Anna clairvoyant? "I... I guess we wanted to give Ginny a show, something she'd enjoy." Ben waited. Did she catch his second lie?

"Hmm... be careful. Ginny's vulnerable. You too. What will you do about Vinnie's decision? He needs help, too."

With a nod, Ben touched Anna's shoulder, his hand underneath her long, silver hair without its customary tie; he pulled her closer. "Thanks. You're right. And I don't know. Maybe Vinnie has a need to help his friends. Maybe I'm just afraid he might get hurt again. I don't think he's in danger, but he might piss some people off pretty badly."

Anna removed Ben's hand from her shoulder, pulling him away from the water's edge. "Come to the cottage for tea, but put on some clothes or my sanctimonious daughters will give me no peace."

"No thanks, I'm on a strict diet. It's late... or early, whichever way you look at it." With a smile, Ben half-turned when Anna touched his back.

"They're bigger than I expected, given your steroid use. It might be a problem. I'll examine you in the morning, and if necessary I'll contact my colleague at the New York-Presbyterian who's a testicular specialist."

Ben looked down, then quickly up, face flushed red, his breathing rate increased. "Anna, I'm fine, really. I have check-ups."

"Hmm. Ben, if your testicles have always been that size, then a lot of women, uh men too, would be very envious of Vinnie." Anna slapped Ben's rear end. "Did that hurt? No? And neither will my examination. I'll see you in my office in the morning."

Ben wanted to explain, but he said nothing as Anna's heels flicked sand as she headed back to Barrow Cottage. He silently cursed Dan for his inadequate preparation about Ginny's mother.

But the old witch doctor had helped him with his decision about Vinnie.

Chapter 27

Ralph Knows

On this beautiful summer's day nobody could have anticipated a traffic jam starting a mile before the Sagamore Bridge over the Cape Cod Canal and continuing north along Route 3. "These fuckers should be fuckin' going to the fuckin' Cape, not heading to Boston." Vinnie's anxiety about missing his flight boiled over. Ben told him to calm down in his big-man, authoritarian voice, and Dan added, "Vinnie, all that cursing doesn't help. We'll be fine." Not one of the men admitted they had cut it short and should have caught an earlier ferry.

If cursing didn't soothe Vinnie's nerves, neither did Dan's cautious driving. Vinnie saw at least three opportunities to pass a slow van in front of them. *Dan drives like he's in a sheep herd. Fuckin' pass the jackass.* "There's a gap up ahead in the fast lane, Dan." Dan replied in an irritated voice that staying in the slow lane gave him the choice to exit at the Quincy split and negotiate Neponset Circle along Dorchester's backstreets, which would bypass delays along the Southeast Expressway. Vinnie's backseat cursing continued and Ben's front-seat silent knuckle cracking didn't help either. They all felt degrees of apprehension, anger, and sorrow.

Reclining on the afternoon flight, in an upgraded, extra-legroom coach seat, headset adjusted and iPhone in flight mode, Vinnie replayed Slider's message that he had downloaded as an audio file rather than leave it on AT&T's mail server.

"Yo, Chime, you won't give this much credence, probably like me, as confused as a goat on Astroturf, but Good'un's takin' R&R. I don't blame her, but she's a goin' to a place where the buses don't run."

Pausing the recording, Vinnie thought, *yeah, well I'm fuckin' depressed. Why should Grace go away alone? That's not what she told me. She was meant to be with Curt, not much better but at least she wouldn't be alone. And why not tell anyone where? And what about the baby? How far is the nearest hospital?* Vinnie pressed play and Slider's voice returned.

"Upper Deck figured out I know as much as the chickens under the porch."

Vinnie pressed pause and thoughts rushed through his brain. *What exactly does Curt know that Slider knows?* Slider's previous cryptic message informed Vinnie that Slider had told Curt he knew where babies came from.

Hitting play again, the message continued. "Yeah, I told Upper Deck I'd be tellin' his daughter. Plum needs to know her daddy's gonna be another daddy, and with her true love... only it wasn't true love but a whole lot of bull honky. Imagine that? And people say I'm the one with a hole in the screen door. Well, I'm not as crazy as normal folk."

Vinnie's smile lasted until the next air-pocket jolt. He wished Slider had never become involved. A big mistake. Slider had entered the big league, this one unfamiliar, and this particular big league had different rules—rules that Slider never learned.

And Slider paid for not knowing the rules. Vinnie's return was sooner than even he had planned. Ben did not try to stop him. One phone call had changed everything, but this was not the message replaying as the plane landed at SFO.

* * *

Twenty-nine hours before Vinnie's flight, Ralph had wagged his tail as the bus pulled away. Alice had him ride unaccompanied this morning, explaining to Al she was late for an early-morning meeting and couldn't reach Slider on his cell—probably needed charging. She wondered if Ralph could ride alone. Al smiled and waved the dog on as if he were a normal passenger.

At the park, Ralph beelined to his favorite corner, and completed re-establishing his territory before a full bladder release. With business completed, he scampered to the empty park bench, finding his leash underneath. He took it in his mouth, pranced a few steps, dropped it, and lay halfway under the bench for the partial shade.

After a short snooze, Ralph strolled across the park to the corner opposite his usual spot. Densely planted bushes with thick foliage formed a sentry line behind two rows of flower beds. Ralph easily crossed the flower demarcation line to reach the smelly object.

Sniffing the dirty shoes and rolled-up pants legs, Ralph casually perused Slider's motionless body. He pawed Slider's shoulders, and pushed his snout into the man's chest. After a few pawings, Ralph barked. He barked several times, then moved back beyond the flower bed to yap from the pathway. Pacing along, he stopped every few minutes to face the bushes and bark again. Ralph's unrelenting yapping was overheard by a jogger outside the park fence. The jogger knew Ralph as the dog that was always with the homeless man. He retraced his steps to enter the park and jogged toward the barking dog.

"What's wrong? What's the matter? You see a squirrel?"

Ralph stopped barking to twist his head.

"Okay, I'm stupid. Why are you barking? Show me."

The man gestured at the bushes and Ralph moved off, again crossing the flower beds. From inside the bushes, Ralph began his nonstop barking again.

The police car arrived in ten minutes, and an ambulance five minutes after that; this was not an urgent call—it was one to retrieve a body.

The policeman squinted at the shocked jogger. "Do you know the man?"

"Uh… uh, by sight. He's here most days. Sits on that corner bench." The man pointed. "He's called Slider. Another guy from around here… no, I don't know his name, well, he called him Slider and said that he used to pitch for the Giants, if you can believe that."

The cop shrugged while another approached holding a cell phone in a clear Ziploc bag. The second cop said, "For a homeless man he was doing pretty good for himself. This is the latest iPhone and he had two hundred on him. Not bad for someone with no job." The first cop gave a short chortle, as if they were sharing an inside joke.

The first cop looked at the jogger then said to his colleague, "Think he robbed the wrong person?"

The second answered, "Dunno. I mean the knife wounds seem pretty serious. Who robs somebody that carries a knife that big? And why not take his cash?"

The first cop nodded his head. "Find the weapon?" The second shrugged and both cops looked at the jogger, who started to back away.

The next day the technical department reported Slider's iPhone call list.

* * *

"Hello, Mr. Chime? Or is it just Chime?"

"Who's this? And why are you calling from Slider's phone?"

"This is the San Francisco Police. I'm Detective David Green. I'm calling because you are the last number placed from this phone."

Vinnie took a seat. He knew hearing from cops meant bad news, but this sounded worse than bad. "What's happened to Slider?"

"I'm sorry to have to inform you, Mister...?"

"Vinnie, Vinnie Briggs. Call me Vinnie."

"Okay, Vinnie... er, I have to inform you that Slider was murdered sometime after he called you. Are you the next of kin or can you tell me how to find them?"

Detective Green heard Vinnie's sobbing. "I'm sorry, I know this must come as a shock. Were you close to the deceased?"

Through fits and sobs, Vinnie eventually provided as much detail as he could manage. Vinnie said he'd fly the next day to identify the body himself, as he was certain none of Slider's family would be interested. He confirmed Slider's affiliation with the San Francisco Giants.

Detective Green whistled. "Jesus, he was good. It's a shame what they did to him."

Vinnie held a tissue to his nose. "Yeah. His murder too. And I know who did it."

"Let's wait until you get here, unless you think the person you believe to be involved is a flight risk."

* * *

Turning the key in the lock, Vinnie stared toward the park. He wanted to believe Slider was slouched on his bench with Ralph on his lap. The police dog pound had called the professors to retrieve Ralph, who had contacted Vinnie as soon as they heard, but he already knew. Ralph had taken his last bus ride.

Vinnie returned to his San Francisco home after a long day's travel, starting with a ferry across Nantucket Sound, a harrowing ride to Boston's Logan Airport, a transcontinental flight, a visit to the San Francisco morgue, and finishing with a long and traumatic interview at the police station. Vinnie's eyes felt like burning coals. He'd need more than a bottle of water to soothe his throat, maybe Niagara Falls. His chin dragged along the sidewalk as he neared his front door. He looked around, angry at the world—people laughing, making plans, and acting as if nothing had happened.

San Francisco's typical fogs were nothing compared to Vinnie's mental fog for not understanding. He had been convinced that after what he had told Detective Green an arrest warrant would have been issued for Curt Peterson. But Vinnie left the precinct station in a cloud of confused thoughts. *I should have fuckin' known better. This isn't over, not by a fuckin' long shot.*

The interview had been very different to the one Vinnie had envisioned.

"We appreciate your help and I've made a note of your concerns. However, we can't arrest a man based on your supposition and your last telephone conversation with the deceased," said Detective Green behind his desk.

"Not 'the deceased.' His name is fuckin' José Rivas, but everyone calls him Slider."

Heads turned at Vinnie's raised voice, but with no alarm signal from Detective Green everyone resumed doing whatever they were doing.

Detective Green held out two hands in an offering. "Look, Mr. Briggs, you're upset. I understand. But keep your voice down, please. As I was saying, you may have provided a motive for Curt Peterson, but we have no evidence to suggest he was involved in the murder. As I've said, I've noted what you've told us and I will follow it up once we are further along in our investigation. For now, leave it to us."

Rather than use the elevator, Vinnie stumbled down two flights of metal steps. He had heard those words before, or good as: "Leave it to us." "Don't get involved." Bad advice then and bad advice now. Vinnie stomped on each phrase with every step. His disdain grew. If he had followed that advice three years ago Dan would have been wrongly accused and possibly convicted of a rape that he didn't commit. Vinnie overlooked that by pursuing his investigation he had inadvertently triggered the murders of two co-workers and nearly his own. Had he recalled this fact he might have taken the detective's advice.

Chapter 28

Putting Out the Garbage

The sunset over Pacific Heights reflected off the garbage barrels outside Vinnie's house with a soft glow and long shadows. Vinnie cursed, stuffing the last refuse bag into the overflowing barrel. Slider had forgotten to put the garbage out for collection the week before. Vinnie felt bad for thinking ill of his dead friend. He had been back six days, and seven since Slider's body had been discovered.

"C'mon, Vinnie, it's not that bad." Grace looked across the driveway separating her garbage barrel from Vinnie's.

"What?"

"The garbage. It's not that bad a job to do."

Vinnie turned to see Grace calmly adjusting the lid on her garbage bin. Their only conversations had been about Slider's memorial, the event they were planning for the weekend. They had anticipated about twenty or thirty neighbors, followed by a buffet at Vinnie's house. Kaelin printed notices and attached them to the park gate, to trees, and on the neighborhood telephone poles. Vinnie had been upset with the rumor—true, so not a rumor—that former Giants teammates planned to attend. They would swell the numbers for the wrong reason—the baseball stars becoming the focus. The professors said they'd bring Ralph and a large bouquet of flowers for the bench. Vinnie said he'd plant a sapling behind Slider's bench, with Grace's help to navigate the city ordinances. Vinnie sent invitations to a few of Slider's Texan friends, but all sent regrets and condolences. Not one of Slider's family had acknowledged the note.

Grace pointed to Vinnie's hand on the garbage lid.

"Yeah, it is. Last week's stink and now the fuckin' lid won't close."

A short laugh skipped across the sidewalk as Grace strolled over to Vinnie.

"Aside from your refuse problem, how are things with you and Ben? How was your return to New York? We haven't had time to talk about it."

"I never heard about your break either, when you vanished without a trace."

A blank stare crossed Grace's face and sagging lower lip.

"Sorry. I'm still upset. Umm… it was good. Ben and I have a decision to make." Vinnie pointed his finger skyward. "This is going to sound terrible… it *is* terrible, but I'll say it anyway. Slider told me of your conversation with Curt. Is it true?"

"I don't want to talk about it. He shouldn't have been listening, and he shouldn't have told you what he thinks he heard."

"Probably not, but he did. I've been thinking about it. A lot. About you, the baby, Kaelin. What a mess. Is it true? I'm guessing that you told Kaelin. That bastard father of hers should be in prison!"

"Vinnie, you're jumping to conclusions. And whatever Kaelin and I decide is not your concern. I don't tell you and Ben how to live your lives. You didn't ask my advice whether you two should have a child." Grace's eyes narrowed. "Besides, you don't know everything."

"I know what I know. Curt forced you into having sex. Maybe it wasn't exactly rape—you're the lawyer—but you had drunk too much, and you can't remember if you said no. Correct? Slider said at the least Curt took advantage, which makes it rape. I'm right."

Grace clenched her hands. "Screw you, Vinnie, and Slider too, even if he is dead. Stay out of my life."

Vinnie stepped back. "Grace, please. I care. Slider did too. All I want is what's best for you, the baby, and Kaelin. I know what lies can do. Eventually your child will ask questions about her father. You'll have to tell Kaelin everything."

Tears formed in Grace's eyes. Vinnie understood tears.

"Grace, I'm sorry. I care so much. I want to be close to the baby too."

The spine of Grace's back cracked. "It's not your baby; she's nothing to do with you, don't you get it? You don't understand—" Grace wiped her tears. "Curt and I had an affair. There, curiosity satisfied?!" With her hands covering her face, Grace sobbed.

A car drove by at thirty miles per hour, passing in the time it took for Vinnie's mouth to open wide enough to reveal his latest fillings. He dragged Grace by her arm to the side of his house, to the basement entrance.

"How is that possible? I thought you and Kaelin were partners."

"We are, but Kaelin is my first… my first lesbian relationship. I'm not like you. I didn't know… I mean about same-sex relationships. I didn't seek it out. Kaelin helped and I enjoyed it. It has been a comfort. But I'm confused."

With another backhand swipe, Grace wiped a few small droplets away. "Curt was kind, just as Kaelin said he would be. She told me he seduces young women and then discards them. Maybe he does but he makes me feel special. And sex with him is different."

Vinnie's mouth opened again and his tongue edged out but didn't move. His head bowed to the sidewalk rather than look Grace in the eye.

With increased strength to her voice, Grace said, "Come on, you've never had doubts?"

Raising his head, Vinnie replied, "Nope. Never. I've known

since puberty. I've been gay all my life."

"Well, that's not true for everyone, at least not for me. I had sex with men before Kaelin. Her too, if you must know. But Kaelin gave me my first orgasm. I was with a guy in college who I thought I loved and would marry, until he had an affair with my roommate. Everything fell apart and I changed after him. I gave up on men."

"But how did you manage to do it with men?"

"You need to ask? Women spread their legs, make appropriate sounds at the right time, and talk about King Kong. It's not difficult to fake. Haven't you ever been excited by a woman?"

Vinnie shook his head no, then thought of Ginny. "Sometimes my best friend's wife gets me interested, but she's different. She's classic gorgeous and her wardrobe is to die for. But not a turn-on, not really." Vinnie thought about his erection a few weeks before, then dismissed it given that Ben and Dan had been in the room; two of the sexiest, hunkiest, and most desirable specimens any gay man could want. With a shuffle he moved closer to Grace. "So, how do you feel about men now? Do you want Kaelin or Curt?"

Tire noise from another speeding car filled the silence.

"Okay, put it this way, where did you go on your break? Was Curt with you? Is that what this is about?"

"No. And I won't tell you where I went. It's my place to be alone."

"But in your condition you can't be alone. Do you really believe Curt will stick around to help after the birth?" Vinnie wanted to answer his own questions. Tell her Curt wouldn't lift a finger to help. Tell her Curt was a loser and would abandon the baby. Tell her to stop acting stupid.

Grace ignored Vinnie's questions, and expanded on Kaelin's persistent, deep-rooted hatred of her father that bordered on psychopathic, maybe even drove her to Curt. "She only agreed to rent Curt's house because I made it a requirement for us to have a baby. She rejects even his child support help if it means him being more in our lives."

Vinnie's mind flashed to his homophobic father and brother, men he hated. He hadn't sought their help, and often paid the price for their entanglement with criminals. *Kaelin's right to be wary.*

Even though he knew that because of his father and brother's help Dan's rape charge was proved false, and that had saved his career, Vinnie didn't care. He brushed aside their eventual acceptance of his homosexuality, crediting his mother's insistence and Ben's two-hundred-sixty-pounds *enlightenment*. And his father had put himself at risk to gain Vinnie's reprieve. Exile had been a better option than the mob's alternative. Yet Vinnie cherry-picked facts in support of Kaelin's view of Curt, especially as he thought that Curt was a murderer.

"When the baby is born I'll take leave from work. I would never make partner anyway, not in a high-pressure corporate law firm. I'll go part-time, but that won't be enough for Kaelin, me, and the baby—not in this neighborhood, and not with childcare costs. We'll never be able to buy a house of our own. Curt's promised to help."

Grace's idiocy was too much, and Vinnie looked away. He sighed and softened his voice. "I can help. I have more money than I know what to do with." Vinnie pointed. "I'll buy Curt's house and you can live rent-free. It'll be a good investment and I can provide baby care."

Grace's bellow preceded her snapping head. Her arms stretched out as if pushing Vinnie away. "No! Who says I want you in my baby's life? I don't—and you can't buy your way into our lives, or my baby."

Vinnie's muscles tightened, he raised his arms, and his shirt spread thin across his chest. "I not fuckin' buying your baby! I'm offering to help, which you're too stupid to realize." Vinnie bent to feel behind the garbage shed for the hidden key box. "So what's your plan? Move in with fuckin' Curt?" *Slider knew more and made notes. I just have to find them.*

"It's none of your, as you put it, *fucking* business, and I'll live with anyone I want. I don't need your permission or anyone's."

Neither Vinnie nor Grace had noticed the moving kitchen curtains. Steam had been escaping from a boiling stove pot. Kaelin shut the window and her mouth at the same time. Vinnie retrieved Slider's key and quickly entered the side door, closing it hard behind him. *Ben and I will have our own baby. Ben was right—it was a fuckin' mistake to return.*

Chapter 29

Big Mouth

Déjà vu all over again, thought Vinnie, smiling at Yogi Berra's famous quote. Slider had often cited this, revealing his inner fantasy that the Yankees' catcher knelt behind home plate while he was on the pitcher's mound.

Taken by surprise, Alice and Mark were delighted by Vinnie's offer to take over Ralph's daytime dog-sitting while he remained in San Francisco. "Won't Ralph be a hurtful reminder of Slider?" Mark had asked. Vinnie had replied it was another connection for him to Slider, who had loved Ralph.

The professors accepted this, at least about Slider's affection for Ralph. The only change was to eliminate Ralph's bus ride. They employed the same taxi that had been used to bring Ralph home from Slider, but this time to take him to Vinnie's. With the amount they paid, the taxi driver didn't care if technically this was against hackney carriage rules.

Ralph's first visit was hard for Vinnie. In the park, released from his leash, Vinnie watched the dog run to sniff underneath Slider's bench. Vinnie's was wiping tears from his eyes. As he deposited the plastic bag in the waste receptacle he caught sight of a man sitting on Slider's bench. Vinnie fidgeted, attached Ralph's leash, and quickly left the park.

* * *

The fog lifted along with the rising thermometer across San Francisco. Sun specks crawled through Vinnie's living room window. Two days had passed since he and Grace had argued and he had missed his New York-bound flight. He paced as he talked to himself. "I should've kept my mouth shut. I had to go on about her and Curt. I can't leave well enough alone..."

To distract himself, Vinnie sat with his iPad to reread Ben's email providing details on his contest preparation—which was to be his retirement contest. Ben had wanted Vinnie to attend, but Slider's memorial had been planned for the same weekend.

Ben posted posing photos on Facebook, but uploaded special photos in a private Dropbox file that Vinnie would have "liked" had they appeared on Ben's FB wall, which decency rules prevented. *I don't even comment on the pictures he does post. I don't know what to say about Ben or any other bodybuilder. They're all big, and except for their faces they all look the same—bloated muscles, each bigger than the other. Besides, Ben's my husband, so everyone would know I'm biased. It's fine for Ginny. She knows exactly what to say. And she doesn't hide that Ben's her trainer, which makes her honest, and that's more than can be said about Ben and me.*

With more finger-flipping across his iPad screen, Vinnie reviewed the series of photos. Maybe he couldn't make a comment on Facebook, but he would let Ben know his thoughts. Vinnie returned to the first photo: Ben's nude muscular ass striated with lines like a cornfield. The follow-up picture showed Ben bent over, his rear spread, and it seemed he was only legs and ass, his upper body ninety degrees to the ground. Vinnie had decided these two pictures were his favorites, making comparison to the Shenandoah Valley caverns in his reply email. Before pressing send, Vinnie heard a car parking at the front of his house. He stood to see Curt walking behind the parked car. *Yeah, go check on Grace and your unborn child. Fuckin' murderer.* Vinnie pressed send.

He walked to the kitchen window, then to the dining room window to follow Curt's passage down the path to his neighbor's kitchen side door. He hated Curt's swagger. *He moves like a fuckin' lizard with a hip replacement.*

For ten minutes Vinnie washed dishes, giving glances out his window to the kitchen opposite. He didn't see anyone, not Grace nor Curt nor Kaelin. No one. But he heard the side door slam, which was just out of view, and heard Kaelin shouting, "Don't come back here again. I don't want to see you. Ever. Understand?"

That was enough for Vinnie. He would add his two cents to support Kaelin. He threw down the sponge into the soapy basin and rushed out of his front door just in time to catch Curt opening his car door. Vinnie moved to the front of the car and placed his hand on the warm hood, as if to prevent it from moving off.

"Oh, you. Fuck off."

"Yeah, me. Haven't you done enough damage? Can't you stay away and leave everyone alone?"

"Like I said, fuck off. It's none of your business if and when I see my daughter."

"Which one?"

"What?"

"You know, the thirty-year-old or the one in gestation?"

"You fucking queer. I should break your neck." Curt stepped back from his car with all ten fingers reaching for Vinnie.

"Go ahead, try. Or do you need your knife, like the one you used on Slider?"

With his arms lowering, Curt shook his head. "I don't know what you're talking about. I had nothing to do with that faggot's death."

Vinnie shook his head like a rattle. "Like you had nothing to do with Grace's pregnancy? I know all about you and Grace. Slider told me. He heard everything. And I'm going to tell Kaelin the truth. Not only did you rape Grace, you've seduced her to

176

make her think she should be with you. You've ruined more lives than a terrorist cell. You're a household terrorist, you mother-fucker!"

Curt moved forward close enough to push Vinnie, except Vinnie was quicker. His weight training paid off as he grabbed Curt's arm, twisted it, and pushed Curt aside before letting go. "Touch me again and I'll break your fuckin' arm."

Placing his arm to his side, Curt growled, "Stay away from my daughter and keep your nose out of my affairs."

"Yeah, how many young, vulnerable women have you fucked this month?"

A sneer crossed Curt's face, and he turned to the open driver's door. The BMW convertible engine ignited on the first spark, producing a smooth hum. The car had crossed the intersection before Vinnie entered his front door.

He held the doorknob, gave it a half twist, and stopped. He reversed direction and marched along the same path Curt had used minutes before. He gave a few raps and waited. Through the slivered opening, Vinnie saw Kaelin's pebble eyes. She opened the door wide and looked past him to the street.

"Hi, Vinnie. This is not a good time."

"I know. I saw Curt leave. I told him what I thought of him, just like you."

"You heard me? I'm sorry. He makes me so mad. I hate him. I should never have agreed to this house rental."

"You have good reason to hate him. Not only for what he did to you and your mother, but because of what he's done to Grace as well."

"What?"

"Kaelin, you don't need to pretend. I know everything, and I know you know. Your father raped Grace and he's the baby's father."

The door swung open as Kaelin stepped back. Vinnie entered like a cat coming in from the rain. He followed Kaelin to her kitchen and glanced out her window to his own kitchen across the adjacent path. From this view, the slightly lower elevation made clear why it was easy to hear and see everything that took place in her kitchen.

Kaelin took a deep breath. "I do know. Grace told me everything before she went away last time, while you were still in New York. We argued. I wanted her to report my father as a rapist. I guess I was so angry I didn't understand what she was telling me." Kaelin's lips bunched, she moved her head sideways, her eyes moved upward.

Vinnie's head also slowly turned from left to right as if searching for a missing object. He touched his cheekbone. "Last time? Has Grace gone away again?"

Kaelin's lips folded inward as she nodded.

"When? Where has she gone?"

"Don't know," hissed Kaelin, no longer needing lips to speak.

"Are you sure? Please, tell me."

"She wants to be alone. I don't like it any more than you."

"Is that what you and your father argued about? You wouldn't tell him?"

Vinnie saw Kaelin's fingers fidget, clawing at her words of denial.

"You didn't have to tell him because he knows, right?"

"Yes."

"How? Oh—his Lake Tahoe cabin, the one you call his 'harem hut'?"

Kaelin hissed her single-word acknowledgment.

"That fuckin' bastard. Tell me where it is. I'll go and check that Grace is okay. I don't want Curt to hurt her."

"Leave her alone. She'll call if there's a problem. He won't hurt her."

Vinnie slapped his forehead with the palms of both hands, then with his left hand he held on to the kitchen countertop. "I'm sorry, but I have to tell you something. I think Curt has

178

convinced Grace to move in with him. He's seduced her. She believes he'll take care of her and the baby. She's confused and won't call you. I have to see her. Please tell me. I'll find out, one way or another, but it would be quicker if you just tell me."

Grace sat at the kitchen table and sobbed her words. "I know all about her leaving me for Curt. That's what our argument was about. He swears he has not asked Grace to move in with him, but he's lying. Grace wouldn't lie, not about this. It's my father who's the liar. He's always been a goddamn liar."

* * *

Vinnie reserved an early morning Zipcar online and called Alice to tell her he felt like a change from the city. He didn't want to make it hard for her and Mark, so, if they agreed, he would take Ralph along on the road trip and keep him overnight.

Alice accepted without asking Mark, adding that Ralph enjoyed the car ride more than the bus. Rather than wait for the taxi, Vinnie arranged to pick Ralph up himself. Alice said, "It's a good idea to get out of the city. The country air always helps a change of mood. Ralph makes a good companion on long car rides, but he needs frequent stops for water and to empty his small bladder."

Chapter 30

Can Revelations

Even with the unusually light I-80 congestion thinning five miles outside the Bay area, there was enough traffic to add over an hour to Vinnie's estimated GPS arrival in Sacramento and the turn onto US-50. Ralph had needed one stop, which corresponded with Vinnie's own need, so that didn't add much. *Fuckin' Bay traffic. People should use public transportation. That's what they do in a real city like New York.*

The original anticipated three-and-a-half-hour journey and one o'clock arrival at the southern end of Lake Tahoe changed to late afternoon. And the rental's GPS indicated another forty-five minutes to travel a dirt road to Curt's secluded cabin. Pulling over at their destination, Ralph charged out of the car to a nearby tree, rejected it, and tried two more before he found the perfect bathroom. By the time he returned to the car, Vinnie had already put his water bowl by the passenger door.

The cabin appeared empty. A few nearby houses peeked through trees. No house was in full view, but neither were any completely hidden.

After ringing the doorbell and a few raps on the door, Vinnie called out: "Grace, are you in there? It's me, Vinnie. Please, let me in."

Ralph explored the perimeter, while Vinnie walked the front porch to peer through a small window. A light was on, but Vinnie didn't exclude the possibility it was timer activated, which he couldn't tell from the outside.

"C'mon, Grace, let me in."

Ralph scampered along the porch, sniffing at the doorway.

"She's not answering, Ralph. What should we do?"

Ralph gave a head tilt response.

"Yeah, we should find a way in. Maybe Grace fell and is hurt. We've come too far to turn back. What do you say, Ralph?"

A small bark gave him all the confirmation he needed.

Vinnie searched for a spare key in the obvious places. Nothing. The night before he had reviewed his private investigator course notes that reminded him to always carry the tools of the trade, which now sat in the trunk of the car. He jammed a small crowbar-like instrument into the window sash until he heard the crack. "Guess old Curt's going to have a repair job on his to-do list. Serves him right. Who doesn't leave a spare key somewhere?" Vinnie waited a second for Ralph's answer.

Inside the cabin, Vinnie verified the light had been on a timer and continued his conversation with Ralph. "Too early in the day to have it set; it's not even dark out. Don't these people know for nuttin'?" He surveyed the living area, looking for a sign of a domestic altercation or evidence that Grace was here. Vinnie moved to the kitchen and searched through the food garbage. The refrigerator had recently been stocked. Fresh milk, a few bottles of sparkling San Benedetto water, and leftover pasta in a microwavable dish stood out. "Someone's been here and recently—"

Before he had finished explaining, Ralph barked.

Unless Ralph's communication skills have increased, it sounds like someone else is here, thought Vinnie, who entered the living area to see a woman in the doorway holding a mop in one hand and a cell phone to her ear.

"I call 911. Who are you? Why you here?" Vinnie heard the broken English from the short, dark-skinned woman; a Spanish accent, possibly Mexican, but Vinnie wasn't good with national differences.

Ralph barked, circling the woman, who swished him away with the mop.

"Stop it, Ralph. Come here. Don't worry, he's friendly. And there's no need to call the fu—I mean police. I'm a friend of Grace's... and Curt's."

"Meester Curt no mention more guests. I make spare bed now," said the woman, but to Vinnie it sounded like a question. "I'm Dolores." She put the cell phone in her cleaning jacket pocket.

Vinnie bent, extending his hand, and Dolores hesitated then gave a limp handshake.

"Hi, Dolores, I'm... uh, Ben." Vinnie liked Dolores already. She reminded him of his best friend Blanca Santos; both Latino women with gentle manners, Dolores more so, lacking Blanca's harsh Bronx accent. *Maybe she's Costa Rican or even Brazilian. I'll ask later.*

"Nice to meet you, Meester Ben. Where's your friend Grace?"

Yeah, Brazilian. "I guess she went out for a walk. I'm late. When did you last see my friend?"

"Other than day she arrive, I not see her. And the night I hear shouting with other woman while I clean house there." Dolores pointed to her left, as if Vinnie could see through the cabin walls. "But I not see her, just hear."

"And who was the other woman?" Vinnie moved a step closer.

"I don't know," said Dolores with a small sidestep, moving behind her mop. "I hear shouting, so I check... you know, see everything okay." Dolores turned her body to face the door. "I knock but woman tell me go away. This not my business, so I leave. But I call Meester Curt. He say not to worry, and he come same night. I know because I see his car next morning." She pointed to the right wall.

182

"So, Dolores, you didn't actually talk to Curt?"

"No. People don't like me bother them. I clean houses, but I think I see other woman from before, not your friend Grace."

"What did this other woman look like?" *Fuckin' spit it out, Dolores. Just tell me everything.* Vinnie gave his best carefree grin.

"I don't see but the week before young lady come, she tall and blond hair. I not judge. People do what want. Meester Curt very good to me. Very fair, not like other clients, if you know what I mean."

Vinnie did. Stingy rich people—give a five-dollar tip when they can afford twenty. Good-old generous Curt gives extra and tongues don't wag. *Curt knows what he's fuckin' doing.*

"Did you hear the argument? What it was about?"

Dolores moved further back. "I make bed. Want me clean up too, or wait until weekend when woman leaves?"

Smart woman. I better not ask more questions. "No need. I'll take care of things and I won't be staying tonight. I have business back in San Francisco. Keep to your normal schedule. And thanks for coming by. I'll let Curt know you are keeping an eye on his place."

With Dolores' departure, Vinnie entered the master bedroom. Inside he opened the chest of drawers, but only the bottom draw held a single piece of undergarment. He recognized Grace's clothes hanging in the closet, but not enough for a long break. And one pair of running shoes. Ralph sniffed inside the closet. "She was here, Ralph, obviously." Vinnie thought it odd he didn't find a suitcase. Grace was gone, and it looked like she left in a hurry.

Ralph hopped into the rear of the car, and Vinnie fastened the dog's seatbelt harness. Vinnie believed in precaution. So did Dolores, who had called Meester Curt to report a man in his cabin and a broken window sash. Did he want her to call the local handyman to fix it? Dolores knew her clients' homes better than they did.

* * *

Returning to San Francisco after midnight, Vinnie shed his clothes on the bedroom floor, omitting his fastidious routine of putting them in the bathroom hamper. Ralph waited outside the en suite bathroom. "Yeah, I suppose I could have peed in the backyard with you." Ralph's head twisted.

Vinnie made himself comfortable on the mattress while Ralph twirled around on the floor. He thought Ralph missed snuggling in his orthopedic doggie bed that cost the price of a good meal. Vinnie missed snuggling with Ben.

The disturbed sleep provoked morning agitation. Vinnie had long ago adopted Ben's habit to weight train at such times as a distraction. Ben told Vinnie that pumping iron and thinking were not mutually exclusive, except in competition training, which was never Vinnie's goal. *He's right again*, thought Vinnie, wiping his face with a hand towel.

After an hour, sweat emerged from every pore on Vinnie's body. His towel smelled. Ben's guideline had been that for long breaks he should have a protein mix, and to refill the water bottle. "If it's not empty, you've not kept yourself properly hydrated."

Looking at the supplement pills in his hand, Vinnie had his first smile of the day and glanced down at Ralph. "Ben made me start these on the first day he taught me to lift. What a joke. I'll never be Ben's size. Why should I? I don't get it, do you, Ralph? No clothing ever looks good on him, not even tailored. It's like dressing the Michelin Man. Fuckin' ridiculous." Finishing his protein drink, Vinnie said, "But I do love him, ya' know that, right?" Ralph responded with a walk around his empty water bowl. "Sorry, Ralph. My bad. Slider would have noticed." Vinnie wiped his face with the towel, but concentrated on his eyes.

With the bowl filled, Vinnie announced it was time for a "visit to the can," to borrow Slider's phrase. Vinnie rarely used the downstairs bathroom other than for a quick pee, but this time he needed to do more. Getting comfortable, he picked up a magazine among those in the rack he had mounted for all Slider's reading material. Slumped on the toilet seat, Vinnie imagined what Slider made of his special magazines and photographs. He wanted to believe he had enjoyed himself one more time before… before…

Flipping through the pages Vinnie realized he was holding the latest gay porno magazine, the one Slider had called "special"; had talked about in his message; had detailed his enjoyment, and suggested Vinnie would too.

"Holy fuck. Look at the pair on this guy. Are they real or photoshopped? He must be with the forest fire department with that schlong." Vinnie smiled while talking to himself. He touched the page with his finger then noticed a small scribbling in the corner.

Big fight outside. GU—UD. Wants to tell P.

Vinnie took a minute to decipher GU, UD, and P, then said it out loud to prove himself right: "Good'un. Upper Deck. Plum. Grace, Curt, and Kaelin."

GU tell P all—she loves UD—UD said wait for baby—UD no—leave P for UD.

What happened? What did Slider learn? Is he saying Grace loves Curt?

Vinnie turned the page. Another hunk, smaller between the legs but with humongous pectorals and inch-long nipples, and a divine face. More notes.

UD tells me to fuck off—same to him—he lies to GU and P. Two lies—P needs to act before the baby comes—I give GU fastball sign— she agrees to tell P tomorrow. If she does a change-up I'll throw a slider. Told her UD is dangerous.

Vinnie realized this was Slider's conversation with Curt and Grace. Curt told Slider to stay out of it—to fuck off—and Grace promised Slider she would tell Kaelin her plans to move in with Curt, but needed a day. Slider agreed, but then he would tell

Kaelin. He believed Curt to be dangerous, but to him and not Grace.

With a suppressed yelp, Vinnie knew he had the basis of Curt's motive in Slider's notes. Vinnie thought about Curt's past. He manipulated women until he held the best position to negotiate. He would lie to both Kaelin and Grace until the baby arrived, and use that to change the dynamics. But not if a homeless queer interfered.

Turning the next page, Vinnie saw an unexciting advertisement for high-quality video streaming, but with more scribbling below.

Big fight P and GU—P hits GU—go over?—GU slams door—bad—GU crying—in morning call UD to tell him its over—call Chime—tell him all.

Vinnie left the bathroom feeling like the stuff he had flushed away. Slider had called him, but he hadn't answered. If only he had. If he had talked to Slider. *If—if I had talked to him, I would have asked questions, gotten the full story. I could have warned him. Advised him to stay indoors. To stay away from Curt. Warned him of the danger.*

Will the cops accept my translation of Slider's message? Why couldn't Slider write in fuckin' English?!

Chapter 31

The Investigation Begins

Vinnie continued his training, his thoughts heavier than the weights. Racking the dumbbells, he said to Ralph, "Gotta keep to the plan. Trap Ginny so she'll agree. Look at these." Vinnie flexed his biceps for Ralph, who walked away. *Even the dog knows that's not the point. Distraction and thinking, that's what I have to do.*

After an hour, pumped and buffed, Vinnie viewed himself in the mirror. He felt a good exhaustion. He needed to pee, and noticed Ralph at the back door. "You need to relieve yourself too? Okay, out you go, Ralph."

A scratching at the door told Vinnie that Ralph had finished. He let him in, and the dog dragged a 49ers scarf into the room.

There was no doubt in Vinnie's mind the scarf belonged to Curt Peterson. The giveaway was the wine stain across the 49 numerals. Curt had explained to Vinnie over the fence, one Saturday months before, at a time when they were still acting neighborly, that he had spilt good wine and ruined his overpriced scarf by leaping from the couch to curse his team's fumbles, a costly error that gave victory to the opposition.

Football's finer points had not interested Vinnie; a game played by brutish men with too much testosterone. But the scarf mattered. He had asked Curt why he would wear a scarf indoors. Curt replied, "Good luck."

Vinnie had thought, *Yeah, some fuckin' good luck. Your team lost. You're the loser.* Vinnie didn't say this at the time, acting neighborly and all.

Taking the scarf from Ralph, Vinnie walked out the back door to the rear garden with Ralph following. Vinnie surveyed the yard until he spied Ralph's latest deposit. "Shit, Ralph, and I mean that literally. Couldn't you wait until our walk in the park?" Ralph's head tilted. Near the deposit was a hole, the kind of hole that dogs make.

From first glance, Vinnie knew. Buried treasure. Vinnie's mind reconstructed what must have happened. Curt murdered Slider in the backyard, then dragged the body to the park. Ralph found the scarf that had fallen off Curt during the struggle, after Slider had been stabbed. Slider weighed less than Curt, but was younger, lean-muscled, and more athletic. His workouts with Vinnie had returned much of his former strength. Killing Slider would have been hard. Curt had used surprise and a chloroform-soaked scarf—something that Vinnie surmised from the faint residual smell.

Vinnie laughed out loud as he said, "As a P.I. in a former life—which you wouldn't know anything about, Ralph—I know chloroform would not have made Slider lose consciousness fast. Curt is too fuckin' stupid to know this." Vinnie gave a snorting laugh. "Curt's scarf would have been blood-soaked. You knew, so you buried the evidence."

Ralph peed on a small bush.

* * *

In the afternoon, Ralph's bark announced a taxi out front. Vinnie and Ralph, San Francisco's two newest P.I.s, caught up with their neighbor on her pathway.

"Kaelin, there's something you ought to see. I want to show you first before I go to the cops."

Two people and one dog entered Kaelin's house. She sat,

stony-faced, without offering either guest a drink.

"Ralph discovered this in the backyard, or I should say he buried it and just dug it up."

Vinnie held out the scarf at arm's length. Kaelin blinked at it, as if each blink would make it disappear like magic.

"You know who this belongs to, don't you?"

Kaelin nodded.

"Probably soaked in chloroform, intending to render Slider unconscious. Ralph buried it. There is still a faint paint-thinner smell. As a midwife, you know that chloroform wouldn't have worked, right?"

A slight nod showed that Kaelin agreed, with her eyes fixed on the scarf. "So, Slider, who you know was strong, struggled. My guess is that the scarf startled him, but it would have taken at least five minutes to make him unconscious, and only if diazepam or alcohol had also been administered. Unlikely, don't you think? So the first knife attack wounded him, letting Curt overpower him. This fits with the autopsy report of a struggle and is consistent with Slider's blood analysis, even if the medical examiner says it's inconclusive... but I know it's true. I wanted you to see this before I give it to the police. I've been right all along—your father murdered Slider."

Kaelin started to cry, and sobbed her words. "I don't know why I'm crying. I've never liked the son of a bitch, but we reconciled a little in the past few years. We never had any real relationship, not since childhood. He treated my mother and me like shit."

Ralph walked around the room, sniffing at the furniture. Vinnie sat next to Kaelin.

"There's something else."

Kaelin wiped her eyes, looking down as Vinnie held her hand.

"More? What else? I can't take any more."

Vinnie's mouth opened, but no words came out. He saw specks of sunlight crossing the table and on the floor across

Ralph.

"You should talk to Grace."

"What? Oh sure. I guess she should hear this."

Vinnie swatted the back of his head. "She's at Curt's cabin, which you knew. But there was another woman there too according to the maid. Is Grace leaving you for Curt? She thinks he'll provide for the baby, but I promised to help, so you don't need Curt."

Turning away from Vinnie, Kaelin's words pushed out. "I know. She thinks my father gives a damn about her and the baby. She won't admit he raped her, because she claims to have consented, even though she was drunk. As a lawyer, she should know that's still called rape. My father doesn't love her. I do. We can manage. So we'll move. My mother and I managed."

Her tears came suddenly like a summer downpour. Vinnie handed her a pack of Kleenex from his pocket.

"Look, I'm sure Grace will come to her senses and let me help with the finances. Eventually."

"You know Slider called her 'Good'un', but he should have called her Stupid One. Grace is too honest for her own good." Kaelin stopped and blew her nose. The silence lasted.

Too long for Vinnie, so he walked away with Ralph trailing. At the door he turned back. "I'll wait a few hours before going to the police with the scarf, which will give you time to tell Grace before she hears from the police or on the news reports. I've rescheduled my flight for New York." Vinnie paused. "I leave the day after tomorrow, which should be enough time for the police to question me. They'll probably want to search my backyard, and talk to you and Kaelin. Call me if you need me."

As he shut the door, Vinnie looked down at the dog. "A fuckin' mess, Ralph, a big fuckin' mess. I shouldn't have returned. Kaelin doesn't know, does she? You know. Grace is having an affair with Curt. It was never rape, was it? Grace has to tell Kaelin, otherwise her honesty goes out the window. Don't you agree?"

Seeing Ralph's wagging tail, Vinnie stopped. *I'm going to miss this dog, just like I miss Slider. I'm never going to be part of Kaelin or Grace's life. Why did they reject me? In two days I'll be back in New York.*

He would have too, if he had made his New York flight.

Chapter 32

P.I. Report

Maybe it's West Coast versus East Coast culture, but Vinnie thought the precinct decor looked like a Nordstrom's fitting room. In New York, dirty gray walls screamed. Here, subdued tints purred. Even the SFPD faux wood table reduced the overhead mini-spotlights' glare, whereas NYPD-issue metal tables reflected light as if promoting a Broadway musical.

Room decor aside, Vinnie sensed the interrogation familiarity. On one side sat Detective Green and Detective O'Brian. Vinnie stared at the scarf in a clear plastic bag on the table between them.

"We appreciate you coming forward with this item. We'll send it to the lab for analysis, which takes a few weeks." Each detective had placed their notepad on the table.

Vinnie didn't respond, trying to decide if Detective O'Brian's raspy voice was from too many cigarettes in the past or too much booze in the present.

Detective Green's lower-pitched voice intruded. "Just so I have this correct, this scarf was found by Ralph? Where's Ralph and why isn't he with you?"

"Well, he sometimes goes by name of Whitey, but everyone knows him as Ralph." Vinnie's eyes never left the scarf.

"So, Ralph has an alias? We'll need his full name, contact information, and cell number."

Vinnie's outburst surprised both detectives. "A dog with a cell! His full name's Ralph Kramden."

Detective O'Brian placed his meaty forearms on the table, pushing aside his notepad. "You fucking with us? Are you saying Ralph's a dog?"

"Yeah, I thought you knew. I mean he was apprehended by the canine squad. They kept him in dog jail overnight. Ralph discovered Slider's body. Isn't that in your fuckin' notes?" *Yeah, you're cursing with the wrong fuckin' guy, you fucker.* Vinnie's grin nearly leaped onto the table.

Leaning back, Detective Green patted his partner's back as he chewed his words. "Tell us, and precisely... from the beginning... what happened. Assume we have no prior knowledge."

With heads bobbing, interruptions, note taking, and statements repeated, forty-five minutes passed before Vinnie said, "Can I get a coffee and take a bathroom break?"

Alone in the restroom and staring at himself in the mirror, thoughts flew across Vinnie's brain. What was he trying to accomplish? The cops were being anal over the scarf location, Ralph, the size of the backyard, fence—everything but the most significant fact.

Back in the interview room, Vinnie looked at the coffee mug on the table with its dishwater-dirty liquid. He stuttered his next words. "I-I-I know who killed Slider, as I already told you over the phone when we first spoke and during my interview a few days ago. You said you needed evidence; well here it is." Vinnie pointed to the plastic bag. "Stop wasting time. Arrest Curt Peterson for the murder of my friend."

Neither detective gave any facial movements, as if temporarily paralyzed. After a few seconds, Detective Green spoke. "And tell us again how you know this."

Vinnie launched into a long, gossip-filled explanation that nearly put the two detectives into a vegetative state. Vinnie ended with hands extended, like a dual handshake.

"Very interesting, Mr. Briggs. We've taken your statement and we'll look into Mr. Peterson's movements."

"Look into him! I'm fu—fudging telling you he did it. Arrest him before he escapes to a foreign country."

The detectives pushed their chairs back in choreographed unison and stood. Detective O'Brian held open the interview door. Vinnie ran his fingers over the tastefully painted pale walls while walking along the corridor.

* * *

Flashing blue lights lit up the trees from three squad cars parked a hundred feet from the cabin. Yellow tape was wrapped around the trees that circled the building. Vinnie sat on the front steps holding Ralph's leash.

"Sir, if you don't put the dog in your car, I'll have to call canine control."

"Wh… what? Uh… uh… uh, what did you say?"

"Put your dog in the car, sir."

"Uh, sure, okay, no problem. Ralph's friendly, you know." Vinnie bent to pick up Ralph, and his outstretched hand touched the ground to steady himself. He took a second before he carried the dog slowly to his car and put him on the back seat. "Cop's a fuckin' loser. You should chew his leg off, the fuckin' dickwad."

At the driver's door, Vinnie operated the switch to lower all the car windows a few inches. Swinging the door closed he caught Dolores' reflection in the side mirror, standing with a policeman and pointing to him. Taking small steps, Vinnie returned to the cabin porch and the interviewing cop tapping his pad. Vinnie sat, his chin resting on his hands.

"Ready, Mr. Briggs? Now, once more, how did you find the body?"

Tears filled Vinnie's eyes, his voice choking. "It's not a fuckin' body, it's Grace Lee and her baby."

The interviewing policeman pointed his pen at Vinnie and

told him to keep a civil tongue. Until identified by the next of kin the body had no name, but the pregnancy was undeniable.

Vinnie began a string of curses, and the policeman reached for his handcuffs. Two men in suits arrived and stood next to the police officer. Detectives Green and O'Brian flashed their badges and told the cop they'd take over.

The policeman stared at their SFPD badges. "Isn't this a little far from your jurisdiction?"

Detective O'Brian answered, his rasp even more pronounced. "None of your fucking business. Get lost."

Before the policeman had replied, his arms already raised, another man in a suit arrived. "Ron, let it go. These two assholes have the Commissioner's approval to take this case. The deceased is a missing person and part of their investigation." Ron and his supervisor understood; the Lake Tahoe Commissioner had relinquished the case as the most expedient way to remove the homicide from official Lake Tahoe inquiry, local news curiosity, and tourist impact.

Detective Green sat next to Vinnie. "I hate copters... make me queasy."

"What?" Vinnie looked at Detective Green.

"The helicopter. How'd you think we got here so quickly?"

"Dunno." Vinnie stared straight ahead.

Detective O'Brian stood over Vinnie but waited for his partner to begin questioning.

"Okay, Vinnie... can I call you Vinnie? Maybe you can start over. Forget the yokel locals. What happened?"

A worm-like grin formed on Vinnie's lips, but it had no impact on his tears. He reported on his previous visit as he glanced over to where Dolores had been a few minutes before. He told of his worry for Grace's safety. "Turns out I was fuckin' right, wasn't I?" Vinnie's story came out between sobs and curses. Both detectives had become used to Vinnie's narrative style. They allowed him leeway with his cursing under the circumstances. He explained he'd broken in on his visit and was about to do it again, except for Ralph.

"Ralph? Oh, the pooch," said Detective O'Brian, expressionless.

Vinnie nodded, thinking Slider would have called him Robo after RoboCop, but nodded before continuing. "Ralph wandered off and I was at the back of the cabin when I heard him barking and saw…" Vinnie blew his nose into a Kleenex he'd pulled from his pocket.

"The body… I'm sorry, I mean Grace, right?" Detective Green patted Vinnie's arm.

Vinnie's upper body bent.

* * *

Four hours later Vinnie parked the car. Ralph awoke on the back seat. Alice took Ralph's leash and hugged Vinnie. "I'm so sorry. If there's anything Mark and I can do, let us know. And don't worry about taking Ralph."

"Thanks, Alice, but I'd like to. Ralph's helped me and he's a comfort. I think Slider would have wanted this too. Ben doesn't arrive for another day, so Ralph's good company."

* * *

A Diet Coke was placed on the faux wooden table in front of Kaelin. The break over, she sat in silence with Detective Green, waiting for his partner to return with coffee for them.

"So sorry for your loss," both detectives had said in a rehearsed monotone the previous day at her home, and they repeated precisely the same sentiment now at the precinct. Their words provided no comfort. Kaelin had nothing to add in today's interview to her previous statement.

"Okay, Ms. Peterson, let's start again. Why do you think Mr. Briggs would make a four-hour journey, twice, to Lake

Tahoe?"

Shrugging her shoulders, Kaelin told them she thought Vinnie believed her father might harm Grace.

"And would he?" Detective Green spoke with measured cadence.

"Yes. Not physically, I don't think, but psychologically. He's a bastard. A selfish man that preys on younger women."

Pushing his cup aside, Detective O'Brian leaned forward, assuming his characteristic position of forearms on the table. With rasping voice he said, "Is your father capable of murder?"

"No. Maybe. I don't know."

Detective Green touched his partner's arm. "What about Mr. Briggs? Is he capable?"

Kaelin gave the same response she had offered about her father.

The detectives alternated asking questions about Mr. Peterson, Ms. Lee, and Mr. Briggs, and the relations between them. The pace continued for fifteen minutes, and then suddenly the sequential interrogation stopped.

Detective Green took over, resuming his measured cadence. "We spoke to the maid—Dolores. Days before Mr. Briggs' first visit she overheard two women arguing. One was Ms Lee—but she didn't get a good view of the other woman. Do you know who she might be?"

"Another woman?" Kaelin's voice rose. "No idea." She paused, then chortled. "Could be any of my father's concubines at his harem hut. Did Dolores describe the woman?"

"So you have no idea? Care to guess?" Detective O'Brian leaned forward, his coffee breath wafting across the table.

"Uh, no, like I said, my father has many women."

"This woman, according to Dolores, had long hair, possibly blond. And she'd reminded Dolores of a woman who'd been to the cabin a long time ago."

Detective Green interjected, "Dolores is vague. Does she

sound like anyone you know? Maybe someone your father introduced to you?"

Kaelin nearly burst into hysterical laugher. "Introduce me to one of his whores?" Kaelin slumped back with dipping chin, her red lips sputtering indistinguishable words.

The detectives looked at each other, neither commenting.

After seconds, Grace straightened her back. "Maybe it was Vinnie? His voice goes up an octave when he's angry. You know he was upset when he learned Grace planned to move in with my father. Vinnie was obsessed with us and our baby. He told me he'd never let my father take Grace and the baby away." Kaelin stopped and looked at her hands. "I'm not saying Vinnie would hurt Grace, but I heard them argue a week ago… garbage collection day. Vinnie has a temper."

The detectives thanked Kaelin and escorted her to the exit. They promised to catch the murderer in their flat, monotone voices, as if providing solace.

Chapter 33

Home Interview

This was Vinnie's third climb of the police station's central staircase. The pale walls no longer soothed. Photos of San Francisco landmarks were tourist clichés. Police chiefs and commissioners, past and current, smiled out from behind mounted, polished glass. Vinnie had never wanted this overfamiliarity with an SF district station, and even less the voices of Detectives O'Brian and Green.

He sat at the table—*I even know my chair*—and declined Detective O'Brian's beverage offer. *Fuckin' waiter. Green wouldn't dare leave waiter RoboCop in a room with a suspect.* Slider would have liked "garçon" better than waiter, or Robo, or Robo-Garçon.

"Thanks for agreeing to come in again, Mr. Briggs. We have a few follow-up questions, I'm sure you understand." Detective Green came close to being cheerful.

"Sure." *Like I had a choice.*

Looking at his notepad, Detective Green read, "You went to the Lake Tahoe cabin twice, correct?"

Vinnie nodded, his lips pursed.

"And the first time you arrived late afternoon. That was two days ago, August 8th, correct?"

Another nod. *Another fuckin' bullshit waste of time interview.*

"Is there any chance you made a night visit, maybe a week or two before?"

Oh, now that you mention it, I traveled four hours and it slipped my mind. Vinnie sneered a loud reply. "What! No. My first visit—my only two times—were like I told you, in the afternoon."

Detective O'Brian placed his elbows on the table, one more thing familiar to Vinnie, along with his sizzling frying pan voice. "You've been working out, haven't you, Mr. Briggs? You're stronger than a few years ago."

"And if I am?"

"I mean how, how much can you overhead press? Two-fifty?"

"What's that fuckin' got to do with anything?"

"You're quite the big size, too. I'll bet it's not all from steak."

"Fuck you."

Detective Green's hand shot up to take his partner's arm. "What Detective O'Brian means is that we've learned you're much stronger than when you first showed up here a few years back. Your weight and strength gain usually means supplements. We know your husband…" Green looked at his notepad, but O'Brian growled, "Ben Hausen. Quite the bodybuilding reputation."

"Yes, thanks Gerry." Detective Green looked at Vinnie.

Yeah, thanks Robo-Garçon—want a fuckin' coffee, Gerry?

"So, you have access to steroids through Mr. Hausen," said Detective Green, looking up from his notepad.

"He doesn't do steroids anymore."

What came close to a smile surfaced on Detective O'Brian's face. "What about you? Needed to match your hubby's muscle? Give him a power thrill?"

Shuffling in his chair, Vinnie pulled down his knitted short-sleeve to cover his bicep.

With a flip of his notepad, Detective Green read, "'Vinnie wants to raise a child.' Is that true, Mr. Briggs? Do you want a child?"

"What! This is ridiculous. What kind of fu—fudgin' questions are these?"

The two detectives maintained their mannequin faces and the clock ticked.

Vinnie forgot his own P.I. training to wait and said, "Yeah, so what if I do? Gay men have rights now. If you came out of your cave you'd know that."

Detective O'Brian's smile stretched his face. "And it would be fair to say you wanted to help Grace with her baby?"

"Again, so what?" Vinnie pulled on his shirtsleeve.

"And her refusal made you angry? Even more when you learned she'd planned to live with the baby's father, Curt Peterson?"

Vinnie's chair screeched on the floor tiles as he pushed back, bellowing out: "It's not fu—fudgin' relevant. Stupid and irrelevant! Curt killed Grace, just like he killed Slider. You're clown investigators!"

He left under caution not to leave San Francisco and Vinnie walked out of the station feeling dejected. *I'll be in this fuckin' boutique-painted room again soon.*

* * *

The steamed windows suggested that Vinnie was preparing a big meal. The giveaway was the kitchen littered with pans and the sink filled with bowls. Ralph picked up scraps fallen on the floor, and by mid-afternoon he was strapped into the back seat of his cab. "You'll see Ben tomorrow. Be a good boy, not a bad boy like me tonight." The cab driver glanced at Vinnie, his thoughts easily deciphered: *people with too much money.*

* * *

"That was great, as always. Want to try yogurt with my promo high-protein mix?"

With no hint of humor, Vinnie said, "No, I'm big enough."

Ben swiveled around the countertop. "What's that mean?"

"You know, not everyone has to be barn-sized."

"Okay, what gives? You don't want the mix, fine. Just say so."

For the next hour, sipping his cheese-flavored protein mix, Vinnie described his interrogation with the implied steroid use. The inference was unavoidable: steroid rage leads to murder.

"And I already solved their case. Me and Ralph. We gave them Curt's bloody scarf and his motive. Fuckin' idiots."

Ben placed two hands on his forehead, moved them over his closely shaven head, his shirt rising, arms bulging. His words ground at Vinnie. "I told you not to get involved. Your meddling has made you a suspect. You're not a private investigator."

"I am. I solved Dan's case, didn't I? And I've taken an online course. Can I help it that the San Francisco police department has two bozo detectives?"

After half an hour a truce was called. They had been apart too long, so they struggled to find common ground but agreed that one area was their love for each other. Ben acknowledged that Vinnie had an innate ability to be loyal to friends, as he had done for Dan years before. Now, loyalty meant justice for Slider and Grace.

Vinnie praised Ben's generosity, like he had shown Dan, and to him when he was in a coma with around-the-clock nursing care.

They had agreed to faithfulness, no one-night stands with strangers. Vinnie honored his words to Ralph—his only "bad boy" behavior had been with Ben.

* * *

Strictly, he wasn't loitering as much as dog walking in the same spot. Vinnie paced in front of the police station with Ralph. "He won't be long, I'm sure. Relieve yourself anytime. They couldn't detect a pile of shit even if they stood in it."

Vinnie had insisted he ride with Ben to the police station.

A desk officer had called to request Ben come down to the precinct to help Detectives Green and O'Brian with their murder investigation. The new cab driver's initial refusal to take a dog changed with Ben's hundred-dollar bill.

"A hundred bucks to indulge your whim."

"And my performance last night was easily worth a hundred." Vinnie's grin stretched over his face.

Ben trundled down the precinct steps like bulldozer in a mudslide. He walked past Vinnie without pausing and out into the street to search for a cab. Vinnie worried that if a passing cab didn't stop Ben would pick one up and carry it home.

"What happened?"

Silence.

A cab stopped, giving no guff over Ralph. *Thank-fuckin'-God* sighed Vinnie.

"So?"

"When we're home." Ben's arms folded as he stared ahead.

* * *

Ben sprawled across the living room couch. Vinnie perched on the couch arm at Ben's feet.

"So, what happened?"

"You were right. Bunch of clowns. Asked me about you, steroids, and suggested I juiced you up because I crave big, strong men. I wanted to show them how big and strong I am."

Vinnie moved behind the couch to rub Ben's back, the way a grand piano is polished.

"I couldn't provide you with an alibi. I should've been here. My stupid guest poser at the Nutri-Supplement Contest. I should've cancelled."

"No. Don't ever change your commitments for me."

With his fist under his chin, Ben continued, his body tense. He never denied using steroids in the past. With arms unfolding,

Ben sputtered an admission he didn't tell the detectives: he had used a little recently, only for his last contest and for Ginny.

"Ben, we agreed. No fuckin' more."

Ben mumbled as he turned on his side, "I know. They make me feel puffed. And I get urges. Not just a hard-on, I get angry over small stuff."

Ben rolled on his back to look at Vinnie, then put a forearm over his eyes. "They said you were obsessed with Grace's baby. Did you say you'd take Grace's baby?"

"No, not take—take her for babysitting. Like with Anthony. I never realized how much I love children."

Moving his arm down, a shadow crossed Ben's face. "Is there something I should know? About your need to be with children?"

With a stagger Vinnie yelled, "What! You think I'm a pervert? Fuck you."

"No, I... I don't. I just don't understand your need."

"Well, for your information, I'm not a pervert. I do not love children in that way. I would never, ever hurt a child," Vinnie spat, fists formed, his neck elongated and crisscrossed with veins.

"Geez, I didn't mean to imply..."

"You did. So did the fuckin' detectives..." Vinnie started to walk away. Ben leaped to grab him. Vinnie tried to pull away but couldn't free himself from Ben's forcep-like grip.

"Stop, please. I'm sorry."

Vinnie's head buried into Ben's shirt.

"I know you wouldn't hurt a child or anyone. You're a good person."

Vinnie nuzzled into Ben's shoulder, his voice muffled. "I can't explain it. I feel a need to give children a good childhood, one better than I had. Make them feel wanted and loved, but not like the detectives implied. Isn't this what every parent feels...? Not every parent, as I know. I just had fun playing with Anthony, is that bad?"

Ben kissed Vinnie, then released his hold. "I had fun too. And you're right about parents. That's how it was for me with Carl."

Vinnie sobbed. "I know what happens when parents abandon their children. A child without a family. When hate sets in. When good people like Slider and Grace are murdered. When I'm all alone."

Their previous night's passionate sex became compassionate sex this night. Love and fear of bad things to come.

Chapter 34

Arrest

With Ben's departure the house felt empty—too much space. The emotional emptiness was bigger still. Ralph was an inadequate substitute. Conversations were one way, and Vinnie's attempt to reply for Ralph unsatisfactory.

"Ralph, I've been alone most of my life so his leaving shouldn't bother me. I guess I had Slider, Grace, and Kaelin… oh, you too. Good boy."

Magic words. Ralph barked, his ears vertical.

"What's that, you want a treat? Sure." Vinnie retrieved a biscuit from Ralph's special jar and held it between his thumb and index finger.

"He had to leave. He wanted to stay—me too. But if I had agreed I would have contradicted myself."

Ralph surveyed the floor for remaining crumbs from his biscuit.

"He's the main guest poser at one of bodybuilding's most important contests. He needs to remain prominent to be on magazine covers. Guest posing is important. I get that, don't you?"

The conversation stopped with Ralph barking at the front window.

"What now?"

A hard knock on the door amplified Ralph's barking. Four policemen along with Detectives Green and O'Brian stood on the doorstep.

The Miranda rights recited by Detective O'Brian sounded like a radio disc jockey announcing a prizewinner. The tight handcuffs bit into Vinnie's wrist as he was marched down the front steps. He'd been permitted to call Professor Alice Datone to collect Ralph, a courtesy extended by Detective Green despite Robo-Garçon's objection. And Vinnie knew the courtesy was for Ralph, not him.

A fourth return to the police station had never been Vinnie's plan. He was in a different interview room, one with dark green walls, a large two-way mirror, and a gray metal table bolted to the floor. Vinnie sat in a rigid chair, also bolted to the floor. The room reeked of guilt and recriminations. The kind of room Vinnie imagined his brother had been in before being sent to Attica in upstate New York. *I'm not a criminal. I'm a fuckin' good guy.*

"Now, Mr. Briggs, do you wish to have an attorney present?"

"Yes."

The two detectives stood. Detective O'Brian, with a macabre tone, said, "Are you sure? Things never go well when a lawyer is involved."

If Vinnie had learned anything from his online P.I. course, it was: a) never believe the police at an interview; b) always ask for a lawyer; c) keep your mouth shut. He'd also learned this from his old man and brother, their one piece of good advice.

* * *

A tall, handsome man extended his hand to Vinnie as he entered the jailhouse interview room, but instead of a handshake he held out a business card.

Drew Stanton, LLD, MsL

Senior Partner

Barrymore, Stanton, Mancuso, Vasquez

Suite 2349

333 Market Street
San Francisco, CA 94104
private number: 425-996-1066
email: d.stantn@bsmvlaw.com

Sitting at the small metal table, Vinnie glanced at the card and appraised the man: fit, by the way he sat upright; successful, from the cut of his tailored suit; fastidious, from his matching tie that was not ostentatious; logical, from his careful placement on the table of a file, notebook, and pen from his leather laptop briefcase. And observant, since he did not remove the computer, a sign this man intended to make close observations.

The lawyer introduced himself as Drew but addressed Vinnie as Mr. Briggs. Vinnie replied, "I didn't have a chance to print up a card, but I'm Vinnie Briggs, just Vinnie seeing that I'm going to spill my fuckin' guts to you."

A smile crossed Drew's face. "Ginny said you were different and that I'd like you. She's never been wrong so far."

Papers spread across the table from the file, Drew adjusted his glasses, picked up his pen, and tapped his pad. "I'm sorry to say, Mr. Briggs, uh, Vinnie, that the prosecutor amended the original arrest charge to first-degree, premeditated murder in the double homicide of Grace Lee and an unborn child."

"You mean when it rains it pours fuckin' shit."

Drew laughed. "Let's begin. I'll take your version of events so you are not fitting your memory to conform to the theory outlined by the police and prosecutor. Then I'll tell you what's in the written report and the formal charge sheet. After that you can add to or modify your statement, or explain what has been said against you. Shall we proceed?"

Vinnie touched his fingers to his lips. *Ginny knows how to pick 'em. Good-looking, good dresser, and good sense.* Vinnie would later learn that Drew and Ginny had met at Harvard, him in law school and Ginny (née Swinburne) at business school. Their common ground began by chance with runs along the Charles River starting at the Harvard athletic facilities. They became running partners, each admiring the other's dedication to fitness and academic excellence. If Drew had had his druthers, he would have gone further but Ginny showed no interest.

On graduation their running partnership ended but not their friendship. Drew joined an upstart law firm in San Francisco rather than accept a prestigious offer from a more established company. Ten years on, Vinnie sat in front of a senior partner with Barrymore, Stanton, Mancuso, Vasquez, one of San Francisco's newest and most prestigious law firms.

Vinnie would also discover Ginny's lawyer choice wasn't for Drew's physical and personality attributes, but his exceptional legal skills and cunning. He was perfect in every way, as befitted Ginny.

Listening to Vinnie, Drew demonstrated his sense of humor, his cheeks widening to produce a dayglow smile. His outbursts were better than any laugh track. He took detailed notes, omitting only Vinnie's citing of all Ralph's toilet breaks. He noted Grace Lee's relationship with Curt and Kaelin Peterson, Slider, and Vinnie. Drew reviewed his notes, requesting Vinnie reconfirm the identities of Plum, Good'un, Upper Deck, Gong and Chime.

"Really? He called you Chime because you're small?"

Vinnie tried to shrink but his pride burst out, just like his pectorals.

"Let's take a break."

The guard opened the interview room door after Drew rapped three times, and pointed him to the visitors' bathroom. Vinnie, in handcuffs, was taken the other way. Drew returned with two coffees, Vinnie already at the table. Vinnie took one sip and pushed the cup aside. *If he drinks his I may have discovered Drew's one flaw.*

Drew thought they should start with motive.

"The prosecutor claims you were obsessed with Grace's pregnancy, acting as if the baby was yours. He says you hounded Grace and Kaelin to take care of the baby—"

"No, that's bullshit," said Vinnie who leaped up and flung his arms overhead.

Drew held up his hand and gestured to Vinnie's chair. "Vinnie, please, just listen. You'll have a chance to respond after I lay it out. So, Curt and Kaelin have provided statements that you offered to purchase Curt's house to ensure the women and baby remained next door. You accused Curt of raping Grace, and wanted her to go to court and declare him an unfit father."

Drew tapped his pen to signal this was the time for Vinnie to respond.

"Of course I accused Curt of raping Grace, because that's what she said, or as good as. And yeah, I offered to buy the house because Grace was worried Curt would kick her out." Vinnie began to alternate between "bullshit" and "fuckin' bullshit" in his speech. Drew's pen tapped methodically during this rant, and after a predetermined number of taps he stopped Vinnie.

"Okay, we'll revisit. Now, the prosecutor claims when you learned Grace was planning to live with Curt you confronted him and Kaelin. They say you became enraged, as if Grace was taking your child away."

No pen taps passed as Vinnie cried out, "Fuckin' bullshit! That's a distortion of my feelings…"

Drew took no notes. He tapped his pen again, but not to mark time. Vinnie stopped.

"The claim is made that you asked Slider to warn Kaelin, which he did. Only you learned that he warned them about you."

"What! A fuckin' lie! A fuckin' fuckin' lie!" Vinnie started to choke and sipped from the coffee cup, which made him gag. "Who said Slider warned Kaelin and Grace about me?"

"Kaelin. Grace too, but hers can be refuted as hearsay."

"What?! Fuckin' bullshit. Kaelin and Grace would not have

said that because Slider never said it.”

Vinnie’s chair screeched loudly as he pushed back from the table. The guard’s face briefly appeared at the door window until Drew waved him away.

“Sit, for God’s sake. Forget who said what. Sometimes people say things in statements that they don’t mean. Or they are manipulated into saying things that can be misconstrued. Or they lie. Whichever, I’ll find out. For now, I just want you to comment if you can provide me with concrete evidence that I can confirm.”

Drew summarized. No weapon had been discovered in connection with Grace. So far, the only evidence was a blood-soaked scarf discovered by Vinnie. Vinnie interrupted to correct Drew. “Ralph found it.”

“Ralph’s discovery, but you turned it over to the police. Or did Ralph?”

Vinnie relaxed at Drew’s attempted joke. And he regretted bringing the scarf to the police station. He should have known better. They had looked at him like he was a weirdo, even a psychopath, when he emphasized his dog discovered the scarf in his backyard. And he should not have harped on about Curt Peterson being a rapist or his loathing of him. He should not have shouted that the scarf proved Curt had murdered Slider. The scarf made him a suspect, and his rant about Curt and the baby most likely produced his eventual arrest.

Drew continued. “So far the bloody rag you discovered in your backyard—” Drew stopped at Vinnie’s cough.

“To be accurate, Ralph first buried the scarf, so technically the second time his digging it up wasn’t a discovery as much as a retrieval.”

Drew wrote in his pad.

“The DA makes a point of your increased size the last few years. He claims all muscle bulk is from steroid use provided by your partner, Mr. Ben Hausen.”

“Ben’s my husband, and he controlled the amount. Besides,

I didn't use much or often. I didn't like the size increase and feeling. But I didn't tell the cops any of this. I don't like being oversized. It's not me. And I never used enough to have fuckin' 'roid rage."

Drew tapped his pen erratically and brought his finger to his mouth, almost hushing Vinnie. "I'm only telling you what the DA says, not that it's true. We have no obligation to mention your steroid use. The burden of proof is on the DA. But he can and will use your spontaneous swearing during your interviews as proof of lingering, uncontrolled steroid effects."

"You've got to be fu—fudgin' kidding me. That's the way I talk. My whole fu—fudgin' family does. Ask anyone. Dan will tell you he almost didn't hire me because of my cursing. I had it under control until two good friends were murdered and the fu—fudgin' cops didn't listen to me. Curt murdered Slider and Grace, not me."

"Then focus on controlling your cursing. I see you have a substitute word. That's good. Start now." Drew made a note.

Seeing tears in Vinnie's eyes, Drew said, "Let's call it a day. The arraignment's tomorrow. I'm afraid you'll have to stay in the holding cell tonight."

"Will I get out after the hearing?" Vinnie wiped his eyes. He listened as Drew outlined the two options: bail denied or bail set very high.

"I don't care how high. Between Ben and me, we'll have enough. Should he be here? I haven't told him, which is why I called Dan for help. He and Ginny promised not to tell him. Was that a mistake?"

"If Ben can help with money, great, but Ginny told me he's bigger than the courthouse. If he shows up he'll give the wrong impression. Dan and Ginny arrive tonight, and they're enough."

Handcuffed and feet shackled, Vinnie shuffled in front of Drew and stopped at the doorway sobbing, "You're going to have a tougher time defending a fuckin' crybaby, never mind the cursing."

212

The guard pushed Vinnie out the door, a push of presumed guilty until proven innocent.

Chapter 35

A Home Gym

People milled around the courthouse corridors as if the Halls of Justice were having a flash sale. Tailor-made suits stood beside off-the-rack basement knockoffs. Baggy jeans were *de rigueur* in Juvie Court, with an occasional butt-crack revealed.

Drew, peering at Vinnie on the courtroom bench, threw a smile as Ginny paraded down the center aisle, with heads turning as her six-inch heels click-clacked on the tiles. Reaching Drew, she threw a hand around his neck and pecked his cheek. She smooched Vinnie with a mint candy smack, and turned on her heels full circle to examine the prosecutor's little table. The California District Attorney's grinning head bobbled, and Vinnie covered his lips. *Not in your fuckin' wettest wet dream, you fuckin' douche bag.*

Ginny sat in the second row, directly behind Drew and Vinnie. She whispered that Dan would arrive after parking their rental car. Called by the bailiff, Vinnie and Drew moved to the defendant's table, identical to the prosecutor's. Ginny now had an unobstructed view of the judge, and vice versa.

The DA's theatrical gestures added to his high-pitched "flight risk" statement. Ginny coughed the way a hacksaw cuts steel, causing the judge's gavel to rise, and diverted his attention from the DA's conclusion. With hammer paused in mid-air, the judge's eyeballs skimmed Ginny's full regalia. She obtained a reprieve of the gavel and gained Vinnie bail.

Set at one million dollars, Vinnie claimed this was the value the judge had put on Ginny's tits. Within two hours Vinnie had handed the county clerk a cashier's check at the same time as his cell beeped, announcing a text. *CU Home.*

* * *

Ben suggested they move to the living room for a recap of Vinnie's case. Vinnie preferred to call the room "a nineteenth-century parlour with twenty-first-century bourgeoisie crap." Ginny and Dan nestled in one of two identical modern love sofas. An eighteenth-century Chinese coffee table with a glass top to protect hand-carved figurines separated them from Vinnie and Ben, crammed together on a sofa.

The conversation flowed uninhibited as all had immunity from testimony; Ben as spouse, and the Livornos as part of Vinnie's legal defense team.

The bail hearing proved that the prosecutor believed Vinnie had succumbed to 'roid rage while developing his muscular body. Ben scoffed as he heard Dan say that the DA called Vinnie "a massive bodybuilder," but Ginny, wincing, stopped him.

"I didn't mean to say…"

"Yeah, I get it," Vinnie said, squeezing Ben's arm.

As if reading Dan's mind, Vinnie dripped his words. "Now that the elephant is strutting around the room in pink posers, ask away. Anything."

Dan leaned on his knees. "So why? You've never liked men with bulging muscles. Sorry, Ben, but I was surprised Vinnie fell for you."

"Me too," laughed Vinnie.

"Fine, but that basement weight room is… well…" Dan didn't know what to add to the comments he and Ginny had already made when they saw the basement gym. It was nothing like they had envisioned from the description they had heard in Martha's Vineyard. Their jaws had dropped touring the house, but their chins nearly cracked on seeing the basement weight room.

Ben cleared his throat. "Remember the story about Seattle? With Freddie?"

"Sure, the homophobic punks beating the crap out of Vinnie and gay Freddie's rescue," said Dan, who felt Ginny's poke and saw her puckered lips shift off-center.

Ben shrugged. "It's the truth, Ginny, even if Dan's version is not PC."

Vinnie's hand covered Ben's mouth. "Wandering."

"Oh, like you don't go off point?"

Vinnie showed Ben his middle finger, which Ben grabbed. "You want to keep this?"

"And you? I seem to recall you like what it can do."

A shuffling noise stopped the two men.

"Sorry, Dan, too gay for you?" Vinnie snickered.

Ginny's hand shot up like a traffic cop. "Enough. Get to the point, as Vinnie put it."

Ben repeated and amplified the Martha's Vineyard story, and the dual purpose for the elaborate gym setup.

"Fine, we know this," said Ginny impatiently.

With a nod, Ben continued to explain Slider's role in what he called Vinnie's "beasting phase." Increased gain, the rush. "He was pretty hot when smaller, but his new body made him what he is now."

Vinnie's middle finger shot up again, and he outlined events: his self-admiration; Slider's approval; Ben's acclamation. He had nothing to do in San Francisco but lift weights. So in a few months he wanted more and Ben found him the extra boost—Vinnie air-fingered quotations.

"And have you stopped the steroids?" Ginny asked.

Vinnie's taut facial skin turned ashen. "Yes. Once I reached my goal—to make Ben jealous over Freddie. To have sex with

Slider." Vinnie didn't add, *and to trap you.* "I didn't want the bodybuilder's bloat and bumps, just better definition. Did I succeed?"

Ginny smiled. "You did, but you were gorgeous the way you were too."

Vinnie shook his head, a small tear forming. *Did his steroid use indirectly cause murder?*

Ginny laughed as she said, "Your posing wasn't too shabby either. But really, aren't you still using? Did you end up having sex with Slider? You might not want to answer now, but you'll have to face it sometime before the trial. I'm sorry, Vinnie, Ben, but we have to know."

Vinnie stood and Ben pulled him down. Vinnie said, "Okay. If we must. Let's go back to Freddie. He proposed a three-way and—"

Ben's response cut Vinnie off. "And I refused. We both did. We confirmed our monogamous commitment."

"Yeah, I had a body to drool over—" Ben lightly punched Vinnie's arm. "Ouch. Anyway, Slider wasn't interested for unrelated reasons, which we'll leave aside. I had no more need to get bigger, to juice up with more steroids. Steroids were just a phase. And, so you know, I've always been faithful."

Vinnie rubbed his cheek along Ben's arm and gave him a light kiss, and didn't ask Ben to answer. He preferred paranoid uncertainty than learning the truth. Stupid too, since it was Ben that insisted on monogamy.

All because of Davis McGregor, Ben's first real homosexual lover, not a good-time fuck-buddy, that gave Ben his remorse. They sat in Davis's parlour, bequeathed to Ben. And by tacitly accepting Davis's promiscuity, Ben felt responsible for Davis's avoiding blood tests and the HIV diagnosis until too late. Monogamy had been Ben's decision, but Vinnie's remoteness for three years had made him paranoid.

From her stare, Vinnie knew Ginny hadn't forgotten the second question. *How to answer? He had stopped the steroids, but started again when he wanted to impress her.*

"Uh-huh. I didn't like how it made me feel, so I stopped." *Yeah, one week before Martha's Vineyard.*

Vinnie felt his soul being dragged across the parlour floor.

Chapter 36

No Proof

At the open front door stood a taxi driver with a yapping Boston terrier. Dan stared out, his loose bathrobe covering his pajama pants and bare chest. The taxi driver unleashed Ralph as Dan fumbled to keep his bathrobe closed with one hand and not spill his coffee with the other.

Ralph sniffed Dan's feet as he trotted past and into the kitchen. Dan entered to see the dog sniffing the floor, followed by a bark.

"You must be Ralph."

Ears stood up.

"You want something, right?"

Ears twitched.

"Food? Water? I'm afraid you got the wrong guy this time. Let me see if Vinnie's up."

Ralph followed Dan up the stairs and scratched at the bedroom door to match Dan's soft taps.

"Are you guys decent? There's someone here for Vinnie."

The door was flung open, revealing Vinnie half-dressed and Ben completely naked bending over. Dan turned around. "Oh, sorry. I didn't..."

"Dan, come on. You've seen Ben nude. Me too. Don't worry, we've finished our morning exercise, haven't we, dear?"

Before Ben could reply, Ralph was jumping up at Vinnie's

legs.

"He needs water. His bowl's under the sink. Would you mind?" Vinnie turned to see Ben, a full frontal view. "Hmm, maybe we haven't finished our exercises just yet."

Dan held up his hands as if stopping a reversing car. "Not a problem. Food too?"

"No, he'll have been fed."

With a nudge, Dan and Ralph walked out, but Dan heard Vinnie say as the door closed, "Ralph's taken care of, but I'm not. Maybe we…"

Ten minutes later Ben entered the kitchen to blend breakfast for him and Vinnie.

"I hope I didn't interrupt… prevent you and Vinnie from…"

"Sex? No. Vinnie sees ass and gets a hard-on…" Ben saw Dan's blinking eyes. "Uh, we're fine—" Before Ben had finished, Dan was gone. He mounted the stairs for a second time, only now appearing to have a pole under his robe. He hoped Ginny was awake but still in bed.

* * *

They stood at the closet behind the basement door, as if caretakers. Vinnie stuffed magazines onto the top shelf and said to Ralph, "You know, in case Ginny or Dan, well Dan mostly, finds them in the bathroom. He's still a bit prudish."

Dan's new eclectic worldview had not completely eradicated his straitlaced perspective. "You saw. We were nude. Big deal. Sure, Ben was bent over…" Ralph's ears twisted. "Okay, that was exciting. Now, let's go out."

Ralph's small paw scratched at the door.

"In a hurry are we? Wait a sec while I get your leash."

The two walked the side path, but only Vinnie glanced to Kaelin and Grace's kitchen window. Then he remembered—there was no Grace.

Ralph strained at the leash.

"Still in a hurry? Well, I had to entertain our company and give Ben his special time. Tell you what, let's make this quicker and we'll go to the lot across the street instead of the park. Just be careful of broken glass."

Vinnie shortened Ralph's leash as they stood at the curb waiting for cars to pass, many above the thirty-mile-an-hour limit. *Commuters late for work or moms rushing to personal trainer appointments to pump iron or get fucked or both.*

"Hold on, Ralph."

A house had stood on the vacant lot years before Vinnie moved to the neighborhood, even before Ben. Destroyed by fire, now wild grass, shrubs, and the usual infestation of urban weeds had reclaimed the land. Surprisingly, a single oak of eighty or ninety years stood at the rear. More surprising, a modern chain-link fence ran around the perimeter. Despite missing an entry gate, there was only a single way in. Few people entered the lot, not even teenagers to drink, smoke pot, or commit other offenses, because the limited ground cover gave patrolling police and neighborhood watchers an easy view—this empty lot should have moved out of the upscale family neighborhood.

Releasing Ralph from his leash, Vinnie smiled as the dog scampered to the tree. *Ralph's modest, like Dan. Oh yeah, Dan's face was something else when he saw Ben's double French door wide-open ass.* Vinnie lost his grin at Ralph's furious barking.

"Now what? Ralph, come here."

The barking forced Vinnie to go to Ralph.

"Another hole!" Vinnie peered into Ralph's excavation. Bending over, he saw what appeared to be a cloth. Lowering himself on to one knee, Vinnie used thumb and index finger to pull from the ground a small, dirty cloth wrapped around a hard object. Unfolding the material, Vinnie saw a serrated fishing knife. He knew.

* * *

The front doorbell sounded odd. Vinnie waited, keeping Ralph's leash short. Kaelin's face appeared at the small glass window.

"Hi, Vinnie. You shouldn't be here, should you?" Kaelin held the door open a few inches.

"Why, because I murdered Grace, right?"

"You should go. I am a witness for the prosecution, even if I don't believe you killed Grace. The police confused me and took my statement out of context. I know you didn't do it."

"Then tell them that."

"I have. And I'll say so on the witness stand."

"Really?" Vinnie lowered his arms. He wanted to hug Kaelin. "I'm so relieved. I thought you believed me a murderer. I would never have hurt Grace or the baby."

"I know. You'll be proved innocent."

Vinnie stopped himself from pointing out that he was innocent until proven guilty. Kaelin opened the door wide.

"Why don't you and Ralph come in?"

In the kitchen, Kaelin filled a bowl with water and placed it on the floor. "So, what's up?" She stared at Vinnie's hand holding out the small package.

"I found this. I mean Ralph found it. In the vacant lot across the street."

Opening the package like a precious art object, Vinnie lifted the knife handle with a corner of the cloth.

"Recognize it?"

Hushed breaths trickled out of Kaelin. "It's a fishing knife. My father has one exactly like it. Me too, a gift from him on my first visit to his Tahoe concubine cabin a few years ago. His first attempt to reconnect with me."

"I knew it," said Vinnie, sounding like a preacher. "Your father killed Slider with this knife. When the cops see this, it'll prove my innocence." Vinnie realized he'd fallen into the same mindset as Kaelin—needing to prove himself innocent.

Kaelin touched Vinnie's arm. "Wait. That's not a good idea. Remember, you're out on bail and accused of Grace's murder. It will look bad for you to turn up with a weapon, even if it's the one used on Slider and not Grace."

Wrapping the knife in the cloth, Vinnie half-hunched. "The DNA and fingerprints won't be mine. I was in New York. My alibi for Slider is tight. This is Curt's."

Kaelin touched the wrapped knife. "Let me take it to the police. I'll say I found Ralph wandering in the vacant lot and thought he had escaped from your house. Coming from the daughter, the evidence is more convincing."

Leaving the house, Vinnie felt like he'd eaten an entire box of chocolate candies. Kaelin believed him. He had proved that Curt had murdered Slider. And if Curt had murdered once, he'd be the prime suspect for Grace.

* * *

"Stupid. Stupid. Incredibly stupid." Ben paced as Vinnie cried, slumped in his chair. "How stupid can you be? Kaelin's a witness against you."

"No," sobbed Vinnie. "I couldn't have killed Slider and she believes I would never have hurt Grace. The police and DA twisted her statement."

Standing next to Vinnie, Ginny held him. "You believe everyone has your best interest at heart, but they don't. Anyway, you're right that they won't find your fingerprints or DNA."

Vinnie's sobbing slowed.

"It'll work out," said Ginny, relaxing her hold. "Ben's worried. You should have given the knife to Drew. He's your lawyer. From now on everything goes to him, okay?"

Vinnie considered Ben's circling like Conestoga wagons preparing for an onslaught.

The preliminary fingerprint results, according to Drew, were negative. With everyone scattered around the room, Drew faced Vinnie. "The blood analysis takes more time." He told everyone that Detective Green had expedited the forensic laboratory analysis and promised a quick release to the defense team for independent analysis.

To further explain, Drew said, "The knife's cutting edge and blade shape are consistent with Slider's wounds and Grace's, so it is probably the murder weapon."

"Does that help Vinnie?" Ginny asked, holding her hands together.

"No."

"Does it hurt?"

"Maybe."

"How?"

"Because of the proximity to Vinnie's house. And Kaelin's claim that Vinnie asked her to give the knife to the police."

Vinnie jumped up screaming. "That's a fuckin' lie! She suggested taking the knife to the police."

The defense team nodded like four bubblehead dolls on the dashboard of a Chevy. Drew made an analogy of the courtroom to a chess game. The DAs would use Kaelin's testimony, and Vinnie on the stand had risks.

"Why? I'm just as fu—fudgin' believable as Kaelin." And everyone immediately knew why: a testimony replete with "fucking" or "fudging" was not a winning strategy.

With pen tapping, Drew continued, "Curt will corroborate his daughter's story, and probably add that an identical knife is missing from his cabin. The DA will point to your visit to the cabin, to the knife being consistent with Grace's wounds, and as evidence for your intention to frame Curt for Slider's murder. They'll have excuses ready for small inconsistencies or bridge gaps that are not fully explicable. The DA will coach Kaelin and Curt. Stay away from her. Maybe the lab results will produce a surprise.”

Vinnie crept out, his innocence hanging on a “maybe.”

Chapter 37

Surprise Talk

Dropping the laboratory's analysis report on the middle of the table, Drew had taken everyone by surprise except Vinnie, who wasn't present. The surprise wasn't the report, but his suggestion that Vinnie take a plea bargain. With his hands on the table's edge, Ben leveraged his body upward. "No fucking way." Dan agreed.

Ginny asked, "Why? There's no real evidence against him. The knife doesn't prove anything."

Drew reminded the group that the knife's significance was to force Vinnie's testimony. The deciding factors were motive, means, and opportunity, and all stacked up against Vinnie. His obsession with Grace's child; his nonstop neighborhood chatter about the baby; his ranting over the baby; his police report of the rape accusation against Curt; the detective's interviews showing Vinnie's rage at Curt being unfit to raise a child; his offer to purchase the house next door; his knowledge of the Lake Tahoe cabin. And his steroid use—believable, since Kaelin provided photos of Vinnie buffed like a brand new Thunderbird muscle car. Even access to drugs was a no-brainer, given that Vinnie's spouse was a professional champion bodybuilder. 'Roid rage and physical strength were foregone conclusions.

"If Vinnie chooses not to accept a plea bargain," Drew concluded, "we'll need more details of Curt's relation to Grace. And a damn good explanation for Vinnie's inordinate obsession with Grace's baby."

* * *

Supper consisted of pizza take-out for Ginny and Dan and a protein shake and a four-pound chicken for Ben, while Vinnie munched on granola cereal. The three friends carried their food to the family room at the rear of the house. Vinnie stayed in the kitchen, alone.

A conversation about nothing took place in front of a black, sixty-inch flat-screen television, more like decorative art than a functioning electronic device. Dan disliked small talk, so he interrupted Ginny.

"Should I talk to him about the baby?"

Dan was looking at Ginny but Ben answered. "Probably."

Taking the empty pizza box with him as he closed the family room door, Dan walked sixty feet into the kitchen. He sensed the difference in rooms: one preoccupied, the other sullen. Dan had liked Drew's chess match analogy, but frowned. The DA was one move away from checkmate.

Vinnie stared into his bowl, ignoring Dan until he heard the sliding of a high stool on the opposite side of the table. Vinnie saw Dan's folded arms, the same posture he'd taken at Vinnie's interview five years before.

It was so fuckin' incredible to get the interview. Vinnie smiled briefly, recalling that the same curse had nearly cost him the job. Dan hired him despite his crude language. *He believed I was a good person. I fell in love with him, his gorgeous face and hunky body. I would have screwed the living daylights out of him if he were gay. And now I love him, Ginny, and Anthony. Through him and Ginny I met Ben, and was saved from a dreary, lonely life. I'm going to lose it all. My life will be more than dreary behind bars.*

"Vinnie, we need to know... I need to know, why was Grace's baby so important to you?"

227

"Dunno. Just was and wasn't."

Dan's hands lifted slightly as his wrists rested on the counter surface.

"It wasn't that I wanted her baby, just to help. I needed to know what it would be like to raise a child. I wanted to prepare myself for when Ben and I have our own."

"So, you never thought Grace's baby belonged to you?"

"What! No. Never. I just wanted to experience a baby from birth, to learn what was needed firsthand to raise a child. To be prepared."

"You've told us this, but you have to admit your offer was a bit extreme. Time, daycare, money, purchase of a house, babysitting."

"Well, Dan, in case you haven't noticed, I have too much fuckin' money. Blood money given to me by DV&N to compensate for the deaths of two good people."

"It wasn't blood money. And you were nearly murdered because of one of their senior employees. And why don't you deserve to have money?"

Vinnie gazed at the gap between his fingertips.

"I'll ask again. What did you want from Grace? What do you want now?"

For fifteen minutes Dan pressed and Vinnie's responses were revelations. He explained his interest in weight training went beyond the Seattle assault and Freddie's encouragement. Not even Ben knew, but Vinnie told Dan all the thoughts he kept hidden.

Dan listened to Vinnie's stuttering explanation. From Dan's tapping index fingers Vinnie knew that he wasn't buying the story as the whole truth. Dan's interruption confirmed Vinnie's intuition.

"So, you thought bodybuilding would get you sex with Slider, then encourage Ben to do something in return. And helping Grace was an educational exercise. That's the gist of it, right?"

Dan's rising voice appeared to lift his eyebrows.

Vinnie stood up. "Fu—fudgin' moronic, I know."

"Right. Nothing is connected. There's more, and it involves your steroid use, doesn't it?"

Vinnie shook his head, feeling disorientated. Wobbling, he said, "Ben couldn't get past Carl's death. I believed my body-building and helping Grace with the baby would give me insight into Ben. Then, just before Martha's Vineyard, Ben agreed, but on condition that..."

Dan encouraged Vinnie to finish his sentence. Vinnie said nothing, so Dan said with raised voice, "What condition?"

Silence.

"Vinnie?"

Walking around the counter, Vinnie took Dan's arm.

"A surrogate mother."

With a head tilt, Dan said, "I can sort of understand that." Vinnie's hand rubbed Dan's arm.

Pushing Vinnie's arm away, Dan's voice deepened. "There's more, isn't there?"

Vinnie's head leaned on Dan's shoulder. "Ginny."

Dan flew out of his chair to the door.

"Dan, wait. Please."

With a turn, his lips parting, patience pushed aside. Vinnie's words inched out, tears dribbling down his cheeks. Dan's anger, Vinnie thought, is nothing compared to his indifference to my torment.

"I'm sorry. It's too much to ask, isn't it?"

Dan moved to the sink and filled a glass with tap water, ignoring the expensive bottled water in the refrigerator. Several gulps later, Dan poured two more and handed one to Vinnie.

"You know how hard this is for me." Dan's words were measured. "You know I'm jealous over Ginny, always have been. I've worried for years about losing her. It took four years of therapy to abate my job loss and false rape accusation, as well as my general paranoia. There was a time that I hated Ben. I blamed him for Ginny's problem and I was convinced she would leave me for him or for another bodybuilder who could fulfill her fantasies. I know, it sounds irrational, probably is."

With the water glass resting against his lips, Vinnie moved his head.

"My therapist taught me to drink water before acting." Dan held his empty water glass in an outstretched arm. "How did Ben react to the idea of Ginny being the surrogate?"

Vinnie rambled while Dan stared into his glass. Dan said Vinnie's explanation seemed incomplete, and relied on the unpredictability of obsessed people. Dan knew about obsessed people—he was married to Ginny after all. He also would never have predicted Anthony's birth could have diminished her sthenolagnia.

Vinnie talked about the similarities between their respective spouses: unintended careers—Ben's bodybuilding and Ginny's fashion world; unashamedly displaying their bodies; sex fantasy explorations; Ben's years of insatiable homosexual partners leading to Davis; Ginny's college lesbian dalliance with her roommate—yes, Rachel had told him.

Vinnie wondered if he could predict Dan's reaction now. He had changed as much as Ginny and Ben.

After all, Dan had had a tryst with Ginny and Ben, the AFF day. Unbelievable, even though Dan confirmed it himself. *It should have been me* he had said with undisguised envy. As consolation, Dan said the event wasn't to do with the exploration of his sexuality but to prove his commitment to Ginny and gratitude to Ben.

Dan revealed he had a psychological breakdown when his worldview disintegrated. Trusted co-workers at DV&N had lied with impunity; believed him capable of rape; his best friend—Vinnie—nearly murdered. He chucked away all inhibitions. His fear of being a homosexual. The tryst not only proved his love for Ginny and gratitude to Ben, but rebooted his psychology. He became renewed, more confident in himself, and did not deny himself pleasure, or the pleasure of his loved ones.

Vinnie wondered. *Does Dan's attitude change have an expiration date? Did the attempt to rekindle Ginny's sthenolagnia also ignite Dan's jealous rages?*

"What?" said Dan on hearing Vinnie's sighs.

"There's more," Vinnie blurted. *I might as well tell him. I'll soon be a lifer in prison, so what does it matter?*

Dan refilled his water glass and returned to his stool, waiting for Vinnie to continue.

"I learned as much as I could about surrogacy. Since Grace and Kaelin had been in a similar biological situation to Ben and me—" Vinnie stopped, with Dan's head tipping back. "Okay, not exactly, but they needed outside involvement, so to speak. I asked Kaelin to teach me about birthing—even to be present when Grace gave birth." Vinnie stopped and shook his head. "I know. The DA will use that against me too. But it was research for Ben and me. So when I heard Grace had been raped I was upset, not only for her but for me. I had lost my chance to learn an insider's experience with artificial insemination."

Dan raised his water glass again.

"It gets worse. When she agreed to live with Curt, I became angry, like it was me who was betrayed and not Kaelin. I had spent a lot of time with Grace. I thought we bonded. I even considered her as a possible surrogate for Ben and me." Vinnie's sigh nearly expelled all the air from his lungs.

"I went to a sperm clinic. Found out that a woman can specify sperm donor criteria. Weird, right? Like going down a Whole Foods aisle for a specific granola brand."

Dan nodded.

"For men, different rules apply. A clinic helps identify surrogate mothers—an entire human being, not protoplasm in a petri dish. They can even implant a fully fertilized egg in a surrogate."

"Wouldn't that be called adoption?"

"I suppose. Anyway, in our case the simplest procedure is for sperm from one of us to fertilize the surrogate's egg. I didn't want to, given my family's criminal genes."

Dan stood. "Bullshit. There's no criminal gene. Look at you, your mother, your sisters."

"I know it's unfounded, but that's how I felt. Anyway, Ben agreed on one condition."

Dan chugged his water, moved to the sink, refilled the glass, and drank deeply again. Dan held his stomach.

"You've guessed, haven't you?"

With a burp, Dan placed his glass in the sink and stared out of the window.

"Fine. I'll say it. Ben agrees to donate but only if Ginny's the surrogate."

Vinnie stared as Dan refilled his glass, then poured the contents into the sink and walked out.

Vinnie looked at the wall, imagining the color of prison gray.

Chapter 38

The Meeting

The baseball playoffs flashed across the TV. Ginny, a loyal Boston Red Sox fan, raised her wine glass to Ben, sitting next to her on a large couch, a token gesture to acknowledge that his New York Yankees held a two-run lead at the end of the seventh inning. Ben's chuckle diminished as Vinnie flopped like a pile of dirty laundry into an empty armchair.

"And?" Ginny said, swiveling her body away from the TV advertisements.

"And what? Your husband needs to think." Vinnie's harsh tone caught Ginny and Ben by surprise.

"About what?" Ginny's tone was equally harsh.

Vinnie deflected Ben's scowl by saying, "I think Ben has something to tell you."

In his UltraFit managerial voice, Ben said, "Shouldn't we wait for Dan?"

A grimace crossed Vinnie's face as he spoke. "He'll be a while."

"Oh?" The O hung on Ginny's lips. "Shall I ask him to join us?"

"I wouldn't."

"That's it. What happened in there?" Ginny flung her arm toward the kitchen.

"I think Dan should explain."

"By telepathy?"

Ben's hand covered his smile, marveling at Ginny's trademark ability to cut men down.

Vinnie's head moved from side to side.

"Care to fetch him?" continued Ginny as Ben's smile widened.

"Hey, I'm not Ralph."

Ben broke into a full laugh.

"Fuckin' retard, Ben. Fine, I'll get him." Vinnie rose to leave.

Ginny pointed at a chair. "Sit. If your first conversation made him need to think, I hate to think what your second might do." Ginny walked out.

Ben turned the TV off just as the scoreboard flashed two more runs for the Yankees, and patted the cushion next to him. Vinnie repeated once again that he wasn't Ralph, and Ben's laugh thundered.

In the half-hour alone together, Vinnie summarized his conversation with Dan, which Ben had already guessed.

When Dan and Ginny reappeared they lowered themselves onto a leather couch facing Vinnie and Ben. Vinnie rambled until Ben squeezed his thigh then raised his eyes to Ginny's.

"You know? So it's all clear, right?"

"Like San Francisco's fog at night." Ginny jerked a thumb at Dan. "Mister Intelligence says I should hear it from you. All I have so far is that this involves Grace's baby and you both wanting to raise a child of your own."

Ginny's arms were opened, her voiced raised. "All clear, right?"

Details rolled out, a scattering from hits off a pinball's flippers: Ben and Vinnie alternating. Ben's approach matter-of-fact and Vinnie's metaphorical. Ginny sat confused. Dan sat motionless, arms folded, one hand under each armpit as if containing an explosion.

As soon as Ben said "surrogacy" the room fell silent. Vinnie didn't like Ginny's look, the bending of Dan's head. He considered pointing out that in Scrabble the word was worth fifteen points.

As Ben had predicted on Martha's Vineyard, once Ginny heard that single word she would know the entire script. Her eyes closed for a few seconds, and opened as she said, "Why?"

Taking on his personal trainer persona, Ben lifted his body, placing two hands on his chest as if locating the center of gravity. "Let's review a few points. It's not so ridiculous—"

Ginny's index finger shot up, a gesture Ben knew well—her intolerance for condescension.

With an apology, Ben continued. "Vinnie didn't see it, not at first, but it makes sense." Ben looked to Vinnie, who nodded.

"We trust you. You're the only person we do—"

Like a tag team, Vinnie interrupted. "You never really know people. I thought I knew Grace and Kaelin. But they never tried to understand my needs." Vinnie covered his face.

Ben's arm crossed Vinnie's shoulder, his eyes on Ginny.

"What Vinnie means is that we trust you with our future family because we feel you are our family, if that makes any sense. The baby would add one more..." Ben stopped, and no one hurried him to speak.

Rubbing his tense arm, Ben concentrated as if he were performing at one of his competitions. "In my opinion... and I apologize in advance for my psychological analysis, but after years of training people, including you two, I have some understanding of human behavior. If I'm wrong, please tell me."

Ben waited, transfixed by Ginny's glare.

"In my opinion, if Ginny agrees then psychologically she'll want me to be the sperm donor." Ben stopped, examining Dan's porcelain gaze. He waited. Even Vinnie remained silent. Ben entered into his trance, his posing mode, the one used to concentrate on each flex of individual muscle fibers to impress the judges. This time he flexed grey cells.

"And I believe Ginny would want the sperm to be implanted

in one of her eggs. Anyone else's and I think she would resent the fetus. I know that sounds presumptuous. Tell me if I'm wrong."

Ben walked over to Ginny, knelt on both knees, his bottom resting on his heels. He took her hand, and tilting his head back he stared into Ginny's eyes, which Vinnie thought looked like a marriage proposal.

"Would you really accept randomness? Not just the identity of the donor but the egg? I'm not being egotistical. I'm stating facts as I see them and as much as I know you. Serendipity has never been your view of life. Am I wrong?"

Dan stood, hovering over Ben. "You are not going to fuck my wife and I don't care how big you are."

Craning and twisting his neck as he stayed kneeling, Ben answered. "I agree. I'm not and would not. I know this is hard to grasp, for me as much as you."

Ginny pulled Dan to kneel on one knee, her arms around his neck. Ben backed away on his haunches to squat facing Vinnie, who kissed Ben's forehead. Vinnie looked over Ben's shoulder. He knew Dan. His jealous anger. His face freshly plastered with fear.

Ben half-turned to see Dan, and said the only words he thought mattered. "Dan, this means everything to Vinnie, otherwise I wouldn't have given it a second thought. Actually I did. I refused at first—"

Twisting around, Dan shouted, "You got it right the first time!"

Ginny rubbed Dan's neck and softly hushed him.

"Maybe," said Ben, "and I still have concerns. Look how messed up Vinnie's become. He's accused of murder. Two people he cares about have died, as well as an unborn child. A baby isn't a whim for him. I love Vinnie too much to turn away. This is his dream and I want to help him. Will you, Ginny? Dan?"

There wasn't a glacier on Earth that could have matched Dan's frozen state. Ben's question hung like a noose around his neck.

236

Ginny didn't look to Dan or Ben, but to Vinnie. "It's a lot to take in. For Dan and me. Ben's psychological profile isn't enough. I'm more complex then Ben imagines, and so are you." Ginny saw Ben's movement. "Ben, don't say any more. You've done enough talking for now."

Vinnie coughed some words, but stopped as Ginny held up her hand to him. "You too." She turned to Dan.

"No one has mentioned the consequence for the baby, which would be mine as much as Ben's." She outlined all their responsibilities, her role, the nine months to birth, and the separation. Ginny ended with a small laugh. "And none of you know the pain of childbirth, no matter how excruciating you think hard training is."

Looking down as she touched her stomach, Ginny said, "And the baby would be Anthony's half-sibling, so he's affected too." She looked at Ben. "With all your psychological analysis you omitted your own state of mind about Carl."

A sinkhole opened in the room. Ginny continued. "Look at all of you. Big, strong men who don't think further than themselves. I would say with your dicks, but even that would credit you with too much intelligence."

Dan walked out followed by Ben, then Ginny. Vinnie burrowed into the couch, crying, holding himself, convinced he was the worst person on Earth. Discussion over. Beginning of the end. He might as well be convicted of double homicide. Acquittal would still mean he'd lose Ben. Would Ginny and Dan still be his friends?

Hours after Ben had gone to sleep, Vinnie slipped into bed and listened to his husband's soft rasping breaths, as if they revealed his dreams. Vinnie buried his face into his pillow, muffling his distress. What should he do? What could he do? He considered asking Ralph in the morning, which was only four hours away.

Chapter 39

Bad Night, Good Morning

The kitchen door swung open, the morning sun flickering on the metal pans in the drying rack. A small crack in the window provided a cool breeze. Vinnie looked up briefly from his coffee as Dan walked across the room, avoiding Ralph's scampering at his feet. Vinnie heard ice from the refrigerator door dispenser clink into Dan's glass, then the door opening, followed by the sound of pouring liquid. Ralph lost interest and curled into a corner patch of sunlight.

Dan's approaching footsteps caused Vinnie to lift his gaze, hoping to hear Dan's soft voice as he placed his juice glass on the breakfast counter. "Vinnie, I'm going to say this once." Dan took a breath. His words riffled like a shuffling card deck in a crescendo: "Fu...UU...CK YOU!"

Tears streamed down Vinnie's face. Vinnie had never heard harsher words directed at him by Dan, and not because they were curses, but because Dan cursed only when he was really upset, on the verge of a breakdown. Vinnie tensed as Dan placed his hands around him, flinched as Dan pulled him forward, and felt his cool fingers from the ice-filled glass. But the hug was warm, tight, the kind of embrace that crushes souls.

With his lips next to Vinnie's ear, Dan whispered, "That had to be said, but my feelings for you haven't changed. You're my best friend. I'll never forget what you risked for me. And as much as I don't like what you've asked, I agree."

The words washed over Vinnie, indistinct like a rapidly spoken foreign language. He stuttered, "Wh... wh... what!"

Releasing Vinnie, Dan stood back. "I tossed and turned all night. I've been up since five, and I can't deny what you want and need."

Like a cat, Vinnie jumped, his turn to hug as more tears filled his eyes. He took hold of Dan to steady him as he gave a full-mouth kiss. Dan gently pushed Vinnie away after a brief hesitation.

"Enough." A grin came over Dan. "I said fuck you, not fuck me."

Now Vinnie laughed, holding his crotch, and said, "You sure? Seems like you're in a generous mood." Vinnie bathed in Dan's laughter, the sunlight a little stronger, and the breeze less cool.

Pouring himself a black coffee, no sugar, Dan sipped before he asked, "Tell me about Ben, his real feelings on this."

"I don't know. Sometimes he gets morose, and I know he's thinking about Carl."

With a trembling voice, Dan said, "It's tough on him, isn't it?"

Waiting for Dan to return to his seat, Vinnie picked up his mug. "Ben has never forgiven himself. On Carl's birthday he goes away and I worry he won't return. I visit the neighborhood Catholic church and light a votive candle. It doesn't help Ben, or me if I'm honest."

Dan's chin moved up.

"You're surprised, aren't you? Me at church. I even go to Mass. Yeah, fu—fudging unbelievable, after the way the church hurt me. But religion is important to me. I thought of trying another brand but realized I'd rather be with the hypocrites I know than start over."

"Being gay isn't a problem?"

Vinnie rolled his eyes as he exhaled. "Turns out not so much in San Francisco. I'm sure once the Bishop learns, Steve—that's the priest's name, Father Steve—gives communion to openly gay men, he'll be seeking new employment. There's a group of liberal nuns too. One is pregnant."

"There you go, our problem solved. Let the fucking nun be your surrogate."

Both men laughed, Vinnie harder than he had in a long time. "I've missed you so much. You've even got the cursing down. Way to go."

"Me too, I mean missing you, not the cursing. Other than Ginny, I have no one to talk to, not the way we talk."

"You mean cursing, rubbing genitals, acting juvenile, and bragging about conquests?"

A fly entered the room, buzzed around, and Dan swatted it. "Very funny, but I'm trying to be serious."

The two men drank their coffee in silence, neither looking at the other nor at anything in particular.

"You know, the final decision is not mine," Dan said in a monotone.

"I know."

"I told Ginny my decision, including that I'm still uncomfortable with the whole idea, but I also stressed she shouldn't feel any pressure. To be honest, deep down I hope she refuses."

"Will you be resentful if she agrees? Ginny will know."

"Sure she'll know, it's Ginny." Both men laughed, unconstrained. "And that's why I've been up since early this morning. I'm sure. I think of the joy a child brings. And I think it would bring joy to me and Ginny too. Like Ben said, we're family. Anthony would have a half-sibling. Imagine the fun! And if this brings you and Ben the happiness that Ginny and I have with our son, then how can I be resentful?"

Tears filled Vinnie's eyes. "When will we know?"

Dan touched Vinnie's shoulder and shrugged his own.

"Any idea?"

"First we have to get you exonerated—we need that not guilty verdict." Dan paused, realizing that if Vinnie was convicted, Ginny had no decision to make. "She'll have questions for you and Ben. And if you think the police interrogation was hard, just wait until she gets started."

"And if Ben changes his mind? Would she take me as the donor?"

This caused Dan to shake his head. "You're jumping ahead of yourself."

"Are you asking if I have the firepower? Want to review the video?" Vinnie gave a pump with his hand in a closed-fist gesture. "Uh-oh, a little too weirdly gay for you?"

A smile came to Dan.

"Yeah, we passed weird a long time ago. But just as a Plan B, if Ben backs out and it has to be me, will it affect Ginny? Or you?"

A frown crossed Dan's face. "I don't know. I guess it's the same to me if it's you or Ben. But Ginny? First, we don't even know if she agrees to the entire concept of surrogacy." Dan gazed out of the window, eyes outward, thoughts inward.

"Ben believes it does matter. But you know Ginny best. What's your gut reaction?"

"I'm with Ben. I think Ginny will agree on condition it's him as the donor," Dan said as his lips scrunched and he rubbed his eyes.

Vinnie face flushed, his hand touching his neck. *The sperm donor shouldn't matter, not in our case. But why not me?* Vinnie wondered if he had vocalized his thoughts, because Dan rubbed his shoulder again.

"Look, it's not that she thinks Ben is better than you, intellectually or physically. That's not her. Remember, this is emotional and she needs an emotional connection. She'll want the baby to be from someone that she understands, and God knows she understands Ben, maybe more than you do. They have history. She believes he understands her. Sort of like me and you."

Another fly entered the room. Vinnie moved to shut the window, watched a few passing cars, then looked to the park. Slider's bench wasn't visible from this angle, yet Vinnie stared.

"It will have to be Ben. But no intercourse. That's my one condition." Dan walked to Vinnie at the window.

"I agree on that point, Ben too. Here's the deal: if Ben and Ginny do get it on, then I let you do me, how's that for a guarantee?"

Dan was smiling. "Any chance we could review the nun option?"

If nothing else, Vinnie appreciated Dan's dry humor. And he loved Dan's Adonis body and face, half hoping Ben and Ginny did have sex.

"What's next?" Vinnie said, washing his mug in the sink.

Dan followed Vinnie to clean his mug and place it in the drying rack. "Ginny's going to talk to Ben during their training session and we're taking Ralph for his walk."

Chapter 40

Legs: Another Way to Talk

Weights clanged as they hit the floor, causing high-pitched vibrations. Ben's leg day impressed bulldozer drivers, unconstrained movement requiring just enough cloth to meet decency requirements. His shorts were short, and his sleeveless, meshed tank top barely enough lint to soak up his sweat.

Ginny didn't train with Ben, which would just waste time by the constant need for weight changes. She opted to exercise her upper body. In contrast to Ben's minimalist dress code, her designer gym clothes proved practical and stylish: Lycra mixed with cotton in matching bright blue and white trim piping. Tight shorts crossed mid-thigh, which pencil-sketched her rear curvature. Her long, well-formed calves glistened, yet were mere pegs compared to Ben's cannons. If his T showed him battleship-wide, her halter top became a mountaineer's wet dream. Even though her clothing was sufficiently discreet for any gym, she would have excited enough old men to burden the local cardiac ward and give twenty-four-hour erections to the young.

Each basement grunt added to already perfect bodies. The effect on emotions was another matter.

Ben spotted Ginny sporadically during his warm-up. This was his training session, not hers. In all their years together, Ginny had never observed Ben work out. She had attended his competitions, had advised him on his show routines, and had watched him practice. He used light weights to show her proper lifting form, but she never saw him train.

His training partner lifted mountains—a man so big he crowded an empty subway car.

Although Ginny knew each of Ben's muscle segments along his legs, she had never seen the manufacturing process: straining, shredding surface layers; loud screams to push one last repetition; a half-ton of iron moved in rapid-fire shots. Ben's skin tightened to the point of snapping. He squatted under a barbell so large it might have been a stolen truss off the Golden Gate Bridge. He exploded power.

After an hour they took a break. Ginny was given first dibs in the bathroom. Water flasks were refilled, and Ben prepared another gallon of protein mix for himself and a pint for Ginny. He drank half before Ginny had brought her pint to her lips.

Ben looked at the weights; he was refueled. He needed another hour on his gluteus maximus and adductor magnus—his ass and inner thigh. Ginny wanted to talk. Ben agreed, not because he felt her need to be greater, but because she had spent her last twenty minutes watching him. He remembered Anna's warning. Luring Ginny was not required anymore—probably never was. He felt guilty, especially if her sthenolagnia had returned.

Ben took Ginny's arm and walked her to facing weight benches, sitting her on one and himself on the other.

Ginny spoke first. "Dan's been up since five this morning."

With a bow of his torso, Ben acknowledged that he knew.

"And did Vinnie tell you what Dan's decided?"

A more pronounced upper body movement provided his answer.

"Good. Then let's talk about my concerns."

"Fine." *That's Ginny, no beating around the bush.* Ben's sigh was barely audible. *She'll press me harder than those weights.*

Ginny started with a prologue about eggs, sperm, insemination, risks, and costs—and she didn't mean payable by cash, check, or PayPal. "We'll each have an emotional reaction, similar and different. I can't even predict how I'll feel, let alone all of you."

Ben said nothing. *She's smart. Anything I say will be BS, and she'll blow me off.*

After a brief silence, Ginny asked, "Is this baby a replacement for Carl?"

The reply was an emphatic "no."

"I can tell you that implanting someone else's fertilized egg in me is not an option. The baby would be Anthony's half-sibling. There's something about—"

Ben reached across to stop Ginny's tapping fingertips. With a penny grin, Ginny said, "Don't you see?" Her voice rose. "The baby has to have a real connection to Anthony, as it will to me. If it's in my body, then one part *is* me."

The emotion in her voice startled Ben. He knew enough not to interrupt, so he expanded his chest as if taking the room's oxygen would stop her.

"Dan feels the same. And it's his choice too," Ginny said with lowered voice.

From her stare Ben thought she mistook him for Dan. *She's acting as if Dan will make the decision, which he has. Is she forfeiting her input? This isn't like her.*

"There's something else," said Ginny stretching her neck, lifting her chin up.

Nerves? Indecision? Refusal? Ben became anxious and drained his protein mix.

"Dan and I have never talked about this, but we assumed or maybe we knew... or maybe felt or... I don't know, just that Anthony was all we wanted. But I've been thinking about a second child and I haven't said anything to Dan."

Her words dropped with more weight than even Ben could lift. She had just changed everything. He and Vinnie had assumed Ginny and Dan were a one-child family.

"We haven't decided. I haven't decided. But if we do, then when?"

Ben's nod hid his feelings. She knew, only Dan didn't. Which made her last question imperative to answer. "Any idea when? That is if you do decide to have another child."

"Not for another year should we decide to go ahead." Ginny stopped.

The hum of overhead fluorescent lights became an annoying buzz to Ben, who thought *A second Livorno child is a certainty, not a "should we decide to." She's already decided.*

Ginny filtered her words. "A lot of parents think siblings should be spaced close together, making them playmates. There's also the philosophical view—get the babies over and done with quickly. But my experience with Rachel proves differently. I'm three years older yet it took until our mid-twenties to become friends."

"Exactly like Vinnie, who detests his brother, who's two years older, and loves his sisters who are four and six years older."

Her eyes narrowed to slits. "Being a surrogate would impact my future family."

Bingo, she absolutely wants another baby—even if Dan doesn't know it. Ben sat up straight, placing his drink on the bench beside him, using his official training voice. "You've decided against surrogacy but don't want to tell me, is that it, Ginny?"

He knew how to take disappointment. Judges had awarded him second-place trophies when he should have taken first. Sometimes they had been right: his gut had been too large; his arms disproportionate to his shoulders. And sometimes they were wrong, so he learned stoicism to remain on the professional bodybuilding circuit.

Ginny shot back, equal in her professional tone. "No. I'm saying I don't know what I want. I'm unsure how this impacts me and Dan, or on our having a second child. I honestly have not decided. How will I feel when I have to give the baby up? Will it change my feelings about having another baby with Dan?"

"But you wouldn't be giving it up. Vinnie and I want you and Dan to be part of the child's life. That's why we asked you and not a stranger. Don't you see?"

A long silence followed. Ginny crossed her ankles and rubbed her forearm and Ben returned to the weight rack. In a soft voice, Ginny said, "You're correct on one score... you have to be the donor."

With a swivel, he saw her eyes grazing on him. He asked her if she worried this might change her relationship with Dan or him. Tears glistened in Ginny's eyes, her nose sniffled, her lips twisted, and suddenly her face was not as beautiful.

He squatted in front of her, both feet flat, and his hard massive ass touching his heels. He rubbed her forearms. "Dan will never not love you because of the baby."

A small smile came across Ben, offering her something he could guarantee. "And we'll always have our mutual perverted interest." He flexed an arm, his stadium bicep closing in to brush her lips.

Reaching out, Ginny cupped her hand over the hilltop bicep, then extended her hand and with her index and middle finger tapped his forehead. "This is what counts."

Ben rose and walked to the power cage. He loaded most of the world's iron ore onto a steel bar. Positioning himself so the bar rested on his shoulders, he spoke to Ginny as if a loan officer at a bank. "Take your time, there's no rush. Vinnie's trial comes first." He pushed his rump back before lowering himself for his first rep.

Ginny replaced dumbbells on the racks while Ben squatted twelve times. She cleared her throat. "It's a joint decision. And we will all have to talk everything through if this is to move forward."

Hearing her words while resting the barbell in a locked position, Ben staggered. Something like a nervous laugh came out.

"What?" said Ginny, rushing to help him, but he waved her away.

"Sounds like we'll need a family therapist. Who would do that?"

With a smile, Ginny's reply wafted across the room. "My mother."

Ben gripped the iron bar tighter.

Chapter 41

Dog Sleuthing

The crisp breeze cooling Vinnie's cheeks contrasted with the early morning September sun warming his back. He, Dan, and Ralph marched into the park, following Dan's suggestion to give Ben and Ginny some space. Vinnie was sure Ralph's motivation was to discover if his territory had been invaded overnight. The small dog moved around to mark his favorite locations, a time-consuming task.

"I'm going to jog, get to know the place. It'll take me at least forty-five minutes with these hills." Vinnie told Dan to take his time, knowing Ben would work extra hard and would need at least three hours.

"Good. This is not like Central Park. Too many hills." Dan stretched, placing his legs on the nearest bench, which caused Vinnie to laugh, thinking he looked like Ralph marking his territory.

"What?" Dan looked at Vinnie, who told him not to wait—they could meet back at the house.

Waiting until Dan disappeared around the block, Vinnie walked to Slider's bench and began to talk. "I meant to bring flowers. I'll do it next time. It's been so chaotic around here. I'll fill you in later. I'll prove Curt did this to you." Vinnie's hand touched the back of the bench and he closed his eyes, willing Slider back into existence, even if a phantom like in the movies.

If only.

Ralph's barking startled Vinnie. "Gimme a break, Ralph. I've got a bag ready."

As Vinnie approached the back of the park, he opened a plastic poop bag. He had noted Ralph's exact location at the time of his bark. As homage to Slider, Vinnie allowed the dog to run unleashed in the park, free to roam where he wished. *Ralph's earned it after he was busted in the pound for a crime he didn't commit. Anyway, who cares about the leash law if the dog's not doing anyone any harm?*

Vinnie spotted Ralph's deposit while the terrier moved off deeper into a bushy area. "Ralph, come out of there. Ralph, come here!"

Ralph barked twice before he showed up with a rag in his mouth.

"What's that, Ralph? I don't have time to pick up other people's mess. Park and Rec employ people to clean."

Standing over the small dog, Vinnie didn't recognize Ralph's possession. He bent on one knee to take the rag, which Ralph was reluctant to give up. As soon as he touched it, he recognized the item as one of Kaelin's dishtowels. Not only had he used this checkered cloth to dry dishes for Kaelin and Grace, he had given it to them among a collection of items as a housewarming gift. He had liked the LGBT rainbow over the Golden Gate Bridge, two iconic symbols.

"Ralph, where did you find this?"

Attaching the leash to Ralph's collar, Vinnie bent and pushed branches aside to walk into the dense bushes. In a few feet he was hidden from the pathway. Moving another few yards, he was able to stand upright in a small clearing, in the middle of which was a hole. To Vinnie it looked like a crater, even if it was no more than ten inches across and typical of Ralph's digging habits. But the hole's shape was without doubt a human construction. *Not again,* thought Vinnie. *Another discovery? This mutt's a better investigator than me.*

Using his cell phone, Vinnie took a photo of the hole before placing the towel in it. The towel placement appeared posed, but Vinnie felt it a reasonable facsimile of Ralph's original find. Ralph barked and Vinnie hushed him with commands to shut up and sit. Vinnie took two additional photos before sending all of them to his and Drew's email box.

* * *

"You've done the right thing this time," said Drew as he took the plastic bag from Vinnie. He called his assistant on the office phone and asked her to contact their private investigator.

"What happens next?" Vinnie was proud of his latest discovery, although he gave Ralph full credit for the initial find.

"My investigator will take this to a laboratory we use for analysis. After we get the results we'll turn it over to the DA if it's relevant."

"But that's blood on it, I don't need a lab to tell me that."

"I agree—it looks like blood, but for the evidence to count we need lab confirmation. And we'll compare it to Slider's DNA samples."

"Wait all you want." Vinnie waved his arms. "I don't need to wait for an official fuckin' lab report. That's Slider's fuckin' blood."

For a second Drew was about to admonish Vinnie for continuing to pepper sentences with the F-word, but stopped seeing his tears. He swiveled in his chair, adopting a lawyer's formality. "The court requires a lab report no matter how long it takes. And remember that a jury won't appreciate your ongoing use of expletives—in fact it'll count against you. Harsh, but true. I know you miss your friend, and again, I'm so sorry."

Vinnie said he knew all about labs and reports, but he also knew that for all the extra time, it meant more opportunity for Curt to leave the country. He also said he would try harder to

251

apply Dan's substitute word and stop his fudging cursing.

"And this can potentially be good news." Drew's smile flashed neon bright, and he was about to add "a game changer," but Vinnie was out the door, muttering what sounded like "Fudge, fudged, fudging, foo."

* * *

Four days passed before Drew telephoned Ginny. She gathered everyone at the house and summarized the lab analysis.

"I knew it." Vinnie was skipping around the room.

"Calm down," said Ben, who sat on the edge of his seat. "Drew only said this was good, but insufficient, and there's a long way to go."

"Sure, but major, right?" Vinnie was dancing, his arms stretched in a stage gesture.

Ben nodded. "Yes, but—"

Vinnie interrupted. "Why the 'but'? Can't you accept good news?"

Ben mimicked an exaggerated patty-cake and Vinnie turned for an ass grind. Ginny had had enough and said so, while Dan continued to eye-polish his shoes.

With the fray stopped, Ginny gave Drew's summary: Slider's blood was on the towel but there was no explanation for how it got there.

"But the towel's from Kaelin's kitchen, which Curt had access to. He was there the day before and after Slider had been murdered. It's obvious: he took the towel to wipe the knife then realized he couldn't bury it with the weapon in the empty lot, so he buried it in the park."

Vinnie zigzagged around the room until Ginny caught him from behind, placing two arms over his shoulders to stop him walking. "What you say may be true but—" Vinnie squirmed, freeing himself from her grip, turned, and gave her a laser beam glare. Ginny threw up her hands in defeat. "Okay, *is* true."

With the palm of her hand, she rubbed one side of Vinnie's face. "The DA and jury will accept the blood is Slider's. And even if we think… um, know the towel belongs to Kaelin, the DA will argue that towel is sold all over San Francisco, so it doesn't necessarily follow Curt stole it from Kaelin."

"Of course he did."

"That's what you believe. We all do. But think about it. The DA will counter that you had as much opportunity to take the towel as Curt. You have a spare key. You live next door. Do we even know Kaelin's towel is missing? He'll say you purchased two, one as a gift for the women and one for yourself. And Slider took yours with him to the park as a head rest or to wipe his bench."

"Great. All on me—again. I didn't do it. How many times do I need to fu—fudging say it?"

Ben joined Ginny and nudged her aside. He embraced Vinnie the way firemen throw blankets to smother flames. "We believe you. We want the jury to believe you as well, that's all Ginny's saying." Ben's tight hug and forehead kiss put out Vinnie's fire.

Hidden behind Ben, Ginny didn't see Vinnie's volcanic reaction as she said, "Drew believes this helps provide reasonable doubt. You don't have to prove Curt murdered Slider, just that he's a plausible suspect, and by extension to Grace. Not the slam dunk you had hoped for, but you'll be free."

The fire Ben thought was extinguished erupted into blue-flame incandescence. Vinnie screamed, "NOT THE SLAM DUNK I FUCKIN' HOPED FOR?!" He choked, and took a deep breath. "I want justice for Slider. Curt's guilty and it looks like I'm the only one who wants to prove it."

The slamming door rattled the windows.

Chapter 42

Dig a Hole

The big house felt bigger without Dan and Ginny; Vinnie moped around after they had returned to New York. The rooms became mere walls enclosing space. He understood. There was nothing for them to do until the trial. He understood their worry about Anthony being left so long without his parents—not that Anna had suggested there was a problem.

Vinnie worried. Would Ben's guilt resurface? Did Ginny connect her missing Anthony to missing a surrogate baby?

He had watched Ginny pack from the open bedroom doorway, thinking her distracted. He offered to help. She thought he meant with her luggage, but he meant her anxiety. *Anxiety over forfeiting her rights; anxiety that Ben and Vinnie would permanently relocate with the baby to San Francisco.*

With the Livornos gone, Vinnie wandered aimlessly around the house. He moved into an empty TV room wearing old jogging pants. At least he could dress shabby, unconcerned. He stopped at the room's rear window, a wide view of Kaelin's house. *Yeah, like us. Empty of real life. Dark rooms. Untrimmed bushes. Unturned flower beds. Grace's job, wasn't it?*

He stared out, aware he was in a temporary home. When the trial ended he'd either be Ben's spouse in New York or bitch to a Benny, Bernie, or Barry in a California prison. Vinnie surveyed the yard next door. *That's a pretty decent-sized backyard for San*

Francisco. It's got to be at least seventy-five-feet wide and hundred-twenty long. A twisted smile came across his face. *Ours is twice as long and wider, practically a mini Central Park.*

"There's a lot of shrubbery to trim, don't you think, Ralph?" The dog had stirred from his basket as Vinnie entered the kitchen. "Not talking, are you? You don't give a rat's ass about the next-door backyard."

Ralph stretched, a bit sluggish. Vinnie believed it was the effect of keeping him on his leash during their walk, constraining his ability to explore every blade of grass or tree stump. *Is being confined more tiring then freedom to roam? Is that how I'll feel in prison?*

The duo went into the basement. Vinnie walked past the weight racks, but training wasn't a priority today. He walked past Slider's bathroom to look out of the window as Kaelin stood at her kitchen side door. Vinnie shuffled back a foot. *Why shouldn't I look out my fu—fudging door?*

From his safe distance, Vinnie watched. Kaelin didn't glance in his direction. She walked her side path with her back to him. Vinnie edged to the window to see her enter a curbside cab. With head pressed against the glass, he caught her midwifery valise. *She'll be gone for several hours, maybe all day and night.*

"Hey Ralph, want to take a walk and explore somewhere different?"

Ralph's ears pricked up, his lethargy vanished. Ralph followed Vinnie upstairs to the front of the house. Vinnie attached the leash to his collar and heard Ben's heavy steps on the cellar stairs.

"Looks like we came up just in time or he'd have seen us. Don't worry: once he starts playing with his iron set he'll be at least two hours."

Vinnie led Ralph out the front door, turned left as the path met the sidewalk, and in a few steps stood at the side gate to Kaelin's property and walked down the side path she had used ten minutes earlier. Passing by the kitchen window, the two entered the decent-sized backyard.

"Wow, what a mess. Even worse when you get into it. You could get lost in here, but you won't, will ya?" Vinnie leaned down and released Ralph from his leash.

The companions moved around the yard, independent of each other. Vinnie found a stick and started to poke at the bushes, swatting at long grass and shrubs. He began at the property line farthest from his and Ben's house. On the other side was an eight-foot, solid redwood fence, a new construction by the neighbor when Kaelin and Grace had moved in. The busybody neighbor didn't want her children to see what might happen at an "all woman's barbecue," or so someone had reported to Vinnie and Slider in the park. "Absurd. Lesbians barbecue food and listen to music, just like straights," said Vinnie. After, when he was invited to one of the women's BBQs, he drank too much and suggested removing all his clothes to serenade Mrs. Tight-Ass with Broadway melodies. Grace talked him out of it, suggesting the nosy neighbor would be in full voyeur mode, ready to dial 911.

Striding along the high fence perimeter, Vinnie didn't see Ralph creep into the shrubs. His low body permitted him to go underneath the branches. Scratching at the soil, Ralph sniffed and, instead of peeing, he barked.

"Quiet, Ralph. We don't want Mrs. Tight-Ass to know we're here."

Either he didn't understand Vinnie or had decided to ignore the advice, because Ralph's barking continued between bouts of digging.

"Shut up already. What's the problem?"

Struggling through the same branches that Ralph had passed under with no trouble, Vinnie found Ralph tensed over a dead squirrel. "Wrong species, Ralph. Nice try. Want a treat?"

The Boston terrier's ears stood upright. These were words he never ignored.

Vinnie pulled from his pocket a small rubber-like substance about the size of a green bean and placed it in his open palm. "Now will you shut up?"

Ralph chewed a few extra treats Vinnie tossed him on his way to retrieve a small spade he saw lying in the backyard. On his return, he buried the squirrel and walked to the fence, tracing Grace's flower bed. She had been so proud of her design, showing him every time she added a new plant. He had admired Grace's work and knew it well, so he noticed the discolored pebbles dislodged from the border.

Kneeling, Vinnie saw the ground had been disturbed. His hand jittered when his short thrust of the spade uncovered the corner of brightly colored material. Vinnie pulled a dishtowel, identical to the one Ralph had discovered a few days before, except this was tied shut with a ribbon. There was no discoloration, no signs of blood, yet Vinnie carefully placed the rag into one of Ralph's plastic poop bags. Vinnie was pleased at his fastidious habit to always leave the house armed with extra bags.

Vinnie scratched a larger circumference, but came up empty. Ralph had joined him in the excavation efforts, but Vinnie put the leash on him and they walked away.

* * *

A long time passed with Vinnie sitting motionless in the room he called an office because of a Mac desktop, ink-jet printer, and a bookcase. Ben called it Vinnie's jack-off room, with the major features being an iPod player, thirty-two-inch TV with surround-sound speakers, a PlayStation, two dozen game cartridges, and more X-rated DVDs than books on the shelf. A professional dartboard with photos of naked men stuck around the circumference was mounted on the wall.

The most dominant item was two tall stacks of Slider's special magazines by the bookshelf. Ben had complained. "Vinnie, recycle. They're not heirlooms."

Vinnie protested. "Hey, haven't you heard of reference material?"

He had nearly every issue, a leftover habit from his East Village bachelor days when money was scare and loneliness abundant. The latest issue lay on top, the one he had retrieved from the basement bathroom before Ginny and Dan's arrival.

Vinnie stared at his discovery. He had not interrupted Ben's workout, but Ben interrupted his thoughts, shouting up the stairs, "Lunch is ready." Vinnie yelled back that he would eat later, to which Ben replied he couldn't wait, his appetite too fierce after his hard workout.

The final shout came up the staircase twenty minutes later. Did Vinnie want to join him for a pantry restocking expedition? Vinnie walked to the head of the stairs and begged off. He waited for the front door to close before he made his call.

On the second ring he heard Curt's voice. Their conversation lasted fifteen minutes. Vinnie hung up, unsure how he felt. He had promised he would wait, give Curt time to speak to Kaelin. A half-hour later he saw Curt use his key to enter Kaelin's house, who had not returned.

Vinnie looked at Ralph. "So! I didn't call Drew as I had promised. But look at what happened last time. Nada. Delay. I'm better at this than anyone gives me credit for. If I had done it their way, Curt would have had time to organize an escape. At least now he's promised to go to the DA as soon as he talks to Kaelin. It's better this way. No delay. *Capisce?* As soon as Kaelin returns this will all be over. Let's hope she's not out all night."

Chapter 43

Willfulness and Regret

Walking the center hallway, Vinnie plodded into the kitchen. He had stayed up past two o'clock and never saw Kaelin arrive home. At the kitchen countertop, Ben greeted him with a cheerful smile. "Good morning, sunshine." It was barely seven-thirty.

Vinnie grunted.

"Bad night?"

"Just late. I've a lot on my mind."

Ben shrugged. Vinnie glided out of the kitchen and returned ten minutes later.

"Plenty of mix in the blender," Ben said, chipper and fully awake, yet staying focused on the iPad's *New York Times* app.

Shuffling around the room in his bare feet, Vinnie pulled on the same sweatpants he had worn the day before, walked out, and a few minutes later appeared clothed in jeans and a long-sleeved cotton pullover.

His squeaking sneakers on the tile floor caused Ben to look up. "You're looking good. What's the occasion?"

"Nothing. Waiting for Ralph. I'll take him for his walk as soon as he arrives."

"I have a pile of emails from UltraFit that need replies, and I have to update my blog, Twitter, and Facebook pages. I'll be lucky to find time for a light workout." Ben grabbed his iPad and laptop and left the room. As he mounted the stairs he turned to see Vinnie staring out the living room window at the vacant lot.

* * *

It was mid-morning before Vinnie returned home. He released Ralph from his leash, and the dog scampered into the kitchen followed by Vinnie. After drinking from his water bowl, Ralph barked, urging Vinnie to retrieve treats from a baseboard cabinet.

After feeling the cold coffee pot, Vinnie put on a fresh brew. He skimmed *The San Francisco Chronicle* web pages on his iPad. Nothing. Vinnie called his lawyer.

"Hi, Vinnie. How are you?" Drew was cheerful. Vinnie used Drew's personal cell, a bonus for being Ginny's friend, which gave him "special relationship" status.

The cheerful tone dissipated with Vinnie's explanation of his previous day's discovery and his subsequent call to Curt.

"What did you do, Vinnie? What didn't you understand about 'everything goes through me'? If you were another client, I would drop you."

"I'm sorry. I can see now I was wrong. I was so angry and confused and I acted impulsively."

"Damn right. I'll call the DA's office now and find out what Curt said to Kaelin."

Ben entered Vinnie's study to see him pacing, one arm swinging his cell phone in circles.

"What is it?"

Vinnie barricaded himself behind his desk. He gave Ben a garbled version of the previous day's events, with key points omitted until he stumbled and mentioned possible new information about Curt being guilty of Grace's murder. Ben roared expletives like a bad comic with no real punchline. Vinnie's forehead touched the desk. "Drew's calling the DA to follow up on Curt."

Ben rushed out. Vinnie cradled his cell phone.

Pressing the cell against his ear, Vinnie answered on Drew's first ring but barely understood his words. "It's not good. Curt never contacted the DA, and he hasn't seen your new evidence."

Vinnie shouted, "He's lying," feeling his universe implode.

"This is what happens when you don't listen to your lawyer. The DA has sent police to question Curt. Hold tight. And for God's sake do nothing without talking to me."

Vinnie walked into his bedroom and lay sideways on his back across the bed, one arm covering his face. If only he could go back in time.

* * *

The local six o'clock TV reporter announced the breaking news. "A man's body was discovered this afternoon in a vacant lot in a Lower Pacific Heights neighborhood. His name has not been released until next of kin are notified."

Vinnie went online with his iPad, and Ben with his laptop. The lot, shown on the Internet, was the same one that had flashed across the TV screen, but they could see it from their front window. They didn't need to wait for next of kin to be notified, because she lived next door.

Around eight p.m. the police disturbed Vinnie's dinner. As he climbed into the squad car, Ben asked the second policeman a simple question, to which he was told, "Mr. Briggs is not being arrested because he is already under arrest. He's out on bail. If I were you, I'd call his lawyer."

Ben left a message on Drew's private cell, and a similar one with Ginny. He sat for two minutes and then went down to the basement, lifted random weights for ten minutes, and then returned upstairs to watch an all-news TV channel.

Just before midnight, Vinnie pushed on the front door with Drew's hand on his back. Drew had spent two hours with the police and made several phone calls to the DA to explain that circumstantial evidence was not the same as Vinnie committing an offense, so was insufficient to rescind Vinnie's bail. Drew had threatened to sue the police force and the DA's office for abuse of power.

Ben hugged Vinnie as they moved to the kitchen. Ben offered to reheat dinner for Vinnie and make a drink for Drew. Vinnie said he had no appetite, and Drew accepted a decaffeinated coffee.

Holding the teaspoon like a pen, Drew tapped his mug. "The evidence is pretty clear. Curt Peterson was found in the empty lot across the street, not especially hidden, so it was inevitable that a passerby would spot him."

"Geez." Ben's reaction was barely audible.

"Curt was stabbed with a serrated fishing knife, the markings similar to the injuries found on Grace."

"What does that mean?" Ben tensed, popping surface veins along his neck, his face a grotesque mask.

"Nothing, so far as Vinnie's arrest is concerned. Or I should say other than the obvious link of Vinnie to Curt. But nothing tangible, only circumstantial."

"Of course there's nothing, because I fu—fudging, no, *fuckin'* didn't do it. Just like I didn't kill Grace or Slider." Vinnie stood up, his chair screeching across the tiles.

"Sit, Vinnie. Let Drew finish." Ben reached out to grab him.

Vinnie listened as Drew repeated what he had heard in the cab ride from the police station—even without charging Vinnie for Curt's murder, it still hurt Vinnie's case. A jury would learn that the man Vinnie had accused of killing Slider had also been murdered in an empty lot just across from Vinnie's home. The inference was obvious, and the jury would fill in the blanks, no proof required.

"But what about what I found?" Vinnie's eyes opened wide, his face mean.

"It's not relevant because the DA hasn't seen it."

"Seen what?" Ben turned to both men.

Drew pointed to Vinnie, who leaned forward and whispered like he was telling a secret. "I was in Kaelin's backyard yesterday…"

Ben's voice thundered, his boom like a supersonic airplane breaking the sound barrier. "WHAT!" He slapped the granite top, the noise and flood of unstoppable curses startling Vinnie and Drew. With anger spent, Ben's voice grated as he said, "Are you really that fucking stupid?"

Tears rushed from Vinnie, and Drew failed to pacify Ben. Vinnie became hysterical, and Ben's hands reached to cover his ears. With arms behind his head, Ben said, "I thought you had stopped playing at your private investigator bullshit?"

Vinnie eventually calmed down, and he thought, *I'm not playing. I made a mistake out of compassion for my friends Slider and Kaelin.*

Waiting until he knew Vinnie had no response, Ben asked in a conciliatory tone, "What exactly did you find?"

"Kaelin and Grace's prenuptial rings."

Ben took hold of the counter as his hurricane-force rant blew. Vinnie's body vibrated and he turned to Drew, who no longer acted as conciliator. "Unbelievable."

Silence descended in the room. After a few seconds, Drew placed his hand on Vinnie's forearm. "Tell him the rest."

"I called Curt."

Ben looked like a grizzly, his arms raised overhead, the moment of attack at hand. His anger replaced words; he roared hard enough to risk a hernia. He stopped, but now the room's silence seemed louder then Ben's rage. Ben hurled more than words. He had lost control. He was about to take off, to rampage until the house collapsed. Drew stepped in front of Ben, snapped his hand up like a traffic cop, and screamed, "STOP! NOW!"

Ben's fists banged into his temples, a volcanic explosion. Drew took hold of Ben's forearms, stopping his self-inflicted violence.

Rushing to the sink, Ben used the faucet hose to spray his face and chest, extinguishing his rage. He knew his dignity, his sanity, his life, lay in a puddle with the water on the floor.

After chugging two eight-ounce glasses of water in rapid succession, Ben returned to his seat, somewhat calmer.

In the quiet, Drew pointed to Vinnie, who said, in a barely audible voice, "I told Curt what I found. He asked me to wait before I called Kaelin and the cops. He wanted a chance to talk to her, give her advice. He more or less admitted to killing Grace and Slider. He promised if I gave him this last chance to speak to his daughter he would go to the DA and confess."

"And you believed him?" Ben's hands were shaking.

"Yes. He was sincere. He wasn't bullshitting."

"And the rings, where are they now?"

"On my desk. Or they were."

Ben jumped up and returned to the sink to drink more water. This time he didn't scream, curse, or throw up his arms. Holding the stainless steel basin, he cried softly.

Vinnie walked over to him, rested his head on his back. "I'm so, so sorry." Vinnie cried too, his head bobbing up and down from Ben's heaving. He held on tight to Ben's waist.

"Hey, it's not all bad." Drew spoke, his voice straining to sound normal. "We can salvage something out of this. It's a setback, especially the missing rings, but this could work in our favor. Leave it to me."

It didn't matter to Vinnie or Ben if Drew was telling the truth. They'd accept false hope. Both men stopped crying. Drew left the kitchen and didn't look back. He knew this all-too-familiar scene—a family in despair over a hopeless situation. Closing the front door, Drew muttered, "Why don't clients ever take their lawyer's advice?"

Chapter 44

Dog Bites

Vinnie sat on the edge of the bed. *Did I sleep at all? Is this really happening?* He had been awake, dressed, and downstairs before Ben had risen. He didn't shower, unsure he could stand for long; and for the same reason he wasted no effort with underwear and pulled up his workout joggers.

He didn't want to be up this early, but his subconscious made sleep impossible. *What happened? Curt said he'd confess to Slider and Grace's murder—or did he? And who would murder Curt, and why? Didn't he say he needed to talk to Kaelin, have it all out in the open?*

For over an hour Vinnie sat in his office, then spent another in the kitchen, and it was barely seven a.m. He knew the best explanation for the buried wedding rings would be the simplest. *Think. You're the P.I. Who would have wanted to bury them? Grace? Why? To prove it was over between her and Kaelin? Did she do this before she went to Lake Tahoe? And how did she get Kaelin's ring from her? Maybe they had a fight and Kaelin flung it at her? Maybe Kaelin took it off before midwifery? Did Grace steal it? Why? And why bury them?*

No obvious answers came to his questions, or at least nothing simple, so Vinnie switched to Grace's murder. *Who was the unidentified Lake Tahoe woman? Is she involved in both murders? Does she have an accomplice? If Curt bequeathed his entire estate to*

Kaelin, does it mean the unknown woman doesn't get a cent? Is this about inheritance?

The doorbell interrupted Vinnie's ruminations. Ralph arrived on time and well rested. The dog trotted into the house, but was stopped by Vinnie, who took hold of the leash handed him by the cabbie. Vinnie guided Ralph down the front pathway and turned right at the sidewalk but his eyes shifted to the vacant lot across the street, crisscrossed with yellow police tape.

The walk was short. Vinnie felt every passing car, every pedestrian, every household had eyes on him. Returning home, he veered to the basement side entrance. He gave Kaelin's kitchen window a quick glance. *Was she watching him too?*

Vinnie moved to the bench Ginny had used weeks before while discussing surrogacy with Ben. Ginny had asked for more time. *Well, she has plenty now—like forever, with me in prison doing a life sentence.*

Ralph explored his familiar territory, his preference for corners away from the weights. Vinnie sat on the bench and faced the wall. Maybe lifting would be a good way to think. Ben said it was for him, the soothing monotony of repetition. Of course, Ben concentrated when pushing five hundred pounds off his chest, with his thinking reduced to the time between sets.

Vinnie pushed the metal up and off his chest, about several hundred pounds less than Ben's, but enough for him to struggle. Between sets his thoughts stirred. Facts reformulated. The simplest explanation was that Kaelin had killed both Grace and her father. But Slider?

His thoughts weighed as heavy as the bar he pressed off his chest. He sat upright curling two thirty-five-pound dumbbells. After two sets he replaced the weights. Maybe he should go up a few pounds.

A small breeze and the clicking side door caused Vinnie to turn. Kaelin slowly approached, the overhead fluorescent lights refracted off her purple blouse, giving the impression that she was more specter than flesh. She had a package in her hand, tied with a small bow. Her other hand held a fisherman's serrated knife.

Ralph ran to Kaelin with excited barks and a wagging tail, begging for his usual treat. Vinnie heard Ralph's yelp, and quickly lifted his head just as Kaelin viciously kicked the small dog. Ralph hunkered down on his front paws, and began to growl. Kaelin cursed while she swung her knife and bared her teeth. The knife missed Ralph by inches, and he snarled and lunged at her wrist. Kaelin dropped the knife and package to rub the trickle of blood. Ralph stood back, legs spread apart, his incisors exposed, a low growl in his throat. Kaelin slowly reached for the knife to slash again at Ralph, this time catching his leg.

The dog yelped as he limped, scampering to Vinnie, who lifted him to his lap and placed his hand over Ralph's bleeding leg. With head bent to examine the wound, a dumbbell connected with the side of his skull. Vinnie dropped to his knees, semi-conscious as he hit the floor.

"You thought you could come in and fuck with us? Take our baby? You're no better than that slut Grace. It's all your fault! Why couldn't you keep out of it?" Kaelin was screaming. She held the knife high above Vinnie's chest, hesitating, as if choosing an exact entry point. In her delay, Ralph leaped off Vinnie's lap and sank his teeth into her ankle. Kaelin instinctively shook her leg, deviating the knife's trajectory to nick Vinnie's arm.

Vinnie remained dazed, and saw Kaelin once more slash at Ralph, who scurried back. She pursued, swiping twice more, with Ralph avoiding each knife thrust.

* * *

Like Vinnie, Ben had endured a night of tossing and turning, only he had woken up late with his rage undissipated. He entered the kitchen, relieved not to find Vinnie and grateful that he was out walking Ralph. Ben wasn't ready to talk, not yet. It was too soon. Although this was a rest day from training, he had decided his best option would be to fling light weights around, giving him time to formulate what he needed to tell Vinnie. During the night, he had reached a decision he never would have thought possible. He had to tell Vinnie this relationship, their marriage, wasn't working, not the way he wanted. Frivolous, capricious, or both, he could not live with Vinnie's risk taking, his subterfuge, his unwillingness to be honest. Ben wiped his eyes. It may have been a rest day, but he was going to the basement gym anyway.

Ben's certainty about his future had invigorated him. His body had never produced so much adrenaline. Of all the drugs he had ever used, none had energized him like this. He was pure emotion, devoid of rational thought.

* * *

Vinnie moaned and attempted to lift himself off the floor. He heard Ralph's high-pitched single yelp as he saw Kaelin's knife penetrate the dog's ribcage. He heard a terrible squeal with Kaelin's next blow, and by her third Ralph was silent.

Through blurred vision, unsteady and disorientated, Vinnie stumbled, outstretched hand seeking the bench. Kaelin stopped cursing Ralph at the sound of Vinnie's banging into the bench. She walked across the gym and was within a foot of Vinnie's back, her hand steady, the knife at shoulder height. Suddenly, a ball-wrecker's blow like that used to crumble multistory buildings hit her somewhere near the third vertebra. Kaelin was propelled twenty feet across the room and careered into a wall, the oxygen in every alveolus of her lungs expelled.

Ben walked slowly across to Kaelin lying on the ground. With one hand he twisted the cloth of her purple blouse like wringing a rag, and formed a handle. He raised her entirely from his shoulder, his arm straight. He looked into her eyes, lifted her overhead as if examining an object in the light. He shook her shake 'n bake style, then his arm reared back and he slung her, a slider pitch.

268

Kaelin hit the mirrored wall; the shattering masked the sound of her ribs cracking. Ben never heard Kaelin's cry, nor saw her elbow bent back behind her. He had no idea she had suffered a traumatic whiplash.

Ben used two hands to cradle Vinnie, placing him gently on the workout bench. Ben's face glowered, his lips rubbery grommets over teeth, his trapezoids flight decks. Ben turned, looking at Kaelin in a blind rage. Vinnie struggled to call out, "No. Ben, you'll kill her. Stop."

Vinnie's words had no impact; Ben understood them as confirmation of his intention, not a directive.

Pure muscle moved forward, devoid of consciousness. The grotesque balloon came within feet of the disfigured rag doll. And a wail emerged, Vinnie's crying out, "STOP!"

* * *

From her hospital bed, two days after her emergency surgery, Kaelin confessed. In her taped statement, she acknowledged that Curt had killed Slider to prevent him from revealing Grace's intention to leave her, not knowing that Grace already had. "She told me everything. That stupid bitch thought I would be pleased with her honesty over admitting she had betrayed me, as if she was doing a good thing. She deserved to die for her betrayal."

She couldn't believe the fortuitous opportunity to cast suspicion onto Vinnie, "another stupid bitch." Even better, not only to cover her tracks, but have him convicted for her crimes. His audacity to intrude on her life with her partner and baby. He even showed her evidence found "by that goddamn mutt" that might free him, and when he had passed under her window, she saw the second opportunity for him to die.

Kaelin's eyes looked to the DA sitting at her bedside, unable to point with her arms in casts or turn her head with her neck in a brace, but obviously she meant him, saying, "so easily duped for a feather in a cap." The DA nodded, but showed no emotion.

He waited.

A break was needed. A sip of water, then Kaelin continued. She explained Curt had waited at her house; told her about the buried rings discovery; knew she had killed Grace. He had conned Vinnie, bartering a confession for Slider and Grace if he was allowed to explain in person to Kaelin—one last time with his daughter.

But to her, Curt gave a different story. He would pay for the best defense attorney, and suggested a temporary insanity defense. And he never intended to confess for Slider.

Struggling with labored breathing, Grace continued. "I had no intention of letting that bastard atone for his betrayal. My mother is unforgettable... and Grace... unforgivable." Kaelin's wry smile was not recorded, but the DA saw from his bedside chair.

She explained her easy entry into Vinnie's basement with Slider's hidden key, the location of which he stupidly broadcast to her and Grace. Her chuckle was short with the ensuing pain in her shattered ribs. She had used the key twice. The first time to steal back the rings, which were easily discovered lying on his desk—the first place she had looked. The second use was to kill Vinnie, which was not as easy as she had thought.

"I would have gotten away with it too, if not for the fact that I didn't have time to better dispose of Curt's body. I couldn't lift him into my car. I barely managed to get him into a wheelbarrow. I needed more time to move him. If not for a busybody calling the police, I'd have disposed of the body the next day. And that dog and Vinnie digging up my backyard. I want them arrested for trespassing!"

Vinnie listened again to Kaelin's taped confession, a concession granted by the DA to circumvent a wrongful arrest lawsuit. Vinnie listened to Kaelin's words, behind them hearing the classic "blame the victim" excuse. He also heard the irrational ravings of obsession.

Is that me? Am I blinded by an obsession to have a child?

Chapter 45

Adult Supervision Required

Moving the curtain aside, Vinnie stood at the bedroom window. Ben called out as he removed his clothes, "Leave it open, please. I'm a little warm and it's about to get warmer."

The sheets rustled as Vinnie tucked himself underneath, throwing the bedcover on the floor. "Is this our celebration dance?"

"You'll see."

At his dresser, Ben caught Vinnie sitting up, his face reflected in the mirror.

"Stop it. Don't ruin the surprise."

Ben appeared to be reading. He moved a wooden chair to the middle of the room, turned the seat back toward the bed footer and placed the open magazine on the seat. He raised one leg up, resting it over the chair's back.

With arms stretched and a quick double-bicep pose, he then flared his tent-wide lats to block Vinnie's view of their original Mapplethorpe serigraphy prints on the bedroom wall. With a half-turn, Ben examined Vinnie's expression, then turned again to bend over. He wiggled his ass high up, his large glutes spread by his hands, then he grabbed the ankle of the foot resting on the chair seat. With his other hand he pushed his penis down.

"Fuck. This is more difficult than it looks."

"What is?"

Ben held high the magazine from the dresser, with a photo and Slider's notes on the side. "This is the guy you and Slider liked, isn't it? I'm trying to reproduce his pose."

A big smile crossed Vinnie's face. He loved Ben so much it hurt. "Except you're a few inches short, which is a major disadvantage for that pose."

"Maybe, but these two are bigger and better." Ben cupped his balls, pushing them up and out.

"Hmm, are those berries? Come closer, I can't see them." Vinnie roared with laughter.

"Hey! These are way above average; they even had Ginny's mother worried." Ben covered his mouth.

Vinnie smacked the bed with one hand, screaming with laughter. "Are you kidding me?" Vinnie took a few inhales. "When was this?"

Ben's smile brought out all the angles in his face. He fell on the edge of the bed, his laughter deeper than Vinnie's. Ben crawled across the bed to lay sidewise to his lover. He recounted Anna's observation, when she met him nude on Barrow Cottage's beach.

"After our fight, remember?"

Vinnie nodded.

"What did she say?"

"Told me these seemed too large given my steroid use, and thought I should have a medical checkup."

"You told her you used steroids?"

"She's not stupid. I didn't get this by eating spinach." Ben flexed an arm.

"What happened?"

"She wanted to examine me. Imagine our best friend's mother twiddling my balls."

The two men gasped for air, faces red. Ben knelt up, fingering his testicles. Looking at Vinnie he said in falsetto, "Now, Ben, dear, I'm going to take measurements and rub my special frog snake brew all around... it won't hurt, but your balls may explode. I'll make a video to instruct my daughter's husbands on testicle manipulation for better impregnation."

Vinnie was in tears, catching his breath between snorting laughs. Ben grabbed the sheet to avoid falling off the bed.

An hour later, Ben huddled into Vinnie's side. With his arm wrapped around Vinnie's torso, he mumbled something about Ginny. He wondered what would happen next now that Vinnie's trial was over. In Ginny's court, there was only one person making the decisions.

* * *

Three time zones away, and a day later, uncontrolled laughter surpassed that of Vinnie and Ben. The women listened to Ginny's explanation of the Zapruder-like replay of Vinnie's ejaculation by her mother. The three women went into hysterics. Sarah and Betsy imagined Ginny's mother's hostage-taking on Martha's Vineyard; her arranged seating of the men; her slow-motion replay of the video clip on the big-screen TV.

Sarah asked, "Did she play it backward too, with Vinnie's sperm entering his penis?" Ginny thought that maybe she did, but didn't say it. She wasn't sure what her mother did or didn't do, with that particular episode ranking in the top five on her "most embarrassing mother moments" list. Rachel ranked it number one.

The approaching waitress veered away to another table on hearing Sarah sputtering, "A twelve-foot sperm shot revealed by Martha's Vineyard's own CSI ace investigator Anna Swinburne... ha ha ha ha..." Sarah slammed her hand on the table. The waitress returned, her words attempting to calm the noise. She went away without taking the women's orders.

"I want copies. I know at least five lesbians that'll pay fifty bucks each for that." Sarah's hands rubbed one palm over the other like a silent-movie villain.

Ginny frowned. Sarah's raucous laughs were joined by Betsy's hiccuping chortles.

With a laser glare the waitress returned to the table. "You girls have been warned already. Lou's about to come out from behind the stove, and he never does that, as you well know."

"We're sorry. If you had heard what we did, you'd be rolling on the floor too," said Betsy with a few small burp-style chuckles.

Sarah covered her mouth with her hand.

"Yeah, sure, honey. Just keep it down or Lou will have you out on your tushes."

With the waitress gone, Betsy looked to Ginny. "That image will stay with me forever."

Sarah kept her hand clamped to her mouth.

"What about me? Rachel? Our husbands, Vinnie, and Ben?" Ginny grinned. "My mother has single-handedly ensured a complex of therapists' tuition for their children's college education."

The three woman roared again and waved to Lou scowling behind the counter. As if he were a sign, Ginny knew this wasn't the moment for a serious discussion. She'd need more time to think it through, alone.

Chapter 46

Last Call

Ginny had left her friends moments before, a warm sun on her back and a strong wind biting her face as she walked to her condo. Her personalized iPhone ringtones alerted her she had a text from Ben. She read his truncated text as she continued to walk. *urg UF bus arrive 2mor 4 1wk wnt 2 mt 4 dnr? V in Sea w F.*

Ginny didn't need to consult Dan. Ben arrives tomorrow for one week's business at UltraFit. He wanted to arrange dinner with them. Vinnie went to visit Freddie in Seattle. She texted as she walked, inviting him to a home-cooked meal at the end of the week. She knew Ben avoided restaurants—too many gawkers, and home would allow more intimate conversation.

For a brief moment, she thought about sending another text to ask why Vinnie didn't rearrange with Freddie and join Ben in New York, but decided it was them maintaining their independence, something they had adjusted to over three years.

Entering her condo, Ginny revised her own answer. Ben's business was more with her than UltraFit. A month had passed since Vinnie's exoneration. *They want a decision and Vinnie doesn't want to be here when I tell them. Tell them what? I've got to stop procrastinating. The longer I wait the more difficult it will be, and harder on everyone.*

* * *

His strong embrace held Ginny tight. She lay on top, feeling Dan's arms around her back. She reciprocated with her fingers skirting his shoulders, then moving between their torsos to reach down to gently squeeze his genitals. The first time Dan had experienced this motion was from Ben, years before. Ginny had watched Ben, and learned. Dan thought she'd become an expert. *Did she ask Ben for instruction? No, she wouldn't. Had she asked her mother? Maybe? No, please God, no.*

Dan giggled with his thoughts, but not for long as Ginny's touch brought sex to the fore. With her one hand jostling his testicles, fingers on the other skated his torso, raising capillaries to the surface. He inhaled her perfumed body, sensing each molecule suffusing his nostrils. Her draping silk negligee tingled his spine with goose bumps. Her breasts moved beneath the fabric, a treasure awaiting; Dan sought to fondle each, and suckle until his cheeks collapsed. But he waited too long. Ginny released his balls and slithered down his hard body to swathe his hard penis in her cleavage. Her full lips assaulted his man-tits. She bathed him in sensuality, whispering love sonnets of a street rapper's rude words. She mixed tender caresses with strong massages. She aroused him now as much as the day they had first met. He could hardly stand her beauty. He wanted her seduction to bring him to climax. Dan felt like a summer's day.

And then it stopped. She wanted to talk. *What!* He was on fire. His testicles ached. His penis throbbed. *Who stops in the middle of sex? Who wants to talk at this level of excitation?*

Dan was sure he misheard. Talking was impossible, not at this point. He needed release. He kissed Ginny's lips; the hot coals burned away conversation. When kissing failed, he moved to pleading as if requesting a death sentence reprieve. Her sigh let him know he had won. She agreed; he was in no state for a serious discussion. Whatever reason, Dan didn't care, his attention gathered in his loins.

He was too far gone, too excited to play around. He entered Ginny like he was fucking the Lincoln Tunnel. In the best of times Dan struggled to be gentle, not for lack of trying but his motorhome penis made subtle difficult. And now, like a jelly donut junkie craving a Sunday morning fix, he moved too fast. His climax cry reached Weehawken like roaring rush-hour traffic. Ginny gave an after echo, and complimented him on a very satisfying journey. Dan believed her.

Despite his pre-sex agreement, Dan struggled to stay awake to hear Ginny out. On his back, Ginny rubbed his arms and chest. She kissed him on his nipples, forehead, and lips while evaluating the situation. Ben's arrival for dinner was her deadline. Any continued delay prolonged everyone's anxiety, and increased Vinnie and Ben's stress—hadn't their last few months been enough? Further delay on her part was cruel.

Dan hugged Ginny, his eyelids closing as he spoke his last sleepy words, "I love you and I'll stand by you, whatever you decide."

* * *

Ginny sent a text to her two best friends, two days before the dinner with Ben. "My place tomorrow night. Dan's away. I'll cook."

Despite her self-denigration of her cookery skills, Ginny was competent. The dinner chatter had covered politics and moved on to the New York theater scene. Ginny had a faint smile as she listened to Sarah give an insider's scoop of upcoming off-Broadway shows. Ginny stopped swirling her knife around her empty plate and interrupted.

"I'd like to change the subject, is that okay?" Ginny's smile faltered. "This is a little delicate… but I may have another baby."

"You're pregnant? That's great," said Betsy as she clapped her hands.

"I'm very happy for you," added Sarah.

Ginny shook her head. "No, I meant I'm thinking about having a baby."

"Oh? Well, that's good too. How does Dan feel about it?" said Betsy as she lowered her hands to her sides.

"He said it's up to me."

The women looked at each other before giving Ginny their sorority stare.

"Of all the things I've heard about having a child, I've never heard that," said Sarah, her head turning left and right.

Betsy added, "I'm sorry, but Dan's mistaken. It's not all up to you. He will have an input, even at the most basic level. He does realize how you had Anthony, right?"

"Of course Dan's included in the decision. He's saying that no matter what I decide, he'll support me."

Betsy moved her plate aside, placing her elbows on the table, both hands supporting her chin. "Once again, oh mysterious magical one, you have confounded the hell out of me. What are you talking about?"

A sigh whistled out of Ginny's lips. "Well, uh, you see… the baby will not be Dan's."

Betsy flung herself backward as Sarah leapt up from her chair. Noises not words came out of both women.

With seconds passing, Sarah sat back down and said, "Repeat, but with more explanation."

"It won't be Dan's baby, it will be Ben's—if I decide to have it."

This time both women screamed, a mixture of cursing with unrecognizable interjections. Sarah raised herself and paced around the room.

Taking hold of the back of her chair, Sarah thrust her face toward Ginny. "You've been fucking your bodybuilder trainer?" Sarah sat. "That's too far, even for you. And Dan's fine with this?"

"When? How often? Start from the beginning," said Betsy, her hands folded in her lap.

After thirty minutes Ginny had taken them through the basics, including Vinnie and Ben's role. Her egg artificially fertilized by Ben's sperm. Dan's initial objection and the reason for his final acceptance. She was the one to make the final decision.

"I was hoping you could help," said Ginny, looking at Sarah, "in that among your lesbian friends with babies I could learn more, the practical side, you know, reputable doctors, agencies, and legal advice."

Sarah's head went full tilt. "It so happens I can. I'll set something up. But are you sure about this?"

Ginny heard in Sarah's voice and saw in her hand gestures her disapproval.

"I don't know. I'll talk to your friends and think it over."

"You're smart enough to realize that two lesbian women having a baby from a donor is not the same as a fully functioning heterosexual couple, right?"

Ginny looked around, as if someone might overhear. "And that is our complication. The big *if*. Will this pregnancy preclude Dan and me from having another child? I mean, I'm not sure I could go through a third, which would kill my career."

Sarah agreed. The time she'd taken off for Anthony had put her professionally at a disadvantage, regardless of the law. In practical terms, she had a high-flying position in the cutthroat fashion world. Her time away with a baby put her at a disadvantage among her competitors. Bloomingdale's would have no choice but to grant her the time off, but fashion was not on hold.

"In essence, you have a few options. One baby or two? Two kills your career." Sarah chewed her words. "If one, whose? Dan's or Ben's?"

"Yes."

A small squeaking cough came from Betsy. "I think a better way to think about this is to ask yourself, what do you want out of life?"

Ginny scratched her chin. "That's what I'm doing. The future for me and Dan, and for Ben and Vinnie."

Modulating her voice, Betsy said, "Think of it this way, and no offense to anyone at the table."

Sarah perked up and glared at Betsy. "I suppose that means me. Go ahead, I'm a big girl."

"Not just you. All of us. My point is that Sarah chose an academic pathway and pursued tenure. She's mapped out her life until she retires. Me? I'm a senior partner in a financial firm. So my pathway's set more or less until I retire. We pursued careers with quick rises to the pinnacle, after which there's not much beyond. Academia is full of deadwood—uh, not you, Sarah—and financial institutions are full of partners freeloading off junior staff. You chose something different."

"And?" Ginny looked at Betsy, then to Sarah, who shrugged her shoulders.

"Don't you see? You took a career that has many directions. There isn't a stopping point. Sure, you could stay at Blooming-dale's forever, and probably please them. But what do you want? Would doing the same thing over and over really excite you until retirement? You're super intelligent... you have drive... you live for excitement. Not like us." Betsy waved her hand between herself and Sarah.

Sarah scowled at Betsy. "Hey, I'm no country bumpkin. As you said, I have tenure at a prestigious university. I do new research and publish new articles and books every year."

"Yes, you're smart, but in all honesty do you think you can match Miss Genius here?" Betsy's thumb aimed at Ginny, and Sarah's middle finger shot up.

"Thank you for proving my point with your intelligent response."

The laughter broke the tension. Ginny poured more wine.

"And, to point out the obvious, for which I could kill—look at her." Betsy again pointed to Ginny. "I wish I had half her looks. She's gorgeous." Sarah forced her breasts upward.

"Don't you dare push your boobs out or so help me I will ground you." Betsy spoke with a harsh voice.

Sarah laughed. "Okay, mom. Finish your point."

"Ginny, compare the pleasure you get from Anthony with your job. You can't because they're different. Both bring something, and you need to decide which you want more of. If you become a surrogate mother, or if you have another child with Dan, you're deciding on a new life and a new career. Maybe a career as a full-time mom. Or a job outside of fashion."

"Betsy, you're lecturing. What's your point?"

"If you let me finish, maybe you'll get my point. Whether to have Ben's child and another one with Dan is not a decision to give up your career in fashion because, and this is my prediction... if you don't change your job within five years, you'll be miserable. Does having one or two or three children reduce your options? I don't know. But I do know that with your intelligence and beauty, you'll have lots of options. Your only real decision is how you'll feel about being a surrogate mother. There's no going back on a child."

Ginny tapped her wine glass and leaped up to hug Betsy. "Once again, you are brilliant."

"Did I miss something? What was so brilliant?" Sarah leaned across the table to poke Betsy's head.

Ginny blurted out, "I know what I have to do."

"What! Tell us," shouted the two friends.

Ginny sat and spoke with her quiet voice. "I'll talk to my mother."

Betsy and Sarah's roars sounded like a Yankee Stadium crowd with the team winning the World Series.

* * *

Ginny followed the Swinburne rule: phone calls were not for

important conversation. Ginny met her mother the afternoon following dinner with her friends. She rode the train from Grand Central to Stamford and was on the return train when she called Dan.

The ringing cell startled Dan from a snooze. He was exhausted caring for Anthony all day and had only managed to get him to bed an hour before Ginny's call.

"Hi, Ginny. Where are you?"

"On the train. I'll be home in forty-five."

"Want me to heat up dinner?"

"No. I had an early supper with my mother. This can't wait. I've made my decision."

"Oh?"

"Yes."

Dan waited until he heard Ginny complete the recounting of her discussion with her mother before he spoke. "Did she really say that?"

"Call her and ask yourself if you don't believe me."

"Pass."

"Fine. I think you should call Vinnie, and I'll call Ben. We shouldn't wait for dinner with Ben tomorrow. And they should both hear my decision—our decision—at the same time."

The next phone conversations brought tears and long silences. Vinnie cried the most. Ben was stoic, like he had learned to be at a contest when he was being judged, only this was a contest he didn't understand. Was this good news or not?

Only time would tell.

Author's Note

A very BIG thank you to everyone who has taken the time to read *Baseball Man.* Readers make a difference to writers. I am grateful for your interest in my books.

If you enjoyed reading this book, then please remember to leave a review at the place where you obtained your copy. I listen to comments and use them to understand what works best for readers. I can't do too much about who the characters are, but they do mature, develop, gain new interests, and find new challenges.

You can learn more about the author and find exclusive content, or sign up to the mailing list and be the first to know of new releases in the Vinnie Briggs Stories series, by visiting the official website: **www.charlespuccia.com**

My stories are loosely based on my experiences, although the characters are fictional. I am fairly sure I can relate to many of my readers' experiences, if not exactly at least approximately. So let me know what you like, something that's happened to you that you would like to see in a story, and what kind of situations you want to read about. Remember the old adage: you have to ask to receive, so please send me your comments.

Share your opinions with others about Vinnie, Ben, Dan, and Ginny and find out what others think in return. And, please, if you enjoyed reading *Baseball Man,* leave a review for others wherever you obtained your copy.